Praise for *Lunch Bucket Paradise*

"A truly absorbing read: the miracle and the horror of America's post–World War II growth, in parallel with the tumult and hilarity of coming of age in California during a time of fantastically clashing ideals."

—Kristen J. Tsetsi, author of *Pretty Much True...*

"Setterberg tells a riveting story and makes you a participant in the booming California of the 1950s. You'll find yourself laughing out loud and wiping tears from your eyes. In the end you will bask in the glow of this great read."

—Ralph Lewin, president and CEO, California Council for the Humanities

"You can't help rooting for the narrator as he plots his escape from Jefferson Manor, the surreal and ultimately absurd suburbia of chemical-enhanced privet hedges, rumpus rooms, electric blankets, and Jell-O molds."

—Clara Silverstein, author of *White Girl: A Story of School Desegregation*

"In electric prose, *Lunch Bucket Paradise* gives us such a sure, detailed sense of what it was to grow up in the late fifties and early sixties—from the music to the name brands to the carbon-copy houses—that we live and breathe the suburban air."

—Judith Kitchen, author of *The House on Eccles Road*

"This is a growing-up story, a family story, and an American story, part banishment from Eden, part escape: a wonderful, wonderful read."

—Mark Greenside, author of *I'll Never Be French* and *I Saw a Man Hit His Wife*

"A brilliantly clear window onto a world that seems alternately seductive, threatening, and intensely nostalgic (and often all three). I love his storytelling and admire his language. But I have no desire to visit Frog Island with him."

—Jeff Greenwald, author of *Snake Lake*

Lunch Bucket Paradise

A True-Life Novel

Fred Setterberg

Heyday, Berkeley, California

Several chapters of this book have appeared in serial form: "The Children of Ike," *American Fiction*; "The Necessity of Maintenance and Repair," *Literal Latte*; "Catechism" won *The Florida Review*'s annual fiction prize; and "Our Golden State" won *Solstice Literary Magazine*'s annual fiction award. "Jungle Music" began as an essay published originally in *The Southern Review* and *The Double Dealer*. It won the Faulkner-Wisdom Essay Prize sponsored by The Pirate's Alley Faulkner Society.

Library of Congress Cataloging-in-Publication Data

Setterberg, Fred.
Lunch bucket paradise : a true-life novel / Fred Setterberg.
p. cm.
ISBN 978-1-59714-166-6 (pbk. : alk. paper)
1. Coming of age--Fiction. 2. Suburban life--California--Oakland--Fiction. I. Title.
PS3619.E86L86 2011
813'.6--dc22

2011014357

Book Design: Lorraine Rath

Printing and Binding: Thomson-Shore, Dexter, MI

Orders, inquiries, and correspondence should be addressed to:
Heyday
P.O. Box 9145, Berkeley, CA 94709
(510) 549-3564, Fax (510) 549-1889
www.heydaybooks.com

10 9 8 7 6 5 4 3 2 1

For Jim Heilborn, Mike A'Dair, Dave Bowlan, Greg Young, Doug Jensen,
Robert Lewis, Nick Kassavetis, Clyde Leslie Hodge III, and Kathleen Krentz

Have you your pistols? have you your sharp-edged axes? Pioneers!
O pioneers!

—Walt Whitman

What was almost never asked was the crucial question, a question that had resounded through much of the history of the frontier. Was this the beginning of something or the end?

—Peter Schrag, *Paradise Lost: California's Experience, America's Future*

Contents

The salesman claws the air and urges them closer. He stands astride a 1951 Ford pickup truck polished ostentatiously to a charcoal gloss. On the collapsed rear flap of the Ford, he fans a dozen mimeographed maps to the fifteen blocks of empty lots.

Young couples gather around the floodlight—all of them, outrageously, expecting to become homeowners.

Within their grasp is a new house with three small, square bedrooms, a one-car garage, the promise of a sycamore blooming someday out front by the edge of the postage-stamp-sized, golf-course-green lawn.

Working people never had it so good.

Several men form an inquisitive horseshoe around the pickup. They still wear their oil-caked work clothes and they chat among themselves, assuming a parity of experience and means, the stuff of neighborliness; and then they suspiciously demand to know more from the salesman about the availability of thirty-gallon water heaters—difficult to obtain after the war; the wattage of future street lamps; the benefits and drawbacks of inclusion in the regional sanitation district. They possess ample credit thanks to the GI Bill and the FHA, and as much work these days as they desire. But they have to ask questions. Twenty years earlier, working people had never had it so bad.

The conversation's escalating energy, its heat and zeal, bring to mind a recent illustration in *Time* magazine. A half-page, black-and-white diagram expounds upon the promise of atomic power—the path of speeding electrons whirring around the fundamental neutron, the implied force of the ordinary. Every man and woman gathered around the pickup truck knows from experience that they shouldn't hope for much, but they cannot help themselves. A slender gold wedding band glimmers from the salesman's ring finger. You can't help thinking: if this character worked in a machine shop or on the factory floor, he would have risked having that ring and finger ripped right off.

One man slips both hands into the frayed pockets of his Ben Davis work trousers, clips his thumbs around the belt. Another allows his knees to sag into a boxer's stance and juts out his jaw.

The salesman's canine persistence reminds folks of the bankers and nervous mortgage men who showed up at their families' farms during the Depression—the accompanying sheriff's deputy morosely rocking on his heels at the far end of the porch; then the fancy stranger would extract from his briefcase the official papers that would turn out to be a foreclosure notice or another court order to vacate another parcel of their property.

Now the world has turned upside down, and the sons and daughters of the dispossessed are shaking the soft hand of the fellow in the white shirt and tie, more than equals. The power of the ordinary. They might even buy his house.

* * * * *

ONE

Children of Ike

Folks in our town talked about the war only as it faded from recollection. Aiming to piece together what had actually happened, we spent Saturday nights at the Alameda Drive-In, absorbing the lessons of *Mister Roberts* and *The Teahouse of the August Moon*. When it finally arrived in the suburbs, my father praised the Rodgers and Hammerstein version of history: *South Pacific* featuring Mitzi Gaynor in Pan-O-Vision. Dad spoke pointedly of Emile de Becque's rich bass as though it somehow modified the atrocities at Tarawa and cut short the bloodshed in Guam.

My uncle Win, a Navy veteran of both Pearl Harbor and the Solomon Islands, complained always about Hollywood's omissions.

In the movies, Win pointed out, nobody ever got sick. But in the South Pacific—not the musical, but the actual theater of operations—Win had contracted malaria, dengue fever, and whenever possible, the clap. In the movies, bullets passed through shoulders, hands, or the fleshy part of a thigh. Win assured me that hot flying metal was just as likely to tear the meat off the arm or shatter the bones or lodge in the intestines or snap the spine or strip the skin from the face and leave the skull glaring back, naked and white.

"Body parts," Win explained in a hoarse and confidential whisper as we stood in line at the snack bar, waiting out the twenty-five-minute intermission between *Hell Is for Heroes* and *The Wackiest Ship in the Army*, "body parts is what they always leave out." Win's half-dollar skidded across the glass counter and landed on the Ben Franklin side. We scraped up two sacks of popcorn, each stamped on red and black newsprint with the terrifying faces of cartoon clowns. "Pieces of men," hissed my uncle, purchasing a twelve-ounce paper cup of Pabst Blue Ribbon drawn from a cold keg underneath the counter. He slowly lifted the cup to his mouth, denying himself its pleasure by quarter-inches, and then he splashed down a mouthful. Pabst Blue Ribbon smelled to me like last night's stale cigarettes and Wednesday morning's fresh white bread straight off the Langendorf truck. "They're scattered here and there," said Win. "My sweet Jesus Christ, you wanted to puke—did you ever, Little Slick." He stroked my head with the same firm, soothing touch he usually reserved for Joe Louis, his dachshund. "Bodies piled up like firewood. Everybody's afraid, that's the plain God's truth. Everybody's afraid, all the time."

After the war, my uncle read more deeply into the events, trying to reconcile his own experience with the historical record. He picked up William Shirer's *The Rise and Fall of the Third Reich* but lost interest around the Battle of the Bulge. He nearly finished *The Naked and the Dead*, though it dragged on far too long, like the war itself. Eisenhower's opus, *Crusade in Europe*, presented a more basic problem. For Win, the war had not been a crusade. He likened the war to a highway pileup, a vast wreck of jagged metal and human guts, a cataclysm.

"During the war," Win once wistfully explained after I had reached the age of nine or ten and needed to know, "things were fucked up bad, boy. They were truly fucked up beyond belief."

Guys shot their buddies by mistake; he had seen it happen.

Ships downed their own planes.

Planes bombed their troops.

Besides the blunders, there were the dumb rumors. Soldiers feared they'd be docked a quarter of their pay if they lost any equipment in battle. Sailors believed Tokyo Rose was really Amelia Earhart and the Watts Towers in Los Angeles were actually Japanese broadcast stations. Even the officers whispered about Allied agents dropped behind the German lines dressed as nuns, about Boston priests with thick Irish brogues working as clandestine Gestapo cell commandos with orders from Himmler to assassinate Harry Hopkins. Berlin was smoldering and Germany was in revolt. Hitler was infected with rabies, insane, foaming at the mouth; he was being treated by a veterinarian. Eva Braun, a secret agent of Eleanor Roosevelt's (and the former lover of Admiral Bull Halsey), had cut the Führer's throat in bed.

The war would be over in a month, a week, by Saturday.

The war in Europe had been over for six months already, but the Army brass wanted to keep marching until they reached Moscow.

When the news finally came about Japan, the tremendous news that the Americans had dropped a big bomb, a really big beautiful bomb, and the war truly was over, nobody could believe that one at first either. Thank you, God, prayed my Uncle Win, crying at his ship bunk, thank you, thank you, thank you, even though I don't believe in you. Thank you for ending this war because it has been truly more fucked up than anybody will ever know.

I listened to every word my uncle told me, and I wondered if I would ever be ready to take my place in the world.

✦ ✦ ✦

"What do you think the worst torture would be?" asked the Mad Professor.

His real name was Philip Barnes, and he lived down the block in a house slathered twice over with coats of fire-engine-red enamel and a team of three-foot-high ceramic Negro jockeys posted at each corner of his lawn. Phil was a year older than me, small for a ten-year-old, with skin the color of paste, an asthmatic with a propensity for pinkeye and bloody noses. But Phil also possessed a Gilbert chemistry set and microscope—and thus, his nickname. We were best friends.

"I wouldn't want to be covered with honey and staked out in the woods on top of a giant red ant hill," I admitted. I pictured ants with crimson faces like savage Apaches. Their giant pincers would be as sharp as lawn shears. "Or get torn apart by German shepherds."

"German shepherds really aren't that bad," said Benny Chang, an expert on dogs ever since his family had brought home a rat terrier from the pound. "But you wouldn't want the Romans to crucify you, especially if they nail you upside down."

The three of us sat Indian-style, feet folded flexibly under our rumps. We plucked longish grass blades from Phil's front lawn.

"I heard about this guy," I offered, "who the Germans, or the Japs, or somebody, tied a wire cage onto his head and inside it they put three starving rats."

"So what happened?" Benny asked. His eyes bulged like a toad's.

"They ate his brain."

"Neat."

"When his platoon found him, two of the rats had their heads peeking out of his empty eye sockets. Like a Halloween pumpkin."

"What happened to the third rat?" Benny wondered.

I shrugged. I hadn't considered the third rat.

"Where'd you ever hear that?" demanded Phil, squinting hard.

"From you," I said. "Remember? At least, most of it."

He thought it over. "I don't think it was the Germans. It was probably the Russians. Or the Belgians. I'd have to ask my Dad."

"Maybe it was the Americans."

"What kind of American would tie a starving rat on somebody's head, Benny?"

"I wish I could." Benny Chang lathered his hands together, one over the other over the other, a miniature ghoul.

"It was the Chinese," Phil definitely concluded.

"Oh, I don't think—"

"Yeah, Benny, Chinese water torture. What about Chinese water torture, Benny?"

Phil and I plugged Benny persistently on either shoulder, demanding the truth. "I don't know," he cried out, "my family never did any of that stuff!"

In matters of water torture, etcetera, Phil was the expert. He had earned his reputation as the Mad Professor through the evil works involving his Gilbert chemistry set, manipulating test tubes, petri dishes, and fat-bellied beakers to conduct various experiments of the demented variety. Phil boiled worms in Pyrex bowls atop his Bunsen burner. He speculated whether a housefly could still fly with sewing pins stuck through one eye (it could not) and where a moth would land once it had been soaked in alcohol and set aflame (it landed directly on the cement floor of the garage, below his father's workbench, a butcher's block of stinking chemicals and tiny gore). It was all for science, he declared. *Mad* science.

Our long summer afternoons of dismemberment and murder were inspired in part by a lavish black-and-white photo book owned by Phil's father entitled *The Horrors of War: Europe and the Pacific, 1939–1945.* "The gory book," as we called it, showed the human damage the newspapers of the era would have never allowed: torsos opened sternum to belly, like wet valises; soldiers holding up for the camera their souvenirs—an ear, fingers, a foot. The image that excited Phil most depicted Japanese infantry standing over ditches with shovels, burying old men alive in Manchuria. One afternoon, he suggested that we bury Benny alive in our backyard. I reminded him that if we buried Benny, we would just be acting like the enemy.

Some confusion frequently arose regarding Benny's identity—friend or foe? But then, our entire neighborhood had been founded upon the complex shifting allegiances of international enmity. Jefferson Manor owed its existence to El Alamein, Monte Cassino, Normandy, Okinawa. We acknowledged this complicated debt through the games we played, aiming a straightened arm like a standard issue M1 rifle, sounding the boom, and expecting from the other side the cooperation of immediate, artful death. For hours we practiced dying, conferring presence upon the battle tales we had heard all our lives from our fathers and uncles.

Most deadly marksmanship involved the upper body; the heart was a magnet for mortal injury. I made a study of grabbing my chest at its misplaced center, shrieking and falling backwards, allowing my head to hit and bounce several times upon the spongy dichondra. I practiced writhing on the cement sidewalk like bacon. We all draped our corpses like strings of Christmas popcorn over the bright young juniper and honeysuckle bushes planted by our mothers, across the new red-brick flower beds erected by our fathers, until watchful parents stormed out of the house to order us back to life and into somebody else's yard for a change. We died all day and into the early evening after dinner. Yet the nationality of the lifeless young bodies scattered across the lawns and sidewalks remained vague and troubling.

Which war, exactly, were we playing? There had been two big world wars, we knew; then over time, we heard about quite a few more. The Chestnut brothers, Vincent and Daniel, came from Tennessee, and they always wanted to wage a Civil War in which the Confederacy improbably won. It was safer to be a dead German. At play in suburbia, a dead German was as common as a dead Indian. When somebody dragged in the Russians or the Chinese or the Greeks because of a grandmother or weird aunt with troubling stories to tell about firing squads, famine, or even more incomprehensible civil wars in foreign places where nobody even spoke English, the results were complicated and unsatisfying, and soon peace was proclaimed. We all returned home for dinner and the war that still raged in tract-home suburbia settled back down until another day.

* * *

My uncle Win despised our most righteous warrior, General Douglas MacArthur.

"Dugout Doug!"

He was shouting over a sirloin steak in our small dining room. My father had just informed Win that MacArthur would have made an excellent president, a proposition Dad believed no more than he expected Win to suddenly sprout wings and flap out the bay window.

"*President* MacArthur!" objected Win. "It turns my stomach to even think about it."

Mom splattered a dollop of instant mashed potatoes on Win's plate, hoping there would not be a fight. I glanced at my father as he frowned to himself and schemed. My uncle believed all the stories about MacArthur drowning his wife's lover in a Philippine swimming pool and evacuating Corregidor with a refrigerator full of wild pheasant and a mattress stuffed with gold coins. A battle, I knew, could not be avoided.

"MacArthur saved you swabbies," said Dad, striking first.

Win gaped at the instant mashed potatoes in horror as though their rising white mounds might contain the General himself. "Like hell, Slick!"

"Don't you swear in my house!" Dad hammered the edge of his plate with the blade of his knife. It chimed raggedly. "Profanity," he explained, slicing off a jagged strip of sirloin steak and waving it in the air like a head on a pike, "is the sign of a crude person that can't express himself."

"That son of a bitch bastard," Win said calmly, "can burn forever in fucking hell."

Mom turned in my direction. "If you're done eating," she said, "you can go outside now and play."

I shook my head and studied Dad, who was studying the situation. He was a keen strategist of the household skirmish, a Rommel of contrariness.

"Slick," pleaded Win, "you think about how he fired on the

bonus marchers back in Washington in 1932. Veterans themselves. You remember that? The bastard."

"Don't you use that word in my house!"

"I didn't mean nothing."

"What *is* a bastard?" I wondered.

"Shut up," explained Dad.

"Can't we just have a nice dinner?" asked my mother, really pleading to herself.

"You don't remember it," argued my father. "You weren't there."

"You saying it didn't happen?"

"Yes, of course it happened. Sweet Jesus, didn't you ever read a newspaper in all those years? Or were you too busy getting yourself in trouble?"

Win gathered his wits; he contemplated retreat.

"Anyway, what do you have against him?" My father set down his fork and knife on either side of the plate, framing the meat and the mounds of instant mashed potatoes, a portrait of postwar dinner perfection. "What personal harm did the man ever do you?" He sensed his brother's weakness and prodded. "*Well?*"

Win took a bite of sirloin and chewed. He swallowed. He turned to me and smiled sadly. "In New Guinea," he began, rousing himself to the effort of recalling the worst time of his life, "everybody I ever talked to—and I swear to God this is true, Little Slick—they all said MacArthur kept a private cow all to himself so he could drink cold, fresh milk when the ordinary soldiers didn't have nothing."

There was the opening. My father grinned in triumph.

"He never had a cow."

"How do you know that?"

"MacArthur had no cow." Dad pushed his plate away, and wiped his mouth with a paper napkin. He drew a deep breath and exhaled his satisfaction, in effect declaring victory. "And even if he did, how could he keep the milk cold?"

"You admit it!"

"Having a cow in New Guinea or not having a cow in New

Guinea, cows being neither here nor there," my father reasoned, "is a big fat NOTHING! I wouldn't have *ever* voted for MacArthur, for better reasons than a cow."

"Name one." His appetite ruined, Win still clung valiantly to the cow.

"Like the man can't obey an order. Like the crazy son of a bitch wanted to run our army over the border into Red China during Korea, despite what Truman told him. Maybe blow up the whole damn world. Win, livestock just doesn't enter into the picture."

My uncle silently regarded my father, this monument of opposition.

"Goddamn it, Slick, sometimes I don't even know where you stand."

"Good," replied Dad. "That's the way I like it."

✦ ✦ ✦

One afternoon, we met in the park directly around the corner from my house to examine the gory book for the hundredth time. We sprawled across the grass beneath a budding elm tree, poring for a full hour over the volume's illustrated atrocities.

The carnage was thrilling: splinters of leg bones erupting through skin like a cracked baseball bat, a head held by its hair—all the body parts Win said they always left out. Then we got distracted when a basset hound dashed past with his owner in pursuit, the dog chasing a squirrel up a branch of the elm. I settled back on the lawn, hands locked behind my head, and examined the clouds scattered across the blue sky like pieces of a puzzle. The ancient world of our fathers receded from interest.

Finally, Benny rose from the grass to affirm his boredom. He produced a jackknife from his jeans front pocket, admitting that he had pirated it from his dad's toolbox. Benny flung the knife into the elm. Cursing under his breath, pretending to have in his clutches Hirohito himself, he attacked the tree repeatedly. He completely stripped the bark off one side, and then I joined him for the remainder. A small, pleasant lifetime passed. Eventually, the Mad Professor located a two-page spread showing the American troops liberating Dachau. He flagged it above his head, attempting to revive our enthusiasm. Phil passed me the book, and I stared in silent disbelief at its pages, the starving, hollow-eyed men and women with arms and legs like broomsticks staring back at me. Bodies were stacked up in the distance, as Win had described, like firewood. My mouth fell open with guilty wonder.

"My uncle was a war hero," I blurted out in response to this horror beyond comprehension, this impossibility. "His ship was bombed at Pearl Harbor."

My declaration seemed to clear the air, the stench of cruelty dissipated amid some vague condition of valor.

Benny leaned into Phil's lap, reached for the book, and flipped wildly through its pages until he found a section titled "Blood-and-Guts-Soaked Sand: The Battle for the Pacific." The chapter opened with a two-page spread picturing the flamboyant devastation of Pearl Harbor.

"There's my uncle's ship," I stated, pointing impulsively to the largest vessel in the photograph. Flames licked its deck, and terrific columns of water thrust up from either side like cyclones lunging up from the depths of the sea. On the shore, Marines pinged their rifles at the Japanese Zeroes, the circles under the aircrafts' wings radiating a nauseating red glow. The skies seemed streaked with paint, buckets of black, white, and gray poured down from the heavens. A brilliant puff of smoke rose to cover the flat, orange disc illuminating the Pacific, and all around the harbor, the water was burning.

"Did everybody on his ship drown?" asked Benny.

I took a stab at how catastrophe actually unfolds. "About half."

Phil studied the photograph, searching for flaws. "Getting sunk," he finally decided, "doesn't necessarily mean you're a hero. My dad was a war hero and he was never sunk."

Benny pried his eyes away from the photographs.

"Does your dad have a bunch of tattoos? Was he captain of a ship?"

"No, but he was once secretary to a guy who worked for an admiral."

Benny's lips puckered into a puzzle of disappointment: "*Secretary?*"

"My uncle was sunk twice. After Pearl Harbor, they fixed up his ship, sailed out into the Pacific to chase the Japs, and he got sunk again. The second time, his ship went straight to the bottom of the ocean."

The phrase hung in the air—*straight to the bottom.* I shifted my eyes towards Phil and saw him silently calculating: did getting sunk twice unavoidably equal a hero?

"So how did your uncle get out of there alive?" asked Benny, still poised for admiration.

The night of the battle, Win had told me, was starless and cold. Twenty months after Pearl Harbor, in the Solomon Islands between Kolombangara and New Georgia, at the Battle of Kula Gulf, a Japanese destroyer hit his ship shortly past two in the morning, firing three consecutive twenty-four-inch torpedoes, tearing off the bow. After the explosion and the sudden jolt, the screech of metal folding in upon itself, Win could see only smoke, gray over black. Then the sky lit up with returning volleys of fire and in the suffocating haze he heard feet tripping upon the deck. Orders to haul down the lifeboats. The wrenching whine of metal, the disintegration of the superstructure. Orders to abandon ship.

In the water, the blackness was relieved only by the light of burning cargo, the percussive eruption of munitions. Win clung to a hot shard of the bow. Pools of oil boiled around him. In another instant, he was swept by the current into the astonishing chill of the ocean. Within twenty-five minutes, the ship tipped, pointed its stern to the cloudy night sky, and sank straight to the bottom of the ocean. Win passed the night in the water, paddling slowly towards the distant shore.

Throughout his life, my uncle was prepared to relate these events in hungry detail. But what happened on the island constituted another matter.

One hundred and sixty men struggled to ground, riding buoyant slivers of wreckage or swimming two full miles to the island of Vella Lavella, north of Kolombangara. They hid in the jungle from Japanese scouts, sheltered by Australian coast watchers who had been protected themselves for two years by the native islanders, who despised the invaders. The islanders instructed the sailors how to catch, cook, and eat snakes and lizards. How to identify the venomous species. How to bury your dead at sea during the night undetected. The skies shone pink and purple, the sea smelled of rosewater. The squawk of cockatoos made sunrise roil with music.

In the late afternoons, Win recalled, there were butterflies the size of both his hands—thumbs met, fingers spread wide. Queen Victoria's birdwings, they were called; splotches of yellow, black, and seaweed-green flitting down from the trees. They looked like rainbows peeled from the azure sky, their paisley patterns melting in the sun. The butterflies' wingspans measured 250 millimeters. Win had looked them up after returning home, to make certain they were real.

A few days before a half-dozen US destroyers dashed up the Solomon slot from Tulagi to rescue the ship's survivors, the sailors at last encountered the enemy. The Aussies had shared their rifles and knives; the sailors killed three Japanese scouts close to camp and wounded another, an officer they took prisoner who chattered day and night in chirpy, agonized English. After two days, the guards drew straws to take the prisoner into the jungle and kill him.

I always imagined that my uncle had been the one to cut the prisoner's throat, though he would never say one way or the other.

I concentrated on the scores of black-and-white images, searching for Win's face amid the legions of young sailors, soldiers, and Marines. I almost expected to find Win smiling back to me through the years—bloodied, vengeful, triumphant, gloriously alive.

"Look," said Phil, reading my mind, "there's your uncle!" His eyelashes batted madly.

"Where?"

Phil had flipped to a full-page photo of four Marines, backs turned to the camera, scrambling in formation across a windswept beach. In the near distance, three spindly palm trees fluttered and bowed, indicating the cover the men sought under fire.

Phil squealed, "He's running away from the Japs!"

You couldn't see their faces. Just four fleeing bodies, backs bent, their long legs in half-stride, arms swinging a spade or gripped around a rifle stock. Desperate young men in uniform: they could have been anybody's uncle, and in another instant they might die.

I craned my neck over Phil's lap and stared at the photograph. Four young men doing what they had to do, which was run like hell. If they survived, they might have returned home to build our houses and pave our streets. They were so foreign and so familiar. They were our fathers and uncles, our neighbors, and this photograph contained some part of their story that could never be conveyed: the indisputable terror borne on the other side of the world when they had been preposterously young.

"Let me see," I demanded, reaching for the book.

"No!" shouted the Mad Professor. He gripped his corner and yanked, and I felt the binding tremble before it separated, the paper screeching like a frenzied animal.

The book tore in two, dividing straight down its center, and we each held half in our hands. Phil gasped, straining to comprehend the mystery of this familiar object now occupying two places at once. Shaking off disbelief, he swept my portion into his own hands, clapped the two halves together, and gingerly set the broken book under the shade of the elm like a wounded bird.

And the next thing I knew, his small, balled-up fist was very quickly and very forcefully driving its knuckles into my face, knocking me flat on the ground.

✦ ✦ ✦

"So tell me, Little Slick." Win grinned at my eye. "Just how big was the kid who gave you the shiner?"

I tried to grin back since I seemed to have something to be proud of.

"I don't know." I shrugged manfully.

My left eye had already swollen shut, surrounded by the immediate blue bruise.

"Here," he coaxed, "like this." Win paced out a defensive stance figuring a three-quarter moon on his living room carpet. He smelled faintly of Old Times. "Hold your fists in front of your face. Don't worry what you look like."

I raised my fists to guard my chin and checked my stance in the picture window mirror. I looked terrific.

"No, no, this way," said Win. His own fists rose like two big cannons.

I had headed straight to Win's house, knowing there would be no sympathy for me at home if I told Dad how I got my black eye. The bruising would have only elicited commentary about the sanctity of other people's property, reflecting finally on my own irresponsibility. Win sized up the world with fewer complications.

"That's right," he instructed, "but higher." My uncle cocked his head, studying my hands.

Then he faked with his right, bobbled his shoulders to either side, thrust his jaw forward with that tricky elastic drop of the head he had perfected as a Navy brawler, and ploughed his left fist into my midsection.

Stretched out face-up and flattened upon the living room carpet, I could not catch my breath. The world concentrated in my solar plexus. I pleaded for air. I tried to shout that I was okay: I was more than okay, I was happy, I was great, I was just a kid sparring with my uncle, a war hero. But I could only bleat gamely and gaze up at the ceiling.

In my airless bubble, I watched my uncle hovering above me—his fat, stinking cigar plugged into his cockeyed grin, his hardy snowman's face rearranged into a lopsided, crew-cut, bourbon-flushed, broken-nosed disaster. Win must have been forty by then. Still trim, fit, rippling with muscles; still working the line at the cannery, stacking boxes ten hours each night during peach and tomato season. He would have enjoyed a son of his own to jab and dodge and merrily punch in the stomach.

I wriggled across the carpet on my back and propped up my elbows on either side, lifting my chest six inches from the floor.

"Now get up and take a poke at me."

I leapt to my feet and swung wildly.

"That's right, but higher."

I swung, and he brushed my fist away.

"Again."

I laughed and swung deliriously and missed by a mile.

"*Again!*"

I swung again, the same wobbly trajectory. But harder this time. I nicked his open palm.

"You know Philip Barnes?" I asked Win, easing into the specifics of retaliation. My chest rose and fell with heavy breaths. It rose and fell.

"No."

"Yes," I insisted, "you do. Phil. My friend."

Win peered down at me over his often-broken nose. "You mean that little goofy kid with the glasses?"

"He's a year older than me," I corrected. And then to make certain that Win was still on my side, I unforgivably added, "Mr. Barnes is his dad."

"Barnes?"

Lloyd Barnes was one of the neighborhood's eternal veterans, a fusty little man with the trim build of a cat and a brown moustache penciled over his upper lip in the exacting manner of Alec

Guinness in *The Bridge on the River Kwai*. Win worked with him at the cannery and he despised him.

"He was secretary to an admiral."

"*Sec*-re-tary!" Win thrust forward his jaw, instinctively baring his teeth, and I knew I had maneuvered him back into my corner. Win hated officers. To my uncle, an officer was any guy in a uniform or suit who gave orders and liked it, who believed that command was his right and duty. Throughout the war, Win had back-talked, taunted, and spit in the direction of the young junior naval officers who passed their time in the splintering shack barrooms of Olongapo and Honolulu. He had cheerfully spread the rumor among local girls in Pacific port cities that the blue sash on an officer's jacket meant he had contracted syphilis.

I delivered a solid little punch to my uncle's ribs and stepped back, dropping my hands, admiring the damage.

"Now that was a nice tap," he admitted, grinning through a flicker of pain. He eased to the ground in a crouch, gently squaring my shoulders in his two big hands. He looked straight into my eyes. "When I know I'm going to have to fight somebody," he explained solemnly, his breathing a little faster, a little deeper, "I hit him first and square on. Then get the hell out." He caressed my cheek with his fingertips, his callused thumb brushing too close to the puckered blue fringe of my eye.

I flinched.

"Did I hurt you?" he asked.

I shook my head.

"I know it's hard to stand up right away when somebody's knocked you down. But you got to do it, or they won't never leave you alone. You understand?"

I tried to envision the Mad Professor as a dangerous aggressor, a threat to our suburb's tranquility.

"You understand me?" demanded Win.

I nodded, realizing that on this point at least my father would have readily agreed. At times, you had to take a stand and what happened next didn't really matter. After that, my uncle was speaking entirely for himself.

"Don't wear your Keds. Borrow some work boots, if you can get 'em. Mine are too big for you, so don't give me that look. Now listen. First step you take, you stomp on the little bastard's ankle as hard as you can, maybe you break it."

This prospect made me smile, it made me breathe a little faster.

"It's fair," Win assured me. "Everything's fair, if the son of a bitch thinks he rules the world."

• • •

The next day, I located Phil in the park, flicking Benny's jack-knife into the elm.

"Your eye's really big," he said, turning from the tree's branching shadow to face me. I stood an arm's length while he scrutinized my damaged face as though it were the map of an amazing country.

"I know." I tried to interpret Phil's interest as a formal apology and I thought for a moment that we could forget the whole thing. The sprinklers were twirling full-blast, the scent of damp concrete rising off the ground. Then I wondered if he was making fun of me.

"You deserved it," Phil said flatly. He pivoted and flung the jackknife into the heart of the elm. The blade lodged in the wood and trilled; the handle vibrated. He had probably already told his father about the gory book, blaming Benny and me for everything.

"You want to fight?" I demanded.

He studied the knife in the tree.

"No."

And then, more obligingly, "Do you?"

I didn't answer.

Along the park's perimeter, at the edge of the lawn maybe fifty yards away, stood a row of white and gray stucco houses with the occasional frantic pastel trim, the aggregate riches of Jefferson Manor—the name itself intended to suggest both patriotism and refinement. The houses faced either west or south but otherwise looked exactly the same. A man ambled across the roof of a gray one, a tool belt strapped around his overalls, a hammer dangling from one hand. He gazed off into the sky, contemplating the clouds or the setting sun or maybe the flock of gulls sailing overhead towards the landfill shore of the bay. He balanced like a sailor on a great ship's rolling deck, rocked by the waves as he gazed out at the ocean beneath the burning sun. He looked like somebody waiting for the enemy, certain they were coming.

"Look," said the Mad Professor, withdrawing the jackknife from the tree's wound. The blade glistened with sap. "Benny let me take his knife home to sharpen it. It wouldn't cut anything before. Now watch."

He selected from a dangling leaf of the elm a fat, fuzzy black caterpillar with a brown-orange stripe running down its back. He tenderly placed the caterpillar on the trunk of the tree and drew the blade across its middle, dividing the insect cleanly. It wriggled with the madness of pain. Both halves still clung to the bark.

The Mad Professor and I had in the past extinguished a small nation of insects. But what flitted through my mind now were the Queen Victoria's birdwings on Vella Lavella, black, yellow, and seaweed-green, with wingspans the size of two hands. In our own living room, Win had shown me the butterflies in the pages of the *World Book Encyclopedia*. He had seen them himself, gloriously alive, when he was young.

"You shouldn't hurt them," I told the Mad Professor, pointing to the caterpillar smeared across the flaking bark. "They turn into something beautiful."

"This one won't."

So I stepped hard on Phil's left foot and struck him somewhere in the face, knocking off his glasses. His nose gushed blood, instantly soaking his cotton shirt. Then I swung at him a lot, though I was aiming pretty wildly. He went down waving his arms, slicing the air and missing me entirely. I fell too, and then more hands slashed at the air, both of us forgetting to clench our fists.

We rolled across the lawn, our legs entangled like trellis vines. When we scraped to a sudden stop, Phil started to cough and wheeze, struggling for breath, and then his face flushed scarlet and he looked terrified.

I threw my weight upon him, pinned him to the ground, my knees upon his shoulders, my hands locating his throat. I could feel the breath of his entire body rasping in my grip, chirping like an insect. I wanted to cry, a rage of tears.

"Give!" I barked into Phil's face. My spittle basted his pink cheeks. I gouged both thumbs into the hard pulp center of his throat.

"*Give*!" I pleaded.

Phil wagged his head, shut his eyes.

I kept squeezing, harder still, and then with a shriek all the air leaked out from my chest and I knew that I was going to be the one who surrendered. I rolled off Phil, collapsing flat on my back alongside him, arms and legs flapped across the lawn. The scent of wet concrete filled the air like poison gas. I didn't know that I was crying until I stopped.

Our chests rose and fell. I listened to Phil breathing and I knew he was listening to me. Later—how many dreamy seconds?—I turned my head towards the row of identical houses, and I spotted the man in the overalls now back on his roof, obliviously inspecting his chimney, not even looking in our direction. I felt ashamed—insufficient to the task that circumstance had set before me. Not a killer. Not yet.

Phil rolled closer to me and whispered, "You're bleeding."

I inspected the small gash across my knuckles.

"I couldn't breathe," he explained. He wiped the damp from around his eyes.

I had wanted to kill him and although I was glad that I had not, I did not regret the feeling. "You're bleeding, too." I pressed one finger against his cheek, holding it there for more than a moment too long.

The moon was beginning to rise over the elm though the sky was still light, the blue melting into indigo, a shade of the South Sea islands. We were lucky boys, beneficiaries of the remorseless young men who had incinerated the cities of Europe and Japan, conquered the world, constructed the present peace.

"If Benny wants to be one of us," said Phil, propping himself up on one elbow, "he'll need to slice open one of his veins with his Dad's knife. Then we'll see." He tossed one ankle over the other, fell back, and folded his hands behind his head, cozy and maniacal. "Blood brothers," he explained.

I could see some stars through the blue wooly sky as it began to fade to black. In another hour, there would be a million more; Jefferson Manor was still too small a place to wash away their glow. The heavens were as bright, cold, and untouchable as the sand-and-plaster sparkles of our living room ceilings. Later in the week, I might ask Win for another boxing lesson, and he would probably knock me to the ground, and I would struggle to stand up, breathless and safe at home.

* * * * *

Every morning, the alarm clock jangles, piercing the heart of dreamy dreams, and the working man reacts to the news of another day with a jolt of dread, his spine arching off the mattress like an electrocuted cat.

In the bathroom, he might forget it's Monday and lazy his way through a Sunday's-length shower, running late from the start.

For breakfast, the wife warms the toast and boils the coffee, letting the eggs form a pool of yolk that adheres to the prong of his fork like Elmer's glue. The clock above the table beats out seconds like a metronome. The working man tucks the lunch bucket under his arm and heads out to the street to wait for his carpool in the rain.

The new guy's driving. Nobody talks. He gets lost, since he doesn't know the shortcuts. For the last two miles, he speeds and corners desperately. The working man imagines what it would be like to die in a car crash on his way to work. He figures that it's better than dying in a car crash on his way home from work, thereby giving the sons of bitches eight hours on a paycheck he'll never see. He tells himself, Don't even start thinking about complaining.

You got yourself a steady job.

You got your own house now, paid for in thirty years.

You got a wife and some kids, and maybe that's a fine thing, too.

Time will pass.

The job is the job.

On break, the working man drinks a cup of burnt coffee from his thermos and reads yesterday's paper. Some clown from nightshift has crumpled up the sports page into a ball instead of folding it neatly and leaving it on the lunchroom table like a civilized human being. So the working man studies an article in the front section about a guy who finds ten thousand dollars buried in a shoe box in his backyard, but now the government says he's got to hand it over to the bank because they're the ones who really own the property.

Back on the job, which is always the job, time fails to pass. It's like watching the grass grow. It's like counting every blade of your front lawn on Sunday for no reason. It's like trimming them with your teeth. The working man just does his job. That's what everybody does except bums, drunks, and mental cases, know-nothings, losers, big-shot phonies, and guys in white shirts and ties who don't really work anyway, since nobody's making them punch a time clock or looking over their shoulder eight hours a day or telling them when to eat, drink, sit down, piss, and get off the pot. For a split second, the working man figures that the rest of the world's got it made, but he knows that's the biggest damn lie anybody could fall for.

The whistle blows. Some guys drop their tools and walk straight off the job without even cleaning up. They're not going to last, no way. The working man swabs clean all the tools he's used today with a fresh rag, returns them to the tool chest, and walks over to the washbasin, where he lathers up and scrubs his hands until they're almost clean too.

Everybody punches out. They file through the shop door. Somebody shouts out something funny and obscene, and the working man nods, raises one finger, and grins with relief because they're all crawling out from underneath the weight of the day. The carpool heads straight home without anybody telling the new guy how to get there.

In the kitchen, there's a hot meal on the table. Maybe it tastes pretty good. After dinner, he falls asleep in his chair with the front page collapsed over his face like a brick wall. He pries his eyes open for as long as he's able. He knows that when he rises from his chair and baby-steps down the hallway towards his bed and wife, he might as well figure it's practically time to start all over again.

That's why they call it work, and he's glad to have some.

TWO

Catechism

"I give that marriage one year," said the priest officiating at my parents' wedding. He whispered too loudly inside the vestry, where he had spirited away my mother's sister Edna, weary and pliable after her fourteen-hour, twin-engine prop flight across country. The priest's breath smelled of perfumed tobacco and sour mash, this old Irishman with the clickety-clack accent from Cork County—unsuitable for my mother's Calabrese family, but unopposable.

"Yes, Father," agreed Edna.

"Mark me," he declared, furious at her lack of fighting spirit. After instructing my father in the catechism for several months, he had come to expect from our family a degree of blasphemy and sacrilege. "Just one year, and then tragedy. But don't you come running to me when it happens."

"No, Father. I live in Boston, Father."

My parents had entered into a mixed marriage, defined in the early 1950s as Roman Catholic and anybody else—non-Catholics bound to stumble over essential matters of faith. To secure the union, my father was required to submit to instruction and raise any children, God willing, within the Church.

"Then you are not planning to become a Catholic?" the priest had asked on their first day together, straining to elicit a twinge of guilt.

"No, I am not," replied my father, flashing a whale of an ungracious grin.

"Then you are a convinced Protestant," the priest explained to both my father and mother, making an instant association between the Scandinavian last name and heresy.

Dad kept grinning. What could he say? That he was a confirmed evolutionist? An admirer of the great Charles Darwin, whose account of the origin of species and the descent of man he had read with eviscerating relish while resident for three and one-half years in the tuberculosis sanatorium? Since he wished to marry my mother, he did not. He withheld exposition on the fossil record, the global extinctions that had nothing whatsoever to do with Noah's flood, the righteous humiliation of Bishop Soapy Sam Wilberforce at the hand of Thomas Henry Huxley.

Nevertheless, my father's religious instruction, lasting twelve weeks prior to the banns of marriage, did not fare well.

"Your fiancé," the priest confided to my mother after Mass one morose Sunday, "has many unfortunate ideas irreconcilable with our faith."

"Yes, I know, Father."

"Does he often speak to you of the Spanish Inquisition?"

"Not often, Father."

"Or the Crusades and the burning of witches—really, such a very long time ago?"

"I know it was, Father. Only occasionally, Father."

During instruction, which lasted two hours each week on Wednesday evenings but seemed to the elderly priest to linger with purgatorial excess, my father would deviously redirect conversation regarding the seven sacraments and the mystery of the Trinity back towards the fiscal and carnal excesses of the Borgia popes. Dad praised Charles Stewart Parnell, modern Ireland's great patriot and adulterer. He speculated provocatively about the state of the souls of the era's famously Catholic tyrants: Batista, Perón, Franco, Somoza, Salazar.

"Was Mussolini a good Catholic?" he asked the old priest, studying the deliberate tick-tock of the large serpent-eyed wall clock. "I mean before the partisans strung him up on a meat hook in Milan?"

Dad's youthful illness had given him an opportunity to investigate the history of the church, which he had formerly regarded only as a vague historical malignancy, an attitude consonant with the low-key anti-popery of his immigrant family. During three years of study in the hospital library, he had encountered numerous specifics to inspire his wonder and contempt.

"Argentina could be rich!" he would shout at my mother over Sunday dinner, as though she were somehow in league with Eva Perón, plotting for the Southern Hemisphere's perennial instability. "The Argentinians have natural resources, labor, good weather. Everything they need, but unfortunately for them, they've got that church of yours, too."

"It's not just my church," she objected.

"Your whole damn family's church."

"It's also your son's church," replied my mother, and the burden of this galling fact toppled him into a bog of Nordic brooding.

The schism between my parents often meant that Sunday constituted a day of dispute, with my father holding forth on the crimes of itinerant friars who sold indulgences to poor French peasants in the thirteenth century, or the devastation of advanced cultures in Mexico and Peru at the hands of ignorant, superstitious conquistadors. When my mother's brothers and sisters visited from the east, he lectured with zest and wit regarding Garibaldi and his Redshirts marching against the Pope, implying that her side of the family must have likewise taken up arms. Too often on Sunday mornings, my mother and I would return home from Mass to find Dad cooking breakfast for the Jehovah's Witnesses, fattening them up for debate. Even these devoted evangelicals seldom stayed for longer than it took to consume a single cup of coffee, perhaps a piece of pointedly burnt toast, perceiving the granite rostrum upon which they would be forced to scatter the seeds of their faith.

"I personally believe that we are all cousins to the orangutans," Dad hollered from the front doorstep as the persecuted missionaries wended their way back down the suburban streets. "Now, what do you all have to say about that?" And then he turned to me, stationed at my mother's side, and he slowly unfurled his fingers, baring his palms in a shrug. I pictured Saint Thomas, the disciple and doubter, his hands probing Christ's wounds. And I knew that I would soon have to choose.

✦ ✦ ✦

In her lifetime's sole act of political conviction, my mother dedicated herself to the election of John F. Kennedy. She had absorbed the saga of Joe and Rose, the arrival of Jackie, the names of all the roving small children: the Luce publications' ideal of the world she had left behind in Massachusetts. Less conspicuously, she snuck glances at the bare-chested captain in the PT boat photo in *Life*, reminding herself that the gorgeous JFK was above all a good Catholic family man.

My father similarly inclined to the straight Democratic ticket, praising the memory of the TVA and WPA, recounting his own stint in the CCC. Nevertheless, he opposed Mom's dedication.

"As a government employee," he argued, "I can't go around electioneering every time I want to. It's against the law."

My father unrealistically pictured Mom passing out leaflets at the front gate of the Alameda Naval Air Station, where he worked as a metalsmith, or speechifying from her soapbox around the corner from our house in General George Patton Park: antics better suited to his own mother. In 1941 Dad's mother, Clara, had led a small part of the crowd in shouting down Charles Lindbergh at an America First rally in San Francisco's Union Square. She carried a placard urging the pilot to drop dead next time over the mid-Atlantic. Germany was menacing Norway, her birthplace, as everybody but that big simple Swede understood.

"It's not electioneering," responded Mom, "it's working for the best man. And *I'm* not a government employee."

"I don't want my wife making a spectacle of herself," Dad said as they argued in the living room, standing up—always a bad sign. They flanked the built-in bookcases stuffed with the volumes of presidential biographies that Dad had been reading in consecutive order since buying the house—self-improvement being the civic duty of all landed yeomen, as he had gleaned from the writings of Jefferson, our great agnostic. Dad was presently immersed in the life of Ulysses S. Grant.

"You can vote for whoever you want to," he said, "but you don't have to go advertising it to the world. That's what I'm saying."

My mother heaved and sighed, the sound of a locomotive whose churning is about to commence. In most paltry matters of national politics and world events, she acceded to the convictions of my father; but in this case, they were disputing an article of faith, her own area.

"It's because he's young, rich, good-looking, and Catholic," she declared, nailing down the point with a tragic certainty almost always held in reserve.

Dad passed a hand in front of his face, waving away the truth as though it were a mosquito. Then he drifted out to the garage and hid under the open hood of the car. Youth, riches, and good looks were bad enough, but when John F. Kennedy's faith and family were also sifted into the mix, Dad could not contain his resentment. Old man Joe Kennedy had been a bootlegger, a get-rich-quick mick whose Druidical grudge against the English had led him to recommend appeasement even before Munich. These Catholics, feared Dad, would plot and pray us all back to the Dark Ages. My father opposed anyone set against the English. They had fought on when nobody else could—a mighty, tight little island; they still made the best precision tools in the world. They had given his mother her first home after leaving Norway.

Even worse, Kennedy, like my mother, hailed from the East—the opposite of the West, and therefore its adversary. The East was where most of this nation's shady deals had been concocted. (You could read about them in *Ulysses S. Grant.*) This domain of the East, with its antiquated privilege and insinuations of superiority, was no place for a working man. Certainly my father would support Kennedy; Kennedy was the best man. But there would be no crucifixes hanging in our front room, no visiting Belfast priests over for Sunday dinner with their malarkey about the English and a republican bomb gripped tight under the swish of their black skirts. No treason, no Pope-kissing. No genuflections to the Eastern temples of finance and theft.

"Well, I don't care what you say," concluded my mother. "I'm going to work for Kennedy and that's all."

Mom joined a campaign committee unofficially formed from the Women's Auxiliary of the Legion of Catholic Decency. At St. Bernard's, our neighborhood church, the congregation took pains not to discuss the election openly. Father McBain, our pastor, had spoken of the spies among us; we need not mention their names. Mom's own family hailed from the toe of the boot and she explained to me who the priest was cautioning us against: the people her parents called "the Americans."

The Americans were Protestants, backyard barbecuers, devotees of the hillbilly ballad. They had occupied this country for three hundred years. They had massacred the Indians, invented the Stock Exchange, covered the nation in billboards and pavement; they owned everything. America was a Protestant nation, but now we were going to have a Catholic president. I tried to imagine my father, technically Protestant, in the guise of our masters—an intimate of Henry Ford Jr. and Dean Acheson; the secret owner of a silk hat. The picture would not hold.

My uncle Win, who had served four years in the Pacific and remembered several courageous Catholic chaplains, did not find my mother's faith malign or ridiculous. Indeed, if he believed Kennedy to be the surrogate of Rome, he still preferred him unequivocally—and not merely because Nixon was campaigning for president as an officer by waving around those pictures of himself in his Navy dress blues. Kennedy had been an officer, too. ("Hell," said Uncle Win, "did you really think they would ever let an enlisted man run for president?") But JFK portrayed himself as a swabby, and so Win also approved of *Life's* skinny, bare-chested photo from PT-109. Kennedy seemed like a guy who'd stand you a drink on leave. Plus, his old man made the stuff. Uncle Win and Aunt Tina were the first in our neighborhood to sink a Kennedy sign into their front lawn.

When Mom brought home a sign of her own, Dad resisted passionately, defending the property like Gregory Peck in *Pork Chop Hill*.

"Half the yard is mine," he reminded Mom. "I won't have you poking around in there and ruining the grass."

"Then I'll put it in my half."

A ridiculous argument: How should they divide the front lawn—top and bottom halves, like a layer cake, or straight down the middle? Did my father get to say whether a campaign sign went into the front lawn because he mowed it, or did my mother control the area because she watered it? Two weeks of undiluted enmity. Finally, they reached a compromise. They agreed that one large rectangular campaign sign, royal blue and white, reading KENNEDY FOR PRESIDENT! would be posted squarely in the center of the backyard lawn, where nobody could see it.

Then Lloyd Barnes, our neighbor who my father despised, plastered four NIXON/LODGE stickers across his emerald Pontiac's fat rear bumper, and Dad thought he saw the opportunity to patch things up. He retaliated against Barnes, moving KENNEDY FOR PRESIDENT! out onto the front lawn and tilting the sign so that whenever our neighbor opened his curtains, its banner blared into his living room. But too much between my parents had already been said, and not said. Mom worked three days a week at the campaign headquarters, while Dad pretended not to notice. Their dispute did not conclude.

✦ ✦ ✦

My mother still talked about San Francisco, her first refuge upon moving west right after the war. Cast off now in remote suburbia, she fondly called it The City—a place lost forever amid billowing shrouds of fog and miasmic fable. Occasionally, she allowed herself to pine for its unmatched glamour, grateful for its willingness to allow a young single woman to thrive on her own.

At the start of her new life, she had rented a room with a Murphy bed and hot plate in a small hotel a twenty-five-minute walk from her job in the secretarial pool at Red Cross. From her apartment on upper Jones Street, the climb to Nob Hill was pitched at an angle so severe that the tiny Filipino women toting in either hand their brushes and rags on the way to housekeeping at the Mark Hopkins looked as though their foreheads might pitch forward to kiss the concrete by the time they reached the top at California Street. On her own way home, Mom passed Union Square and regularly crossed Stockton to window-shop at the City of Paris, thrilled like a child every Christmas season by the glitter of the forty-foot tree rocketing up from the department store mezzanine—chastened only by the dome's stained-glass illumination of a galleon sailing forlornly across the ocean, as far as could be imagined from home.

On Sundays, she attended High Mass at Old Saint Mary's, with the perfume of charred incense so sickly sweet and coagulant that she had to cover her face with a cotton handkerchief and stifle a cough when the priest passed her aisle swinging the censer by its plump gold chain. She beat her heart three times and bowed her head as Mexican altar boys rattled their bells and challenged the congregation to awaken and be born anew amid their lustrous surroundings. After Mass, the Wyman Club served black coffee and jelly doughnuts in the arctic basement, and invariably a recently demobbed soldier or sailor asked for her phone number—who could afford one?—and so she wandered unaccompanied down Kearny or Grant, rapturously mute amid the heathen Chinese and their gobbling commerce, the screech of their two-stringed violins and the sidewalk smells from their kitchens like sweet sticky rice and soiled laundry, which is to say unfamiliar and enthralling. In North Beach, she listened to harsh and affectionate words bellowed in the household rhythms of Naples, Catanzaro, Reggio, Palermo. Old men like her father back in Boston's North End perseverated all morning over an espresso and a slice of *cuccia* on Saint Lucy's Day. Old women in black like her dozen aunts, fierce widows by the age of forty, crossed themselves against *malocchio,* the evil eye, their index fingers and pinkies extended quakingly like a pair of horns to signify the *mano cornuta,* their feat of spell-breaking punctuated by a sudden gob of spit on the sidewalk. In the evening, even on a Tuesday or Wednesday, she might sieve through the theatergoers crowding the sidewalk in front of the Curran on Geary Street, enraptured by their selfish, stylish whirl, privileged to feel a part of the anonymous city and never guessing that another person—my father, for instance, who she had yet to meet—might be piling up resentments over the fancy men and their women in ostrich-plumed hats who didn't have to rise for work the next morning and punch in before dawn.

In fact, once discharged from the TB ward, Dad went to the theater on his own whenever opportunity and two bucks extra made it possible. He saw John Barrymore in *Richard III*. When Barrymore launched into his closing soliloquy amid the carnage of kingly ambition, bodies strewn about the stage, his realm in ruins, he cried out in a voice like tempered steel: "A horse, a horse, my kingdom for a horse!" The fellow sitting next to Dad—a portly schmo in a seersucker suit, stinking of gin with every rasping breath—laughed. He laughed at John Barrymore. The great actor glared in their direction, prompting my father to sink into his seat as though it was a pit of quicksand, and

Barrymore thundered: "No, by God, no horse this evening. I will saddle yonder braying ass!"

"Such language," remarked Mom whenever Dad told this story, which he had in truth merely read and lifted directly from Gene Fowler's 1944 biography of Barrymore. He wagged his head, another two inches of distance separating their view of what in this world might be worth remembering and what had to be confabulated.

✦ ✦ ✦

At St. Bernard's, the priests and nuns remained scrupulously noncommittal. Addressing a classroom of nonvoting elementary school children, Sister Henrietta, the fat and sad Portuguese nun whose own personal cross was teaching the public school boys whose parents did not love God enough to send their children to St. Bernard's parochial school, nevertheless stipulated that we should never, ever visit a Protestant church—the presumptive recruiting grounds of the Nixon campaign. And why would we want to? Didn't we belong to the one true faith? What possible reason (what perverse desire?) would tempt holy young Catholic boys and girls to spend any more time than they already must among the Protestants, those weaker vessels of Christian duty who replaced study of the Latin breviary with Sunday school coloring books glorifying the antics of John Wesley; who divorced one another right and left like slavish imitators of Elizabeth Taylor and Eddie Fisher, whose movies were proscribed by the Catholic Index; who had precipitated hundreds of years of completely unnecessary religious war to prove a minor point or two; and who now voted Republican?

"There was a young boy," said Father McBain, lecturing our catechism class one Saturday morning in the crisp days of early autumn, his voice already froggy with the season. "And he was a very holy and pious young boy."

Father McBain did not look at me. I presumed he knew something of my patrimony.

"He was so holy," explained Father McBain, "that when he was delivering his newspapers each day on his daily newspaper delivery route, he would with every newspaper he delivered whisper to himself, very piously, 'Jesus, Mary, and Joseph.'"

Father McBain removed a white handkerchief from the billows of his gown, draped it over his huge red bugle of a nose, and blew tremendously.

"Now this very holy boy," Father continued, "he had—oh, I don't know, he had three hundred homes to deliver newspapers to each day. And with each and every house, he said quietly to himself, 'Jesus, Mary, and Joseph.'" Father McBain repeated: "'Jesus, Mary, and Joseph.' Three hundred houses."

We nodded piously, and waited, and stirred.

"Now all of the newspaper delivery boys in this town had entered a contest," Father finally explained, "and they were in the contest to see who could get the greatest number of new subscribers and thereby win a trip to Disneyland. Now this very pious young Catholic boy had never been to Disneyland. But he very, very, *very* much wanted to go. Still, he knew that his parents were ordinary people like us all, and what money they did make had to go first to feed and clothe the pious young boy and his six brothers and a sister and send them all to a very good parochial school."

"Father, Father!" exploded Nicky LeRoux, waving his hand under the priest's crimson nose. "Father?"

"Yes, my child?"

"What was the school called, Father?"

Father McBain looked puzzled. He withdrew his handkerchief, mashed it into his face, and issued another blast. When he turned to Sister Henrietta, she winced—assuming she was supposed to know.

"It was called Saint Henrietta's," explained Father McBain.

Nicky laughed, but the rest of us kept quiet, since we could not tell if Father McBain was making a joke. Father did not usually make jokes. Sister Henrietta appeared pleased and confused.

"So this very pious and holy young Catholic newspaper

delivery boy—did I mention all the other delivery boys were Protestants?—he got up an hour earlier every morning so that he could get all the subscriptions he could manage."

"Father, Father!" demanded Nicky, stretching his hand towards heaven.

"Yes, child."

"What time did he get up, Father?"

"He got up at five," said Father McBain.

"Father, Father!"

"What?"

"You mean he went around to people's houses at five in the morning and asked them if they wanted to subscribe to his newspaper?"

Father McBain froze. He paused for a moment to consult himself, his own great authority, and then answered sharply: "Sister!" Sister Henrietta strode to Nicky's desk, strapped her large, fleshy hand around the boy's biceps, and elevated him from his chair. Nicky's legs scissored in space. The pair moved quickly across the room, the door slammed, Nicky was gone.

"Every morning," explained Father McBain, "this very pious and quiet and obedient young Catholic boy got up an hour early to pray to Jesus, Mary, and Joseph to help him do better each day, after school, which is when he would go to people's homes and ask them to subscribe to the newspaper. He prayed for a full hour. *Before* he went to school."

We all nodded mutely, very piously and obediently.

Sister Henrietta slipped back into the room, alone. Father McBain continued: "Now for many months, this young boy worked hard to increase his number of newspaper subscribers. Soon he was saying 'Jesus, Mary, and Joseph' four hundred times." Father repeated: "Four hundred subscribers. 'Jesus, Mary, and Joseph' four hundred times. Any questions?"

Sister Henrietta ordered: "Say, 'No, thank you, Father.'"

"No," we chanted, "thank you, Father!"

"So the pious and holy young Catholic newspaper delivery

boy wins the contest," Father McBain rolled on, growing impatient now with the time it took to apprise public school children of the facts of Catholic life. "He gets the most subscriptions. He gets many, many more subscriptions than the young Protestant delivery boys. Now he is saying 'Jesus, Mary, and Joseph' six hundred times. Every day. And he is especially thankful because he knows he will get to go to Disneyland soon. But two days before he is supposed to leave on an airplane with all the other newspaper delivery boys from his state who had won the contests in their own towns—and they were all *Protestants*!—the pious young boy was delivering the last newspaper on his route when his bicycle's front wheel skidded on a banana peel. The boy fell off, and he broke his leg."

We gasped. How could this happen?

"How could this happen?" asked Father McBain, establishing priestly intercession with our thoughts before they floated off to heaven. "The young boy wondered, too. At first. But then he told himself, while he was waiting for the doctor in the hospital to fix his leg—and it was very, *very* painful—if Jesus, Mary, and Joseph don't want me to go to Disneyland, then they must have their own reasons and it's not my place to question them. And his leg stopped hurting right then, even before he was treated by the doctor, who was a very handsome young Catholic doctor and a graduate of Notre Dame."

We all waited, and then we waited. It didn't seem like Father was finished. He just stood there smiling. Since Nicky wasn't around, I raised my hand.

"Yes, child?"

"Is that the end of the story, Father?"

"No, child, it is not." Father McBain took this opportunity to again trumpet his nose—one, two, three brassy heralds! "Because the next day, when the pious and obedient young Catholic delivery boy woke up, his mother rushed into his bedroom with that morning's edition of his very own newspaper. And sitting up in bed, he read the front-page story telling all about how, the night before, the airplane flying to Disneyland had crashed into a mountain. And all of the Protestant newspaper delivery boys were instantly killed!"

"So who put that banana peel under his front tire?" asked Sister Henrietta.

"Jesus, Mary, and Joseph, Sister!"

* * *

After her mother died, my mother could not stop crying. She was thirty-five years old, living in Roslindale, Massachusetts, the family's last unmarried child left at home after the end of the war. She cried every day and night for eight months, indulging in long showers during the morning to hush up the sound, taking long, winding, tearful walks alone at night after work, where she had spent much of the day unproductively crying at her desk or crying in the bathroom during breaks and lunchtime. She was employed by the Veterans Administration, shelving files containing accounts of the soldiers and sailors who for want of their arms or legs or something less tangible could not readjust. Her office friends told her that all this crying just wasn't normal. A Jewish girl she hardly knew more helpfully handed her the name of a psychiatrist. My mother visited the psychiatrist three times, but she did not stop crying. Finally, the psychiatrist suggested she talk to a priest.

The priest was a middle-aged Ulsterman named Father Keneally. At some point during the early 1940s, members of Father Keneally's congregation had complained to the bishop that they too often found their priest hiding in the confessional with a bottle of scotch, refusing to acknowledge their presence on the other side. "Bless me, Father, for I have sinned"—but he would not slide open the window, no matter how persistently they rapped on it. Father Keneally spent much of the war in the thin air of the Rocky Mountains, where priests from around the country were sent to dry out. He was drinking again, even now as he spoke with my mother in Roslindale, a coffee cup in his grip three-quarters full of J&B.

She explained that she could not stop crying. That she felt like she was falling through space. That she had never married and never would. That her brothers, with their wives and their children, their lives, wanted her to stay at home and care for their father, who was himself now old, old. And she could not stop crying.

"Flee," he told her. "You must flee to someplace where you can find somebody who will love you just a bit and then allow you to start all over again. Our faith is about the resurrection," he explained. "Please do not forget this. We celebrate the rising of the dead and buried. Jesus returned to earth before ascending to heaven. His body bore the marks of excruciating tortures. You must follow our Lord's example. Flee this particular world."

She fled to San Francisco. Her brothers declared that she would be back in six months. But she knew somebody there, a tough old hen from the Veterans Administration who had headed west after the war and married an Aussie veteran of the guerrilla campaign in New Guinea; they had settled down peaceably on Telegraph Hill. Alice Delaney, my mother's friend, stepped gladly into the role of mother superior. She located a small studio apartment on the edge of the financial district, and then a lead to a job at Red Cross. My mother was resurrected in San Francisco.

When she met my father at a Knights of Columbus dance, Dad was just out of the sanatorium, unexpectedly delivered from TB, and he wanted to marry immediately. The season was Lent, marriage unthinkable, and so they waited. He attended Catholic instruction at Old Saint Mary's and spoke to my mother of Savonarola and the Crusades.

Up until this time, my father's religious training had been limited to the quack medicine shows and traveling spiritualists who set up their tents outside of Eugene, Oregon—where his family had settled after losing their farm in the Saskatchewan wheat crash prior to the Dirty Thirties. There Dad was introduced to the disciples of Madame Blavatsky, the Swedenborgians, and the entrepreneurial descendants of the clairvoyant Fox sisters who toured the West with a stuffed baboon and a pledge to heal every variety of illness.

These tent shows were all for fun and free, too, if you knew how to negotiate and when to volunteer. My father's spiritual indoctrination consisted of a hodgepodge of outlandish pleas and confabulations: rubbing the stuffed baboon's matted skull, watching tables knock and float in midair, listening to the séance music of rattling iron sheets presenting backstage thunder. He absorbed the mumbo jumbo of the old patent medicine fakirs recently out of the big city drunk tank, who also read the stars for a price and predicted an end to his family's troubles, attributing their present condition to a recent hex or an ancient curse or just plain bad luck, which seemed undeniable. Tongue-talkers, snake-handlers, and all manner of holy rollers plashed the children in their wooden washtubs or submerged them to the gravel bottom along a narrow piece of the McKenzie River during the warm summer months. It was all a game, doing little harm and no good.

+ + +

Most Sunday mornings, I would be sitting in the middle of St. Bernard's third pew, my mother on my right, patient and alert, receptive to the transactions of the altar. To my left ran the long line of indistinguishable stiff, silent men in their one dry-cleaned Sunday sport coat and their wives, in bountiful floral dresses, their arms overflowing with mewling, screeching, scrabbling children. And all our busy hands would be kneading the rosary or fumbling with change, sealing the collection envelope with a furtive, soggy dog's lap of the tongue, the dimes and quarters and half-dollars clinking into the wicker collection basket as the usher on the far end of the pole grimaced at the jolt of each donation's tidy bounce.

Father McBain lectured us about eternity.

We would burn forever, he informed us, suffering unspeakable, unimaginable torments, our flesh seared, our muscles and sinews roaring with flames, our bones crackling and our marrow sputtering, if ever we should occasion to sin without the benefit of confession and thereby fail to achieve a state of forgiveness, grace, and redemption. We risked eternal damnation if we missed Sunday Mass, ate meat on Friday, took the Lord's name in vain, even once.

"Imagine your brand-new shiny station wagon," instructed Father McBain, his voice fluttering with deceptive good humor, slyly suggesting relief from God's constant and awesome irritability.

I held my breath. We did not own a station wagon.

Uncle Win did, but like Dad, he didn't attend Mass.

I tried to concentrate on the martyrs. Sister Henrietta had told us on multiple occasions that we should pray very hard to the Holy Family for the privilege of one day becoming a martyr to the faith. "To be a martyr," she instructed, "is the most glorious opportunity that God could ever send you."

It seemed to me upon reflection that this assertion was demonstrably untrue. According to our catechism, martyrs were likely to be tied to a tree and pierced with arrows, like Saint Sebastian. Or broken on a spiked wheel, as happened to Saint Catherine. Or barbecued like a flank steak in the fashion of Saint Lawrence. Martyrs might be dismembered into a half-dozen pieces, which I initially presumed to account for the Christian name of Saint Sixtus. Today martyrs were still being fricasseed and devoured by savages, an end that doubtlessly befell many of the missionaries whose fate my mother had sealed along with Sunday's special collections envelope for the Propagation of the Faith in Heathen Lands. God, who was everywhere and knew everything, could not be relied on for protection.

I wished I were at home with my father.

Not Our Father who art in heaven, but my dad residing in Jefferson Manor, who believed none of these priests' tales, with their power to render flesh into ash and cinders and compel every one of us to kneel howling before God in penitent regret.

"And now imagine a great mountain of sand ten thousand times higher than the most towering mountain in all of California," ordered Father McBain. "Imagine Mount Whitney, if you've ever been there on vacation." He surveyed either side of the aisle, concluding that none of us had. "Consider that you drive your brand-new station wagon to this gigantic mountain only once every million years to remove from the pile a single grain of sand. And when this enormous mountain has finally been hauled away, and all of your travels have at last been completed over millions upon millions of centuries," said Father McBain, erupting into a gaping, carnivorous grin, "removed grain by grain, mound by mound, eon by eon, then you still will not have spent even one second in the tormenting hellfires of damnation everlasting."

I exhaled, exhausted. Guilty. Terrified. I wondered what Dad was doing this moment at home. Sipping his coffee, munching on a waffle, perusing Dagwood and Blondie in the Sunday *Tribune*. I imagined my father courting the flames of perdition by thought, word, and deed—a martyr to his own faithlessness.

"'As flies to wanton boys are we to the gods,'" my father had said, spouting off one afternoon in a moment of autodidactic intoxication about something I did not comprehend. He peered deeply into my gaping, alarmed eyes to see if I appreciated the rhythm of his words, his invocation of chaos. "'They kill us for their sport,'" he chuckled proudly—a sin in itself. I knew that he wasn't speaking about boys or flies or sports or even, finally, God. I fretted for his soul.

Try to imagine eternity, as Father McBain demanded, the boundlessness bordering either end of our lives: no start and no conclusion.

I tried. *Per omnia saecula saeculorum.*

Forever, forever, forever, and forever.

My father was a rebel, a Protestant, an outsider, the opposition. But something else, too. Something I could not yet fully appreciate or even entirely perceive. Dad's sin, as Father McBain would have surely called it, was to fashion himself into someone as confounding and contradictory as faith itself; he was a model of civic doubt overshadowing the merely capacious administration of the Church. Did he harbor suspicions of immanence? Might he have experienced somewhere in a distant moment, now resisted, a pang of ecstasy? In the woods, perhaps, alone—tracking a deer with his rifle gripped pleasingly around the nut-brown hardwood stock? In his hospital bed, as he drew the first breath that confirmed his survival? In some boundless private moment in the arms of my mother? He revealed nothing. He chose loneliness.

I pressed my back rigidly into the fold of the bench, bone against oak, and I reeled through space and time.

Did my father fear punishment, forever and ever?

Per Dominum nostrum Jesum Christum, Filium Tuum, Qui Tecum vivit et regnat in unitate Spiritus Sancti Deus: per omnia saecula saeculorum.

And what did it signify that I was his son?

• • •

I fell into bad company.

One Saturday afternoon, I picked up my best friend Phil and together we trudged down Harvard Avenue to attend confession with Nicky LeRoux, who was waiting for us on the church patio. Nicky liked to torment Father Witalczwyz, Father McBain's second-in-command, an incomprehensible ancient dispatched to our parish in the California suburbs from Warsaw. Father Witalczwyz appeared to be deaf, seemed to know no English, served mainly as an obstacle to the apprehension of the faith. After the last adult finished his acts of contrition at the front pew, Nicky, Phil, and I quietly slipped into the confessional booth together.

The window slid open.

"Damn me to hell, Father," declared Nicky in a pious whisper, his voice threatening to crack with the herald of adolescence, "for I have sinned. It has been two hundred years since my last confession."

From the other side of the confessional: some mumbling in Polish, the shadow of Father Witalczwyz rattling his head up and down in adumbrated boredom.

"These are my sins, Father. I robbed a bank yesterday, and I pulled down my pants and showed Sister Henrietta my hairy butt. I smoked a big fat cigar in church. And I'm going to go to a strip show where there's a bunch of naked ladies with big boobies as soon as I get old enough."

Phil started to giggle. I jammed an elbow into his ribs. Phil was a Protestant, but he covered his mouth.

More mumbling from the other side of the confessional, the volume rising now, more mumbling. And then: *something something something,* five Hail Marys, *something something,* an Act of Contrition.

I enjoyed this ritual, but I understood that I could never regale my father with tales of our adventures. Dad might cite the formation of the Church by first-century Jewish mystical sects; the Albigensian heresy; the billion Chinamen who had never heard of Jesus Christ, yet still managed to invent fireworks and civilization—but he nevertheless insisted on paying respect to a man doing his job as best he can; even a priest. Father Witalczwyz, Dad declared (calling him Father Vitallis, or Father Watchacallim), this old Polack who nobody could understand, was free to believe whatever he wanted, just like the rest of us Americans. At least until JFK put Cardinal Cushing in charge of the State Department. Father Witalczwyz might not be a working man—just look at his hands—but he had his rights like anybody else.

Dad required no signs and portents. No revelation regarding the deep-set unknowable and righteous order of all things. No transcendence, blessing, or grace. He just stood up for the guy.

✦ ✦ ✦

On the day of the inauguration, our teacher brought in her own portable Magnavox television set so that we could watch the new age begin. She told us how this president represented a fresh start, another chance for a nation now practically two hundred years old. "What else lives for two hundred years?" she asked, trying to carve out a lesson from our unauthorized leisure.

"An elephant," I suggested.

"No, a parrot," said somebody else.

"No, no, no, a tortoise!"

"Good effort," she coaxed, but nothing on Earth lives for two hundred years. She was talking about something else.

"What about a tree?" asked Nicky.

"Okay," she conceded, maybe a tree. But she was talking about an idea, something you couldn't actually see. She furiously blinked her eyes, and then she laughed and wiped away her tears and told us she was fine.

It was snowing on television, 20 degrees Fahrenheit back east. They had recruited three thousand sailors and soldiers with seven hundred trucks and ploughs to shove back the snowbanks, thereby effecting clear sight lines for the entire nation.

In California, the January sun baked our school-yard blacktop, though the air remained chilly, bristling with the bay breeze. We studied the television with scriptural intensity.

The Kennedy family had gone to Mass early that morning, the television announcer informed us. The camera drew a bead on his church in Georgetown—a grand cathedral pleated in snow up to the stairs, icy white upon a fresh coat of ivory.

The new president walked down the stairs towards the podium and everybody clapped their hands. He wore a silk top hat. The Marine Band played and the officers in uniform saluted. They sliced the fixed plane of their flattened hands across their foreheads for a long, long time and I suspected for a moment that they had frozen stiff. The mysterious East.

An old man with white hair, glasses, and a heavy scarf

flapping in the wind read a brief speech. "A golden age of poetry and power," he said, fiddling with his glasses. The new president stood up, slipped out of his overcoat. Everybody seemed amazed by the cold. He raised his right hand and swore, and now he was officially in charge. His pretty wife smiled.

* * * * *

The suburbs thrive and then quickly spread, new homes fixing a fresh grid of rectangles atop the bracken and duck sloughs, the oceans of stucco washing over acres of cherry orchards. Men laboring weekends in their yards and gardens witness their dreams come to fruition: a sycamore seedling now arching across the front sidewalk, the shade splashed upon a small patch of emerald lawn, the homeowner lolling under the fluttering canopy with a bottle of Lucky Lager clasped in hand. Men patch up their old canvas hunting jackets with iron-gray duct tape and sell their .308 Winchesters and 16-gauges, declaring themselves partisans of the Canada geese that now wing their way north since the sacrifice of their marsh. Weekend gardeners and carpenters settle down to the business of propagation and improvement.

All this is to say that they cannot believe the good fortune that has come their way.

"The reasons for the rapid growth of suburbia are easy to understand," explains a lavish color supplement to the Sunday paper. "They are but the fulfillment of the unyielding rules of economics and the inexorable laws of supply and demand."

"First Advantage—Strategic location." (The newspaper calls the new suburbs "irresistible to the industrious man and woman who seek an affordable house, an opportunity to labor honestly, and a good, decent place to raise a family.")

"Second—All the year-round climate and the low city tax rate." (As though weather and taxes are twined together in an aspect of natural selection.)

"Third—Splendid opportunities for employment, and unexcelled potential for the opening of even more factories."

Sooner or later, it all comes down to jobs for working people—but something else, too. Something hardly ever mentioned.

If you're halfway honest, you've got to thank God for the sheer dumb luck of being born in such a time and place. You can tell yourself that hard work and smart choices made all the difference, but why lie?

For those acquainted with Thomas Jefferson—and every subdivision has a few citizens equipped with curiosity and a library card—there is a passage in *Notes on the State of Virginia* that feels pleasant to ponder at the foot of a blossoming pear tree when Saturday afternoons turn too hot to work. The homeowner sinks into the foam pad of his chaise lounge and reflects, as had Jefferson, on the landed yeoman as the ideal citizen of the new nation. He reflects upon his neighbors and himself.

"I view large cities," Jefferson declared in a revelatory passage that any sly burgher will pounce on, "as pestilential to the morals, the health, and the liberty of man. True, they nourish the elegant arts, but the useful ones can thrive elsewhere..."

They're thriving right here, wrested from the ground and pieced together at the workbench. Maybe you could pat yourself on the back just a little for everything that seems to be going right.

* * * * *

THREE

The Necessity of Maintenance and Repair

"What's that I smell?" demanded my father, cracking open the kitchen door. His face materialized by the jamb, his wide eyes ravenous, lordly, insatiable.

Mom glanced up from the countertop, her right hand clenching an enormous blue sponge coated with Ajax. Already the butter yellow tiles were gleaming in tribute to her labors, the hacksaw motion of her elbow and shoulders.

"You *know*," my mother whispered, momentarily the coquette.

"Cake," said Dad, sticking out half in the kitchen, half in the garage, sniffing the air, growling like a rapacious household bear. He pounded his chest with one hand, a grease-pocked socket wrench dangling from the other. "*Me want cake*!" Tarzan of the Suburbs: He was kidding around for my benefit, I figured. Mom swayed back and forth on the linoleum floor giggling, actually giggling.

Cake because it was late Saturday afternoon. Cake because he loved it. Cake because he had come to expect it, even though he still could not quite believe his good fortune—this cake so readily available and exclusively his own.

At forty-two, my mother looked ten years younger, her olive complexion bathed in the pale overhead light of the kitchen's single milk-glass fixture. She wore her thick ebony hair drawn back and bracketed by a pair of North African ivory combs that had belonged to her Calabrese mother. Dad towered over her by nearly a foot. He was trim and bald, like an ancient Greek athlete or philosopher—his remaining fringe of curly brown hair cropped close to his skull cannonball fashion. His cyan eyes radiated reckless hope, along with the usual doubts.

"Do I get just a sliver?" he asked dreamily.

"You clean up in the basin outside," ordered Mom, "and be sure to wipe your shoes." She glanced down at me as I stamped the floor, feet switching. "I suppose you want some, too?"

"Yes, yes, yes, yes!"

"Then you wash in the bathroom, and take care to sponge up your mess."

My mother hadn't been a baker until her marriage, the most surprising event of her life. Jolted into new habits of domesticity, she now luxuriated over the oven, conceiving every imaginable shape, flavor, and decorative variation of the basic American cake.

Take two eggs, water, a stick of margarine, one box of Betty Crocker's instant cake mix and another of her frosting. Then consider the hidden possibilities, and select judiciously from your rack of Schilling's spices, your Heinz food colorings. Employ your imagination.

Mom baked ginger cakes, spice cakes, angel food and devil's food cakes. Cakes with creamy egg whites whipped into frothy Swiss mountain peaks, cakes dyed scarlet for St. Valentine's Day. As her confidence grew, she deviated from the pathways of Betty Crocker to fashion from scratch the delicious black licorice and bubble gum cakes that marked my birthdays once I could be trusted to chew and not swallow the embedded morsels. My mother baked cakes that relied on the juices and the zest of lemons and tangerines. Still others from the pairing of peaches and pineapples, apples and raisins, apples and oranges.

On Saturday mornings at the grocery store, my mother and I wandered the produce aisles while she sang to herself about her own good fortune, this limitless abundance, the miracle of California. Life was so easy now. I pushed the shopping cart and together we discussed her bright ideas for new creations—an Independence Day sheet cake in the form of a frosted white flag with fifty red stars fit into the upper left corner: When you cut the first slice, you saw that the inside was colored patriotic blue. Mom mulled over the possibilities as she stroked the stalks of asparagus and polished the softball-sized grapefruit in her palms.

"So moist," said my father, shoveling into his mouth this Saturday afternoon's first slice. His gaping maw was filled with an undercooked, liquescent chrome-yellow cake pitted with tart wells of gelatinous goo that caused his lips to stick and smack with each bite. He eyed my mother rapturously.

"What's this green stuff?" I wondered. To me, a cake was just a cake and I could not hide my doubts about some of her improvements.

"Lime Jell-O. Do you like it?"

"I guess."

Another bite, my tongue dabbing uncertainly at the metallic taste of chemical innovation.

"What's this stuff on top?"

"That's imitation citrus Dream Fluff frosting, dear. Don't let it bother you."

"So light and refreshing," observed my father, endorsing her latest masterpiece. He wiggled a dollop of sweet plasticine concoction on the prong of his fork. "With that sharp little afterbite on the tip of the tongue."

"I'm glad you like it, honey."

"It's all so creamy, I don't know if I can stop myself from having more, I can't seem to get enough."

"You go right ahead, dear."

"Makes me want to take a little midday lie-down with my wife."

Mom cut him a second sumptuous slice. The cake yielded,

coating the knife blade with a moist smear of vegetable oil. "We could do that," she agreed, her voice fluttering a provocative half-tone higher. My father regarded me out of the corner of his eye, wondering if his good fortune would hold for another precious thirty minutes, and then he scooted me out into the front yard and firmly closed the door.

✦ ✦ ✦

Mom wrote to Betty Crocker.

> Dear Betty Crocker,
>
> My husband enjoys all your cake mixes, and what I do with them, but he sometimes wonders if they couldn't be even richer. I've wondered too, and I think I've solved the problem. I now substitute half the water in your recipes on the back of the box for two cups of sour cream. The sour cream makes the cake even creamier and moister, the way my husband prefers. I know that not every person would want sour cream in large helpings with their cake, but my husband is still very thin from a serious illness of some years past, and his appetite is remarkable. I hope you will feel free to share my suggestion with other housewives.

Betty Crocker—who was really forty-eight different women working in the home service department at the corporate headquarters in Minneapolis—wrote back and thanked Mom. But General Mills did not acknowledge my mother's recipe in their newsletters or apply her helpful hint to the back of their cake boxes. Nevertheless, we continued to be a Betty Crocker family, dabbling with both Pillsbury and Duncan Hines but ultimately rejecting them in the same way that the men of our town might trifle with a Pontiac or Rambler but finally have to come down on the side of either Ford or Chevy.

Aunt Tina did not bake, but she had her own tricks in the kitchen that astonished us all. She molded patties of ground round into the shape of T-bone steaks, coated them with Wheaties, and inserted a sliced carrot lengthways to impersonate the bone. She mashed potatoes for Christmas and sculpted them into the form of a squatting chicken or a snowy alpine peak sprinkled with a forest of parsley. Her Jell-O molds were constructed in layers, jiggling ensembles of pineapple, grape, and strawberry riveted together with a dozen maraschino cherries.

In the new world, everything seemed possible, the ingenuity that won the war now lavishing its innovations on the home front.

Uncle Win purchased vinyl flooring, wood paneling, and a portable phone. On alternating paydays, he set money aside against a new washer/dryer, electric blankets, electric floor polisher, electric can opener, and matching electric toothbrushes. Win bought Aunt Tina a new refrigerator the size of two linebackers, but colored pink; later they acquired a tan freezer for the garage. The door to their new stove featured a glass window: you could watch the food cook. Perhaps due to all this timesaving technology and convenience in the kitchen—not to mention the end of his own cooking once he married Tina—Win put on an extra twenty pounds; then ten more.

Dad called him weak, fatso, incapable of self-discipline. But with so much of everything now available, Dad put on fifteen pounds too. That year in the Christmas photographs, the two brothers crowded the dinner-table turkey like rival snowmen.

"Franklin," asked my mother one Saturday afternoon, serving him an oversized slice of raspberry-fig cake. "Franklin, dear," she repeated rather stiffly, allowing all this new possession to tempt her into forgetting the basic nature of my father, "when do you think we might be able to buy a dishwasher?"

At first, Dad really did not understand the question. How did you "buy" a dishwasher? His mother, Clara, had been a dishwasher, as well as a cook—but no, of course, that was not what she meant. Dad first pretended that he hadn't heard the question, and later, following numerous repetitions and clarifications, he simply uttered with momentous conviction: "Never!"

But along with our household's Kenwood automatic food

mixer, the Westinghouse portable steam iron, an RCA AM/FM radio alarm clock with snooze control, and the Ronson cordless electric shaver (used for one week, and then Dad returned to his Gillette injectable safety razor), we soon added to our own collection of luxuries a fully automatic, front-loading, roll-away dishwasher on sale for ten days only at Wards.

We were not competing with Uncle Win and Aunt Tina: Dad said so repeatedly, with exasperation and hints of savagery. Nevertheless, our dishwasher was bigger than their dishwasher, newer, too, and we should never forget that it cost less. ("I recognize a bargain when I see one," crowed my father, hinting that my uncle could be bamboozled by those sharpies on the appliance floor at Sears.) America offered so much more than anybody needed of everything, he rhapsodized. Dad spoke passionately of nylon, Dacron, rayon, Zylon. His eyes bulged like pies, his heart beat faster with the utterance of each improvement. We were becoming new people in the new nation without even trying. The dangers were immense.

✦ ✦ ✦

"You have tested positive for tuberculosis," the doctor informed my father. It was 1938, and he was twenty-four years old. For three months he had been losing weight, down to 145 pounds though he stood nearly six feet tall. The doctor explained that he would have to go to a sanatorium until he recovered; or not.

The California state legislature had passed a statute pertaining to all individuals infected with the tubercle bacillus. If citizens did not adhere to a system of laws, my father reasoned, anarchy might prevail. In Madrid, Mussolini's Fiat fighter planes were strafing civilians. In Baton Rouge, they had gunned down Huey Long on the courthouse steps, proving that even the Kingfish could not survive by his own lights. Still, Dad knew he could not submit without a struggle.

He had arrived in San Francisco looking for work, aiming to enlist with Harry Bridges on the docks, or join the seamen's union with Lundberg, Larsen, and the rest of the Swedes. Anybody could see that a war was coming in Europe. Everybody would be working soon, shifts around the clock, more sweat and good pay than you could hope for. But some days all he could do was sleep.

His joints pained him throughout the mornings, and at night he broke into fever sweats. Then came the cough: his blood spit up suddenly, tattooing the sidewalk. His voice echoed and rasped, like somebody blowing through a long hollow reed, and the growl deep in the center of his chest, with its subsequent frantic gasping for breath, startled him awake every night.

At his rooming house in the Mission District, he planned to lie low for a spell, get better somehow. For the landlady, he invented a kidney ailment. He bought his own plate, bowl, glass, and silverware, determined not to infect anybody else. For weeks, he thumbed through old copies of *Life*, never leaving his bed, howling up blood into pages of newsprint that he threw out the window on mornings before the street sweeper arrived.

The landlady told her husband that she suspected he was a "lunger." Dad paid his second month's rent, and a few days later, the county public health nurse showed up at his door, insisting that he turn himself in to the sanatorium.

"But I don't have any money," he argued. "I've spent every red cent I've saved over the past six months."

"Then the County will have to pay for you to get better," she said, stressing his added contribution to the common burden. She was a sharp, pointed stick of a woman, pink-faced and squint-eyed, furious at my father's debility.

Dad checked into the county hospital, where they X-rayed him repeatedly. A brawny male orderly with a boxer's flat face and broken nose inspected him for lice and then scrubbed him down with lye soap in the huge porcelain basin that served as the institution's bathtub. He clipped Franklin's hair short enough to suit the Army and issued him a barracks-green bathrobe, baby-blue pajamas with a pocket stitched at the belly like a marsupial's pouch, and a pair of surprisingly well-made slippers with sewn leather soles—meant to last the life of several patients.

On his first day, my father padded down the zigzag corridor that served as a feeding tube into the TB ward. The walls were painted flat white and the rails of overhead lighting hummed softly, allied in the unnatural pursuit of perpetual, indeterminate day. He would not make the return trip for nearly four years.

Between noon and four, the supervising nurse permitted no talking, whispering, walking through the grounds or loitering in corridors, no visiting other patients, reading, or writing letters. Crying was strictly forbidden at any time. The head clerk ordered him to sign a statement declaring that he understood all the regulations and agreed to obey them. He stored the rule book in his locker, which was stamped with his patient number: 01789.

In the public hospital's TB ward, my father met other men who had vanished from the world, captives of illness who had neglected to inform their families and friends of their descent into public charity. Everybody had a story to tell about how they had contracted the disease, with the point always being that it had not been their fault. Patients grasped that the world outside regarded their infection as proof of a moral lapse, the fevered mark of negligence, ignorance, indolence. In truth, tuberculosis was most frequently a disease of the underfed and the exhausted. Once perceived to be a malady of the oversensitive—the poet's disease—TB had more realistically established itself among unemployed bricklayers and overworked stevedores; tramps, migrants, and job seekers: ordinary people, such as my father. The dispossessed.

At first he believed, like all the young men and young women who took up temporary residence in the public TB ward, that he would recover and return to the world. But he quickly learned to stop talking and even stop thinking about one word in particular: tomorrow. Tomorrow was no longer part of his vocabulary.

The present absorbed my father's future. He rose, walked, slept, ate, read, slept a great deal more; always in the tedious, endless present.

At the conclusion of his first month, my father wrote a letter to his mother, then working as a house cook for a wealthy family in Portland.

> Now, Ma, don't you worry about me, just take care of yourself, and I will be just fine. Always have been, always will.
>
> Your loving son,
>
> Franklin

The effort wore him out for another day. Had he slightly more energy, he might have been tempted to tell his mother about how he had accidentally contracted the disease. How he had picked up a hitchhiker outside of Klamath Falls, some ordinary Joe scratching around for a job like everybody else. How the man had coughed all the way to San Francisco. How it had not actually been his own fault that he was now almost certain to die.

+ + +

"You choose your tools like you choose your friends," my father first told me. "For their worth and their weight. You understand what I mean?"

"No."

Dad glanced down at me to see if I was smarting off; and then, with a deliberate flick of his head, he returned to the task of wiping out his sockets with a dry, clean cloth, figuring: no, not just yet.

"A house is like a machine," Dad lectured, knowing my mother couldn't bear to hear another word on this subject. His voice climbed and then cooled, indicating that we were embarking upon a truth I should take pains to absorb. "A house looks like it's just standing there, sure, that's a fact. But deep inside, beyond those corners you can't see your way around, far up in the nooks and crannies, there's a secret life taking place that you can't hardly imagine."

Everything outside and inside our house, my father explained, from the furnace, pipes, and plumbing to the exterior woodwork, wiring, and paint job, all required constant vigilance, repair, and general maintenance.

"General maintenance," he proclaimed, "is one of the secrets of life."

I nodded and ran a whisk broom lightly over the workbench; then I sorted through the contents of my father's toolbox, his treasure chest.

A hammer and a rubber mallet. Screwdrivers, wrenches, and sockets. Hand drill and bits. Several grips, awls, picks, and gouges. An auto-roll metal measuring tape, spirit level, and miniature T-square. A vice and a clamp. Plumb bob, soldering iron, tin shears, pliers, file, wire snippers, rubber cement, razor blade. I allowed the claw end of a hammer to cleave my palm and then dangle from my fingers, getting a feel for its heft, speculating on its usefulness. I liked the way the nails and bolts and washers rattled around in their ancient mayonnaise jars as I plucked them down from the wall of cabinet shelves—each container segregated by size and purpose, labeled with an ink-pen scrawl across a strip of tan masking tape.

Dad could no more imagine hiring another man to plumb the toilet, rewire the fuse box, or patch the roof and refasten the aluminum gutters than he could picture himself taking a taxi each morning to work or investing his paycheck in pork belly futures instead of US government savings bonds. People did these things, it was true. Just not our people.

"You ready, boy?" Dad returned the fresh-swiped sockets to their steel case.

I nodded, and then I strapped on my leather tool belt, that Christmas's best present. It included a child's-size hammer, screwdriver, and measuring tape. I wore the tool belt all year, thinking it much finer than a gun and holster.

As he closed the garage door, Dad warned, "You keep every one of those tools where they belong and out of mischief."

"Sure, sure," I said. "But let's get going."

We launched ourselves down the sidewalk, the morning breeze stiffened by the fragrance of spring. Slender young plum and cherry trees, trellised jasmine, Saturday's fresh-mowed grass, one yard after another after another, down the street and around the block, property lines dissolving and then binding together our neighborhood into an emerald stream of uninterrupted lawn. Working men on their day off labored in their t-shirts, watering their rhododendrons, clipping their privet hedges. A pitcher of iced lemonade set out by the wife perspired in the shade of the juniper bush as the Giants game blared from a transistor radio the size of a pack of Camels.

Everybody in Jefferson Manor puttered. Uncle Win had built a slatted redwood fence for the wisteria in his backyard and planted tea roses in redwood boxes running up the front walkway. Dad forged master plans: rows of Mexican mock-orange to blot out the neighbors' view into our living room, puddles of concrete to serve as steps across the muddied yard in winter, a hummingbird feeder suspended from the fiberglass awning come spring.

The first generation of suburban pioneers: they replaced the tar roof with wooden shingles, added on a rumpus room, and built a red-brick fireplace out back with the handprints of both parents and each small child impressed into the wet cement of its foundation.

We had plenty to lose, Dad often told me, meaning to frighten and instruct—but merely baffling me.

Work hard, he warned, stay lucky.

We were all lucky as hell.

Things couldn't possibly stay this good—because they never did.

We walked in silence until we reached the Jensen family's house, on the corner of Pond Street and Princeton Avenue. My father wanted to study their hole in the ground, the source from which an additional bedroom would rise by the end of summer. By dint of the time and labor invested, this hole now belonged to Mr. Jensen; the hole was something he had made and he had done a fine job of it, too. He could feel proud of that hole, said Dad, and he offered Mr. Jensen help with framing and then pouring the concrete. They shook hands on it.

After we got home, I asked Dad, "Aren't we ever going build a bomb shelter?"

He was scrambling around on his hands and knees in the side yard, placing the final touches on the four-foot squiggle of a fishpond carved into the clay outside our living room.

"Of course not."

He scoured the fiberglass bottom with a Brillo pad, refining it to peach-skin perfection. Then he draped a hose over the edge and filled the pool two inches higher than normal to test for cracks.

"Phil Barnes said his dad is going to build a bomb shelter in their backyard because of the Russians."

Dad glanced up from his fishpond, giving his arm a rest. "Don't forget," he said, "old man Barnes is an idiot." More scrubbing and polishing, smoothing the ultramarine glaze. And then Dad's head whipped back up: "Now don't go telling your mother I said so."

Over time, Dad dotted the perimeter of the pond with ferns and grasses, cultivating a wild, tropical skyline that resembled King Kong's island. At the far end, he installed a two-foot-high pumice mountain and a motorized pump to power the waterfall. A half-dozen goldfish purchased for a dime apiece from the big tank at Rexall's swam in rotation.

My father enjoyed watching his dime-store goldfish pass their lazy days in the pond he had constructed, nibbling at their ruffled carpet of green algae and then rising suddenly to swallow a mosquito skimming the surface. When one fish was perceived to be pursuing another in tireless, moralizing circles, day after day, Dad took to calling the pair Jean Valjean and Javert.

"Who are they?" I asked.

"Prisoner 24601," he answered, "and his nemesis, who might as well be in prison himself."

• • •

Win visited Franklin only once during the three and a half years he spent in the TB ward, and then only to ask permission to borrow his tools.

"Man, this is the life of Riley," Win told my father. "You got nothing to do but sit back and relax. There are some pretty nurses around here too, Slick. When you start noticing, you'll know you're getting better."

In the tuberculosis wing at San Francisco General, many of the nurses and doctors turned out to be former TB-ers themselves. None admitted it directly to the patients, but word circulated since they were usually the stricter, more demanding staff. "It's your job to get well," one of the nurses lectured my father and the other three men who shared his dormitory alcove. She was one of the old lungers, bulky and wide-bottomed in her recuperated good health, intolerant of malingering and weakness.

"This is my brother," Dad explained to the nurse on the day of Win's visit. Win was grinning like crazy, determined to impress.

"Well," she admitted with a scowl, "it would be"—and Franklin had to agree.

Dad didn't believe his brother was suited to survive tuberculosis. Bumming around the country, getting into trouble, that was more Win's speed. My father never resisted orders, as Win would have. He slept dreamlessly for fifteen hours at a stretch, erased from the world, sufficiently disciplined to remain immobile and mute. Win couldn't have done that either, not even for two weeks.

In his third month, my father started to wander more extensively around the TB wing, meeting his fellow patients. Some of them were interesting people, he now told his brother, characters outside his previous realm of acquaintance. Before getting sick, several could claim distinction, even titles: Professor, Police Sergeant, Chef.

On his floor resided both an FBI agent and a counterfeiter; they had each met Al Capone on Alcatraz. He talked for hours with a professional jockey who had served with the Abraham Lincoln Battalion in the debacle at Ebro. They discussed the Catholic Church, Spanish wine, and Uncle Joe Stalin's betrayal of the Republican forces. He made friends with a pickpocket who spent two months wising up his fellow patients to all the tricks of his trade before he died.

"It takes a backbone to get out of here," Franklin told Win. "You got to be determined, you got to sweat. And you better plan to take care of yourself, you understand, because they can't cure you here, they really can't. You do it yourself, or it don't get done, right?"

Franklin acted as though Win was the patient, a suggestion Win abominated. Win was younger than Franklin, always the healthy one. *Stronger* than a horse. He wasn't the fellow who had picked up tuberculosis.

As the months passed, Dad began to read, distinguishing himself from his brother, who never read anything before the war except the racing form and then later maybe a Zane Grey or Mickey Spillane that he might have found aboard ship. The hospital maintained a library of two thousand volumes. Once a week, he made his way down the winding, flat-white corridor, up a flight of stairs, and into the anteroom that housed a collection reserved exclusively for the residents of the tuberculosis ward. He vowed to read every book in that room if he did not get better soon or die first. During his three and a half years of removal from the world, he read most of Mark Twain's books, Superman comics, and copies of *The Daily Worker* smuggled into the hospital by members of the maintenance staff, who were eventually dismissed for their enterprise. For the first time in his life, my father couldn't work. Doctor's orders; he could only rest. He could read.

He read Charles Dickens's ghost stories and *Our Mutual Friend*; and then Francis Parkman, the Old Testament, Sinclair Lewis, Lewis Carroll, and *Les Miserables*.

My father read omnivorously, ferociously. In the country of the white death—the phrase that the jockey had taken from the Spaniards to describe the fluttering bedsheet finality of tuberculosis—in this waiting room for the worst to come, his incapacity meant opportunity. There were always books in his hands now, rather than dirty old tools.

My father sped through Darwin's account of the voyage of the *Beagle*, he absorbed H. G. Wells and Jules Verne and occasionally pondered what the future would look like tomorrow after tomorrow after tomorrow.

He introduced himself to contrasting visions of our Republic as propounded by Thomas Jefferson and James Thurber. He read the illustrated biographies of Tecumseh, Crazy Horse, and Geronimo.

He pursued the lurching, pot-holed trail of the self-taught, never quite confident about what he should master. Years later, he would quote *Othello* and recite long passages from *Cyrano de Bergerac* to the mailman, mocking the neighbors who had never heard of Baku or Samarkand.

Franklin figured he might as well loan Win his tools when his brother asked for them. Win declared that he had a chance to join the merchant marine—a job that never did pan out, though it propelled him into the Navy. "Take them," said Franklin, "but take good care of them, too. I might need them myself someday." Both Win and Franklin knew the odds of that happening.

* * *

My father devoted his two-week summer vacation to driving us around Oregon's backcountry, touring what seemed like a thousand miles of mountain loops and zigzag shortcuts to bear witness to what he had accomplished during the Depression.

Dad had joined the Civilian Conservation Corps several years before contracting TB, and in the riotous good health of his youth, he cut terraces into hillsides, strung telephone lines, and helped his crew run roads like needles through the backwoods, patching together the state's small counties. The CCC planted thousands of trees, carved hundreds of hard-clay drainage ditches, bushwhacked acres of forest shrub to cut firebreaks for the smokejumper crews training at Skagit and Mt. Hood.

On our last day in Oregon, my father got lost for a couple of hours in the mountains and swore up a blue streak—at himself mainly, for being so damn forgetful. Finally, he negotiated the most circuitous route possible to our destination, his New Deal stone bridge.

Our Chevy eased into a fat turnabout and Dad flicked off the ignition with a rough snap of his wrist. Then he opened the door, stepped outside, and strode silently toward the riverbank. I caught up with him and we walked together. We mounted the bridge. I could feel the platform wobble from the rush of waters below.

"Smell the sockeye?" he asked, turning his face to the wind off the river. I nodded vigorously though I had no idea what he meant.

Dad leaned over the faded whitewashed rail, straining to wet his face with spray. He ran his hands over the pillars, observing the smoothness of each stone. If I listened carefully, he said, I could hear the roar pitched back from two hundred miles downstream where the river hitched up with larger waters and turned all this rushing into practical power. He was talking about progress. Progress and FDR had brought electricity to the dark corners of Oregon. For farmers and loggers—"families like ours," he said, though I understood he wasn't talking about my mother and me—this intervention by the government had resulted in a spider web alliance of electric lights, the front room blare of the radio, an aperture to the rest of the world. It had been the start of everything getting better and better in this country, the dawn of promises that maybe promised too much.

"You got any idea how many of us there was in the CCC?"

I pressed my back flat against the guardrail and squinted out the answer.

"You told me more than two million yesterday."

"Two and a half million," Dad said, his voice dwelling on each syllable to suggest that my own answer lacked precision.

Two and a half million: I found the figure meaningless. But Dad continued to spout his precious numbers, a preoccupation with quantity, size, and proportion streaming through his speech. His company of 181 young recruits, aged 18 to 25, had during a single month in 1935 devoted some 17,000 man-hours to planting 25,000 pine and black locust seedlings. His voice grated against each number, notifying me to pay attention. Never forget the 200 cubic yards of earth they had moved to flatten the mountain. The 600 small dams his crew had erected. The innumerable hillsides they sloped, inserting Bermuda grass sod along a dark line of endless ditch banks. Dad had committed his entire 18 months to memory; he still relished reciting the details to anybody who would listen.

I tried to let it all soak in. But I just couldn't. At my age, I saw no point in the past, everything exhausted by duty and resignation. His splintering oak and stone relic seemed like a burden, a ploy. If I had had the words, I would have called it sheer vanity.

We studied the waters and failed to speak.

At last, my father turned to me, settled the hard calluses of his hand on my soft shoulder, and pressed his fingers into my flesh. "You got to be something, you see? You got to learn everything you can or otherwise you're just going to be a prisoner, like we were."

"You're not a prisoner," I informed him, weary of his history, his adamancy. A station wagon stalled at the foot of the bridge. The driver honked and waved, and my father signaled back for him and his family to forge ahead. My father, captain of his bridge.

"I was a prisoner," he said, "and you'll be one too, if you don't learn enough to make you different from every other son of a bitch out there scratching around for a job."

I shrugged. I wasn't worried about anything I couldn't see. I certainly didn't worry about the future and a life of regrets.

"There's just not a lot of room for mistakes," Dad said. "Not for people like us."

Too little time had elapsed between Dad's last laying his hands, in triumph, upon his New Deal stone bridge and this present moment of prosperous uncertainty. Tomorrow would arrive because there was no holding back tomorrow. But tomorrow could bring eviction, trouble, and despair just as easily as another chance.

The station wagon sputtered along, the waters roared beneath us. I could hear him, but I didn't understand yet. We eased away from each other, leaned against the railing, and let our eyes follow the leaves skimming downstream.

✦ ✦ ✦

Halfway into his third year, my father stumbled into the most important book of his long stay in the TB ward.

The Star Rover by Jack London chronicled the exploits of a Swede from Minnesota, presently a San Quentin convict. In the novel, the Swede learned through rigorous self-discipline to induce a trance that could send his mind sprawling from the lockdown of solitary confinement into a universe of previous incarnations. In the privacy of his cell, the prisoner relived past lifetimes as a medieval court jester, monk, Elizabethan soldier, shipwrecked sailor, Viking mercenary, lawgiver, and judge.

My father read the book as simple truth. He had himself experienced a sudden transportation from his own cell of sickness into other lives, this new world of books.

Dad thought about Achilles. He had encountered the ancient Greek hero in an illustrated volume by Bulfinch; then stumbled upon him again, nearly two years later, in Homer's *Odyssey*. Achilles was dead and reigning over Hades, a shade of his previous existence. If he only were alive today, he told a visitor to the underworld, he would happily forego all his past glories. There is nothing like life, Achilles proclaimed, prisoner of the gray light of the dead.

Achilles made my father think of simple things: wet grass mashed under bare feet—he could feel its knife-edges, prickly and cool, even though he hadn't run across a lawn or walked through a field in three years. The sound of rain on a river. A cold beer drawn from the tap in a smoky tavern with the jukebox blaring and people dancing. He knew he was going to die. After three years, almost nobody got better. The doctors agreed that he showed no signs of improvement. Some weeks, the cough grew worse, his joints pained again; all he could do was sleep. Still—remember Achilles—even this was better than death. The thing was to be alive; then something was possible. Achilles was nothing, air and reputation. He wanted to live.

In his third year, my father began to imagine himself getting better every day. He didn't daydream about a miraculous recovery, but like the prisoner in the Jack London novel, he applied the possibility of a new life to himself, a regimen of maintenance and repair. He invented in these moments of absolute, fabulous concentration an existence beyond his cell. He ordered his mind's eye to envision his lungs clearing, his body growing stronger. He had been right all along: they could not cure you here, they really couldn't. You had to do it yourself. Some days he could only work up the energy for five or ten minutes of will power. He did whatever he could. There is nothing like life.

In three months—performing on cue for the nurse—Franklin could expand his lungs like rubber bags and they didn't hurt, he didn't cough. The doctor told him that he was very surprised, very pleased: Franklin now tested negative. There are no miracles, my father decided, but there is the miraculous triumph of a man determined to survive—which he can do, if he's willing to make an instrument of his own mind and commit himself to the job. Without self-discipline a man didn't have a chance. You worked hard all day, and then the next day you got up and did it again.

When Franklin was released from the hospital, Win had already shipped out for the Pacific. He left Franklin's tools with

Clara and she sent them promptly to San Francisco. A hammer was missing. Franklin asked his mother to write Win, find out where the hammer went to. Did Win gamble it away or sell it, did he simply lose it somehow? Clara wrote to her younger son, but in his letters home, Win never mentioned the hammer.

Dad heard the news about Pearl Harbor while driving over the Bay Bridge, hurrying home from weekend overtime at the Alameda Naval Air Station to his studio apartment in the Mission District. He had been back in the world four months, fully employed for almost three. He couldn't believe the Japanese would attack Pearl Harbor. Win's ship was stationed at Pearl; he had told Clara that he loved Hawaii. The Japanese must be crazy, thought Dad, foolish beyond belief. They couldn't hope to win the war. Everything my father had read about the Far East, the history of naval conflict, the physics and chemistry of munitions manufacture, and the economics of industrial capacity told him so.

My father's car approached the magnificent arc of the Bay Bridge, traffic running in either direction on the top span in those days. Some cars pulled over after hearing the news on their own radios, the drivers compelled to alert their fellow citizens. They flagged down other motorists, screaming nonsense into the deafening wind. Dad's blue Hudson reached the cantilever's peak, the bridge swaying above the water, the city revealed. He drove slowly enough to inspect the Ferry Building and the ships docked at the port, and he imagined them shrouded in flame with Jap Zeros flush in the skies. He thought about Pearl, his brother, the inconceivable stupidity of it all, and he wondered whatever happened to that hammer.

✦ ✦ ✦

At the end of our two-week Oregon vacation, we drove out to the Alameda Naval Air Station to pick up Dad's paycheck. Every summer, I accompanied my father and afterwards we toured the hangars, visiting the airplanes scheduled for repair. Already I knew that I would not come again.

At the main gate, the Marine guard grimly inspected Dad's pass and then allowed one eye to roll up suspiciously to settle upon me.

"That's my boy," my father grumbled, annoyed by the red tape and military idiocy. Still, I felt proud. There was no question in his mind: I was his boy.

Aircraft were stationed along the runways, Navy planes lifting off and roaring above as we trod from the parking lot along a series of flat-gray hangars. The exertions of the air base, the F-11s screaming overhead, the rumble of Jeeps, personnel carriers, and armored caravans, reminded me that at any moment terrible things might again strike us and we must always be ready. I could feel the heat of the blacktop radiating up through the soles of my white high-top Keds.

In the distance, Marines drilled parade routines on the pavement between a set of antique cannons, and crews of workmen in blue coveralls dashed across the tarmac to inspect a Phantom jet flickering down from its test flight. We strolled into Dad's hangar, and I surveyed the damaged machinery scattered across the workbenches and suspended from the rafters. A fuselage from a downed Convair, the partial wing of the latest McDonnell fighter jet, a dozen Wright engines waiting to be rebored and fitted.

They were flying F-104s that year, the Starfighters later shipped to Taiwan. One plane stood tail-up, its needle-nose pricking the tarmac. Several armored slats were missing from the side. Dad strode decisively towards the nine-step metal ladder propped against its frame and fit into the hole. He shook the ladder once to establish its balance and gripped its sides with both hands.

"Climb on up," he invited. Dad had filled out the papers in the office and received his check. His mood was buoyant and unbelieving. He had just picked up two weeks' wages without working.

"Up the ladder?"

"That's right."

We clambered into the airplane, sliding through a crawl space that seemed too small even for me. My father maneuvered instinctively, shifting his weight, easing into each vacancy like a droplet of mercury. He balanced on the balls of his feet and burrowed through the fuselage with the speed of a groundhog, leading our way into the cockpit. Numbers adorned a thousand dials radiating from the pilot's control board.

"Should we take her up?" Dad asked.

My smile hung crooked across my face. "You mean in the air?"

"Yeah, you want me to fly us back to the Manor? Once we get a few thousand feet up in the clouds, I can radio one of the guys in my shop to drive our car home."

His eyes settled upon my own with deliberate stillness, his hands effortlessly capping his bended knees.

Of course, I knew he was kidding. "When did you learn how to fly?" I kidded back.

"Oh, hell, I bet I can figure it out. What do you say?"

I said: No.

I knew that he was fooling with me. Just the same, I should have said: *Yes, yes, yes, let's go, let's fly right home.* Then Dad would have needed to say something else, something sharp and funny that would have got us both laughing, our spirits lifted by the prospect that one day after tomorrow, or tomorrow, anything might be possible—if not for him, then more probably for me. But I had understood for some time now that my father would not have been allowed to fly the plane home or even remain inside the cockpit for much longer without the good excuse of fixing something. Dad's suggestion of flight only pointed out what he could not do, what he certainly did not know—the limits of even workmanship and diligence. I felt the sudden closeness of the cockpit, the slope of the shell rounding so low over the control panel and nearly touching my shoulders that I could not stand for more than a few more moments. I turned towards the hole, wanting to scramble down the nine steps of the ladder to gasp in the sweat and oil-sweet air of the hangar, ashamed and elated to leave the confines of my father's cell.

"Next time," I said, my back turned against Dad, whispering over one shoulder, lying to us both.

* * * * *

The handheld camera, flitting from face to face. The focus muzzy, the shots choppy and curt. Bouncing from the floor to somebody's knees and back again to meet an uncertain smile with the eyes squinting directly into the light bar's glare. Shooting with a 16 mm Kodak on Standard 8 and then a few years later, Super 8. But the technique improves only slightly—the unsteady hand, the long snout of the lens snuffling from subject to subject every few seconds. A crisscross of impatient arms waving the man away, go away!

Each family cultivates its solemn routines. A bevy of presents under the tree with the children pouncing like weasels on Christmas morning. (The baby discovers a toy drum, an illustrated book about making way for ducklings sent from a godmother in Boston, the oddity of a wool cap in California: everything delightful and now captured on camera!) Some rituals require documentary evidence: first communion, significant birthdays, confirmation, important anniversaries, graduation. Everyone displaying a pained self-consciousness in front of the camera in the years before everybody owned one. Posing. Hiding. Pretending not to notice. Waving under the glow of unbearably bright lights a favorite panda bear nearly as tall yourself. Whacking your brother on the arm—birthday surprise!—and for the next thirty years, it's proof you never got along. The succession of squalling, squirming children wrapped up in mother's or father's arms—the camera indicating their wary astonishment at the latest kid's existence. Early marriage, its unblemished pleasures. The camera catches a coy smile and a brush of the hand. Put on your Davy Crockett imitation coonskin cap, your Cisco Kid chaps and bandolier, your Marshal Matt Dillon badge, sidearm, and holster—and then parade down the side yard walkway, and then do it again, and this time let's see a smile on your face, and once again so that the camera's actually rolling this time...

What do we seize and memorialize?

Neighbors long gone. The gaunt bodies and thinning spirits of relatives growing older and soon to depart themselves. Excursions to Golden Gate Park, where your little sister gets lost among the rhododendrons. A trip to Lake Merritt, with its cormorants, mallards, and the old gray goose who bit the baby on his ankle and made him cry—his first betrayal imprinted on celluloid. Home movies enable us to remember the kids down the block who moved away, the girl who would be crippled the summer before the Salk vaccine, a best friend from fifth grade killed years later in a beery teenage car crash—that same wise guy nine-year-old towhead who swoops into the camera frame on his Stingray bicycle, his mouth open and cawing like a demented raven, though we don't hear his voice in these decades before sound, and never will again.

And later, years later, the unnatural absence of speech on the bright white screen as the 16 mm projector whirrs and crackles on the dining room table while the family devotes a night to recalling all that happened over a procession of neatly spliced four-minute reels. An in-law on the couch sleeping it off after another Christmas Eve bender—but you can't hear his snoring or the curious snap of his bones as bad dreams and the DTs whip and ripple through the sprawl of his emaciated limbs. Without sound, we miss the children shrieking, the baying of old dogs, the meow meow meow meow of a kitten freshly rescued from the pound and driving everybody crazy. We can't even hear the voices of mother and father, our sisters and brothers. Just the mute entanglements—holding hands, grinning with heartfelt pride and gooniness.

If some little doubt has arisen, some suspicion that all this won't last forever—well, the camera can't pick that up, either.

* * * * *

FOUR

Our Golden State

"Now pay attention to me..."

Dad towered above, hands on his hips, sunlight filtering through a cross-hatch of sycamore branches, his smooth, pink scalp illuminated and glistening with sweat. He wore grease-pocked tan chinos savaged at the knees from planting radishes and carrots all morning in the backyard. His canvas hunting jacket was fastened together at the unspooling seams with a foot-long patch of silver duct tape.

"*...You can't just cut their heads off.*"

I shifted my weight, working the flat of one palm into the wet grass, adjusting my gaze so that Dad's shoulder obscured the sun. Several score of yellow dandelions lay scattered across the lawn where I'd neatly severed them mid-stem.

"Why not?"

"'Cause they grow right back, that's why. These weeds ain't no Marie Antoinette and King Louie, you know." He hitched up his trousers by the belt loops and grimaced, estimating my acquaintance with the events of 1789, and then ploughed ahead just the same. "You can't go decapitating these fellas like some crazed Jacobin."

Dad was in a fine mood this Saturday morning, the cool spring air sharpened with the scent of bay salt and arsenic swept in from the landfill at the edge of town. He'd been up since dawn, relishing several hours of complete dominion over the yard. In his hunting jacket's inside pocket, he kept a small notebook and pencil stub, ticking off the chores and projects as they fell one by one.

Crazed Jacobin: Almost certainly, this was a compliment.

"Here. Try this." Dad flung a nine-inch screwdriver into the lawn. It thronged. I would have heard all about it if I'd been the one playing with tools. "Dig 'em out. Every one of 'em. By the roots."

He stalked off and I rolled back on all fours, retracing the zigzag of luminous yellow petals beginning to wither and curl in the glare of mid-morning. Basically, he was saying, "Start over." I stabbed the screwdriver into the lawn, imagining it to be the fat belly of Superman's archenemy, Lex Luthor. Only this morning in bed, sheets pulled up to my neck, I had started reading the latest issue of *Jimmy Olsen Comics*—a three-part exploit in which Superman's pal is mysteriously transformed into a human porcupine. I suspected Luthor was behind these shenanigans. *Shenanigans,* meaning mischief, pranks, monkeyshines, or tomfoolery—whatever that meant. I'd come across the word in a recent issue of *Action Comics* in which an inexplicable energy burst from inside a scientist's laboratory strikes Lois Lane and gives her X-ray vision so she can spot Clark Kent changing into Superman in the men's lavatory. Comic books can be very educational. On my third try, the screwdriver found a soft spot amid the gristle of Luthor's belly and sank up to the handle.

My father did not object to comic books, but he argued that greater satisfactions could be obtained by making a necessary contribution to the household. I plunged the screwdriver into the heart of a headless dandelion, which squirmed under pressure, its stem mashed and slivered, but the root wouldn't budge. I leaned into the tool and we sank another inch. Working from the wrist, twisting and flicking, I up-ended the weed at its tip and it flipped out of the ground and into the air like a little man in a flowery hat shot from a cannon. Its crisp tail had broken off. That made me think of a carrot chomped a third of the way up, like Bugs Bunny would do on Saturday morning cartoons. I was hungry. I wanted to go inside, get out of the sun, eat Frosted Flakes, watch TV. Maybe spend some time later with Jimmy Olsen, cub reporter for *The Daily Planet*, a great American newspaper in the city of Metropolis.

A blast of water rattled the pipes along the side of the house. Almost immediately, my nostrils throbbed, registering the tang of iron. My throat burned. Dad out back spraying the roses.

I sank the screwdriver handle-deep into the lawn and hurried into the backyard to watch him work.

Dad was leaning against the compost bin, cradling a brown plastic bottle like the head of a snake slinking out from a dirty coil of sun-baked hose. When he fingered the release valve, the fine, acrid mist of Ortho Home Orchard Spray doused a platoon of aphids tramping across our butter-yellow roses and I gagged. Insecticides, said Dad, had won the war, along with plastics and light-metal alloys and radar and jet engines and a thousand other inventions and improvements. Insecticides and herbicides had saved the bacon on Saipan, flushed Japs out of the bush on Guadalcanal, mowed down mosquitoes and chiggers and tiny blue flies that laid eggs in your eyes and killed men in twenty-four hours and otherwise would have cut a swath through the best army in the world. They probably saved my uncle's life in the Solomon Islands, said Dad—though Uncle Win pointed out that he seldom got to land unless it was by swimming there after being sunk at sea and it was the sharks he had to worry about then.

Yet my father did not apply Ortho to our front lawn, where it might have done some good against the dandelions. Mom disapproved. Dad could do whatever he wanted in his backyard, but the front was public property—at least in the way it got used every day by us kids slithering through the grass, grinding ourselves into the dirt, soaking up through our open pores the lurking vestiges of modern science's most recent realignment of the ordinary molecule, the polychlorinated hydrocarbons and biphenyls that made life out on the patio pleasingly free from gnats, that caused California's Central Valley to blossom into the best-spread fruit and vegetable table the world has ever known, that gave the citizens of suburbia the green gushing pleasure of backyard horticulture, the companionship of flowers, fruits, grasses, shrubs, and trees all year long.

"You done in front already?"

I shrugged, sniffing the air. The scent of Ortho was both repellent and delectable, like the rot of your own athlete's foot.

"I guess so."

"Why do you have to guess?"

"I'm not finished yet," I explained more judiciously. "Not nearly. But I want to help you massacre the snails."

Dad peeled back his lips to expose a faultless set of alabaster false teeth. The Army had yanked all the originals, saving him a fortune in dental bills for the rest of his life. "Okay. Go get the Bug-Geta. It's under my workbench."

When I returned with the green and orange cardboard box featuring a menacing gargantuan snail on the front, we sprinkled its contents across a patch of beets, onions, and spinach.

"Dad, can this stuff hurt people?"

We both studied the russet carpet of petrochemicals.

"You an aphid?"

"No."

"A snail?"

"No."

"A slug?"

"No."

"Well, then..."

"But you wouldn't want to eat it," I asked innocently enough, "would you?" Soon as we stopped talking, I'd have to return to the dandelions.

Dad cocked his head. "Look," he said, his voice rising in faint exasperation. "I know what your mother thinks, but there's people in India and China and whatnot now that've got enough to eat two and even three times a day thanks to Bug-Geta and what-have-you. There's even a scientist, and this fellow's got himself a Ph.D. from the university—a doctor of plants or animals, or insects maybe. And every morning during his coffee break, along with his Nescafé, he treats himself to a nice little meal of a bug poison with a funny name. I believe they call it 2,4-D. And what do you think it's done to him?"

"Nothing."

"Not a damn thing. Said he's even got to enjoy the taste." Dad grinned bumptiously at the audacity of learned men, at progress itself, and then he suddenly tightened his lips and his expression straightened like a clothesline. "Now don't you go snacking on this stuff yourself. It's for snails only. At least," he said, clapping me on one shoulder, "you wait until you get a laboratory of your own."

I laughed along as though I thought I might actually grow up one day to be a scientist, or a farmer, or even the guy at the nursery who sold us the box of Bug-Geta. It seemed the perfect moment. So I asked him.

"Can I have a dog?"

• • •

Gil was the youngest brother of Mrs. Bingham, the butcher's wife. After two years in the Army and an honorable discharge, Gil decided not to return to Mitchell, Nebraska, so the Binghams let him move into their garage. "Just until something opens up somewhere," Mrs. Bingham explained to my mother. Gil owned a primer gray '55 Buick that he planned to repaint sky blue and cherry out with chrome mags, headers, and a tach once he started working, but for now it sat on the curb outside the Binghams' house and seldom moved before noon. On the driver's side above the gas tank, in four-inch ivory block print, Gil had hand-painted the name of his former girl friend: *Dee*

Dee Dinah. They had been engaged back in Nebraska, but the girl found an older man who worked in a bank while Gil was fulfilling his military obligations. Gil was stationed in Germany the same two years as Elvis.

"You ever see him?" asked Benny. The Changs lived three houses down from the Binghams and Benny had talked me and Phil into tagging along. The garage seemed far too dark for the middle of a Saturday afternoon because the Binghams' new boarder had covered the lone side-door window with several layers of the *Oakland Tribune*'s help-wanted section. Mrs. Bingham said Gil was still exhausted from active duty.

"More than see."

Gil sprawled the length of his canvas cot, a relic of family hospitality that staggered and whined on its spindle legs every time he shifted his weight. He sparked up a fresh Marlboro and puffed lazy smoke rings into the rafters.

"What do you mean?" demanded Phil, fanning himself with splayed fingers.

"I'm not saying I was his closest friend, you understand. But me and Elvis, sure—we hung out together. Now and then. You see *G.I. Blues*?"

"No."

"You remember the part in the barracks, everybody singing along?"

"We didn't see it," explained Benny. "None of us."

"That's me. Standing next to him. My elbow's leaning on his bunk. He didn't mind. He's a cool head."

Elvis Presley was a cool head. Who could dispute it? At our house, my mother only paid attention to the radio when she heard "The Theme to *Exodus*" by Ferrante and Teicher or anything by Connie Francis (whose real name was Concetta Rosa Maria Franconero—she changed it so the Protestants would buy her records, too). Dad preferred the news or a Giants doubleheader with Gaylord Perry and Juan Marichal pitching. It was Benny's older sister Bernice who owned a copy of *50,000,000 Elvis Fans*

Can't Be Wrong with Elvis on the cover wearing a gold suit that hung on him like damp sheets of cellophane. If anything happened to his sister, Benny said he'd inherit all her albums.

"You ever see Elvis fight?" demanded Benny.

"Nah, he kept to himself. Colonel Tom Parker ordered him to. Didn't want no bad publicity when he got out of the Army like me." Gil groped blindly under the cot until his fingers located the dial of his plug-in table radio. Its vacuum tubes warmed to cast an orange glow on the underside of the canvas so that it looked like its occupant was being pan-fried. Twisting the dial through a hail of static, Gil settled finally on "The Battle of New Orleans" by Johnny Horton.

"I heard he knows judo."

Gil yawned, his lips forming an infant's perfect O. He was twenty-two years old, long and sinewy like a knotted rope. He wore thick black frame glasses in the style of Buddy Holly before his plane crashed, and they made his eyes look like steelies, the chrome-plated marbles we prized above all others as the most devastating shooters. After the service, Gil had let his hair grow, lubricating the sides with Butch Wax, an indolent chocolate-brown wave teased over his forehead like the horn of a unicorn. He clapped a hand over his mouth when he saw me staring.

"Do you know judo?" persisted Benny. Sometimes Benny was like a little mutt with a rubber bone in his mouth that he wouldn't let go of for anyone.

"Judo's for babies." Gil puffed a smoke ring in Benny's direction. It landed and dissolved on the tip of his nose. "I learned karate."

"My dad's got a black belt in karate."

"No, he doesn't, Benny."

"Benny lies like a rug, Gil."

"I bet your hands aren't registered as deadly weapons with the police."

"I still got to do that," admitted Gil. He cranked himself up on the cot and surveyed the three of us. "You kids want to trade or not?"

"I got some *Archie and Veronicas*," said Benny.

Gil nodded his approval. "Where are they?"

"In my sister's drawer."

"Go get them."

Benny threw open the side door, flooding the garage with the light of day.

"What about you two?"

"My dad doesn't let me read comics," said Phil. "He says they make you stupider."

"I got Jimmy Olsen," I admitted. I didn't feel like I had any choice.

"*Jimmy Olsen, Superman's Pal,* or Jimmy Olsen appearing in *Superman?*"

"Both. I just read the story where Jimmy gets amnesia and thinks he's an orphan and he only wishes he were Superman's pal. But Supergirl's living in the same—"

"Go get it."

"Okay. But what do you got to—"

"Go get it. Then you'll see."

I hesitated. It wasn't that I didn't want to trade, but I knew that my parents were bound to ask where I was going if I rushed out with an armful of *Jimmy Olsens* and I suspected that Gil's garage was not the right answer. Nobody had said anything directly against him. Still, my father had a way of tilting his head whenever Gil got mentioned, while my mother nibbled her lips as though discretely swallowing some uncharitable comment before it escaped to run riot in the world. Gil was too old to trade comic books, even I could see that. And the last time, all he had were two issues of *Casper the Friendly Ghost,* both of them smudged with grape jelly. I was summoning the courage to ask if he had any *Green Lanterns* when the kitchen screen door flew open and crashed against the wall.

"Gil, can I have a ride to the store? We need some things for dinner."

Sandy Bingham lined the door jamb, her torso a seesaw of

triangles fastened loosely at the corners—the head of blonde curls bobbing across one shoulder, her hips filling out a pair of green-striped culottes and jutting the opposite direction. Sandy was only three years older than me and Benny, and for as long as I could remember we had all played together on the neighborhood's front yards—Freeze Tag, Simon Says, Mother May I? But ever since starting junior high the previous fall, she had begun calling us "the little kids."

"What're we having, cousin?"

"Pork chops. But we don't have enough."

Gil turned up the volume to "El Paso" by Marty Robbins. He ran his hands down the front of his t-shirt, ironing away its wrinkles. "Then we better get enough, shouldn't we? You know I love my pork chops."

Sandy laughed way too loud and I didn't see the humor. Gil read my mind.

"Elvis loves pork chops. You know that?"

"Uh-uh."

"Sure you do."

Gil shoveled his legs off the cot and reached under his bunk to pluck a midnight blue satin jacket from a nest of littered clothing. He slowly rose, shook the kinks out of his legs, and with a serpentine shrug slipped both arms into the sleeves. A half-moon of hand-sewn gold letters spangled the jacket's backside: DUSSELDORF U.S. ARMY.

"You come back later with that comic book," he told me, "and I'll give you a *Prince Valiant* for it."

"I don't like *Prince Valiant*."

"Come by tomorrow. I might be busy tonight."

* * *

"What should we call him?"

"He's so..." Mom ransacked her polite vocabulary for the proper word. "Huge."

"A whopping big name then," suggested Dad.

"He's great!" I squealed and knew I sounded just like a girl.

"Did you have to get the biggest one?"

"The biggest and the best," said Dad. "Am I right?"

"Right!"

"Oh, I don't know..."

"We'll name him after your people," Dad offered. "After some dago."

"We will not call him that."

"One of your emperors. Caligula."

"Who?"

"Or Nero. Nero means black in Italian. Black as sin." Dad drummed both hands on the flat pan of our new family member's rump and his tail switched like a whip of steel cable lacerating my legs. "I bet your mother didn't know that."

"Why is he drooling? Are they supposed to drool?"

"No, not Nero. Nero had a black heart. Fiddling around when he should have been governing. Let's call him—oh, I don't know...How about Gaius Julius Caesar Augustus."

"Your father was reading the encyclopedia all last night. I don't know why."

"It's kinda...long."

"Augustus."

"Franklin, really. What kind of name is that for a dog?"

"Rome's finest emperor. Of course, they had given up on self-government by that point."

I lay my hand across his forehead as though taking his temperature through the thick coal carpet of fur. The distance from my thumb to little finger wasn't long enough to span his two rheumy brown golf-ball eyes. Part Labrador, part mastiff, part hound of indefinite origins. "A mixed breed," my father had explained at the pound as I pressed my face against the wire mesh cage and allowed his wet, pink, six-inch tongue to marinate one cheek and then the other. "Just like you." Our new dog was eight months old. Seventy-five pounds. Almost big enough to ride. The animal control officer said he had the rest of the day and if nobody took him home, then that was that.

"Augustus!"

"So be it."

* * *

Dad planted a bountiful Valencia orange as the sun shone intermittently between winter's rain and spring's drizzle. Alongside it, he placed a Meyer lemon of the improved dwarf variety. In the shade he tended columbine and in the sunlight rockrose, geraniums in a red brick planter box and pyracantha for the springtime rattle of scarlet berries. He lavished care upon carpets of lamb's ears surrounding the hop seed bush and phlox selected to attract butterflies and hummingbirds, along with stalks of crimson amaryllis and towers of agapanthus cast in shades of virgin pale and heliotrope. Our backyard remained treeless, but bushy—red azaleas stationed amid eggshell-white and lavender rhododendrons, the redwood fence corners flush with sticky, saucer-shaped ocher flowers branching from the flannel bush, a *Fremontodendron* named for John C. Frémont, who drove out the Mexicans, served as the state's first senator, and now had a suburb christened in his own name down the road from ours. Dad told me all about him as we watered, turned the compost, and poisoned our enemies. Everything, he said, grew better in the West.

That was one reason they were pouring into California from everyplace now—our neighbors, our future fellow citizens. Seventeen million already and we drew another thousand, another fifteen hundred new people each day. We had become the biggest state in the union, more populous than New York, which hardly seemed worth imagining now, or even Texas—where cowboys still roamed, where Davy Crockett had died defending the Alamo, a place that just *sounded* big, but we were bigger. Bigger and better than anyplace that anybody had ever seen before.

Mom collected magazines that trumpeted the good news and piled them on the end table in case relatives from Massachusetts should come to visit: evidence that she had made the right choice. *Newsweek* put us on the cover, declaring: "No. 1 State: Booming, Beautiful California." *Time* called California "A State of Excitement." *Life* said "California Here We Come—and This Is Why." We were building houses, highways, hospitals, new universities up and down the state and the best public school system in the country. Just stand at the kitchen sink and you could see the scope of our collective ambition emerging from the stainless steel faucet, a reminder of the California Water Project with its eighteen pumping stations, nine power-generating plants, and hundreds of miles of canals and levees. There was nothing like California back where folks came from, nothing to match us in distant forgotten Kansas, Missouri, Arkansas, Iowa, Alabama. California was a desert, but we were making it bloom.

I concentrated on the dandelions. Every afternoon after school, I plucked at least fifty from the ground. But they kept growing back. Perhaps I'd miss one or two—even Dad admitted that you couldn't get them all—and they'd explode the next day into starry blossoms, thousands of taunting yellow flowers arcing towards the sun only to collapse overnight, turning into prickly globes obliterated by the slightest breeze, their seeds and parachutes unscrewed from their cushion heads and sailing, lofting, floating, and finally descending into the hundreds of hospitable perforations I had created in the moist ground with my screwdriver. The more I picked, the more grew back. A half-dozen sprouted from a hole where a few days before I had evicted a single weed. Each night as I fell asleep, the dandelions etched themselves onto my eyelids, their green-stem plumbing, their flattened yellow helmets, their wicked beige taproots and insinuating tendrils that I could never, ever extirpate for good.

Our neighbors sought long-term solutions for their front yards. The Sandersons paved over their slope of Merion wonder grass and painted it green, calling to mind a pool of lime Jell-O. The Changs introduced ivy and then sat back to watch it run rampant through the course of a single thirsty summer. Some homeowners did nothing at all, allowing their property to revert to a state of nature, which entirely missed the point of living in Jefferson Manor, where our lawns were meant to be aligned as indistinguishable patches of one-and-one-half-inch tufted emerald carpet reconstituted as a garden of endless duty: as Eden.

In March, Dad and I drove to the nursery to purchase three twenty-pound sacks of Scott's Turf Builder. In April, Dad sowed grass seed in the spots that had parched and spoiled, sousing the soil with a frothy ammoniac blanket of Cope to suppress grubs. In May, we layered more fertilizer and inspected the ground each evening until the seeds sprouted. We watered once in the morning and again at night during the summer—then spread around Weed and Feed to bring the clover to its knees and replace the gobs of nitrogen it otherwise drew from the air and injected into the ground. We attacked the crabgrass with Clout and Kansel and pummeled the remaining insects with another aerial barrage of Cope. When in doubt—it was like washing your hair with Prell—we lathered up and did it all over again.

But mowing and feeding and watering and mowing again had no end. To my father's way of thinking, this was the price you paid, though sometimes he spoke of a devil's bargain.

Leaves had begun to yellow and fold on the Bearss lime—*Citrus* x *latifolia,* also known as Tahitian or Persian lime according to *Sunset*'s *Western Garden Book*. The culprits appeared to be ants. Dad pinched his thumb and forefinger at the crown of its slender stalk and watched a dozen misdirected workers scramble across the back of his hand. He had worried about lime blotch or scab or greasy spot or even red algae, but the man at the nursery said he'd probably just over-watered, flushing the ants from their nest and weakening the tree until it turned ripe for invasion. We purchased a half-dozen Grant's Ant Stakes. Active ingredient: 1.0% hydramethylnon. The buggers died quickly.

Two weeks later, they were back—and twice as many.

+ + +

"Is *Dagwood and Blondie* all you got?" asked Benny.

Gil sparked up a Marlboro, inhaled rapturously, and blew the smoke directly into Benny's face.

"Why? You don't think Blondie is bitchin'?"

Benny shrugged. Augustus was sprawled across the cold concrete floor close to the door, where a slim margin of light leaked in through the crack. In the gloom of Gil's garage, my dog looked like a big black boulder, dense and immovable, except when he was licking himself.

"Think about it," advised Gil. "Blondie is bitchin'—that's a fact. And you can have her for two *Betty and Veronicas*."

"How come two?"

Gil swiveled around on his cot and squinted in my direction. "What about you, kid? What'd you bring me today?"

I made a face that I was glad Gil couldn't see in the dark.

"Speak up. Whaddya got?"

I rolled my copy of *Jimmy Olsen, Superman's Pal* into a periscope and casually surveyed the garage. I'd read the issue three times already, but I still wasn't sure about trading it. In the featured story, Jimmy drinks a vial of serum that temporarily gives him the ability to stretch every part of his body like a rubber band that will never break. As Elastic Lad, he can peek over tall buildings like the world's biggest giraffe and tie villains all up in knots with his rubber fingers. Once he grabbed a bank robber down the block without leaving his chair (and then he made a crack about the long arm of the law). Serums had previously turned Jimmy into a werewolf, a giant turtle, a Bizzaro World version of himself, and an incredibly fat freak.

"Betty and Veronica," purred Gil, his voice syrupy and spit-filled. "I wouldn't kick either of 'em out of bed. Ronnie's got those big tits, man...I'd come all over them and she'd probably lick it right off."

Benny's head tipped back like he'd been winged by a slingshot. "Eeww! You hear what he said?"

"Betty's not so bad, either. Little Catholic girl, probably.

Wearing her uniform all innocent-like. Hell, they can't keep it out of their mouths. You know what I'm talking about?"

Benny and I glanced at one another, admitting that we probably did not.

"It's just," said Benny, easing away from Gil's cot, "that I already traded you this one before and I'm not really interested in reading it again."

Gil flopped down on his back and sighed. His head rolled my direction and we locked indifferent gazes.

"I bet you two would rather fuck Little Lulu."

"No, we wouldn't!" I objected.

"I bet *you* would," sniggered Benny, the traitor.

"You don't even know what it means, Benny."

"I do too. My sister told me."

"I don't even like Little Lulu," I protested.

Gil kept puffing on his Marlboro, his puckered lips surrounding the glowing red dot. His waterfall was greased thick with Butch Wax.

"You two are a couple of real poker players, aren't you? Holding out on me until I bring out the good stuff."

Benny and I didn't say anything.

"You're pretty smart, aren't you? Be honest."

"I am," admitted Benny.

Gil wiggled his way to the edge of the cot and sat up straight from the belly, like he was still in the Army. He muttered to himself about how we had really pulled one over on him this time.

"You," he ordered, pointing to Benny. "Get my duffle bag from underneath."

Benny dove for the concrete, slipped under the cot, and hauled a big duffle out from the shadows.

With two hands, Gil yanked open its string purse and sank one arm down deep, blindly fondling its contents.

"Here it is." He flapped a magazine onto the cot.

I could hardly see anything except Gil's ball-bearing eyes vibrating above the glow of his dwindling cigarette. He reached for the flashlight he kept under his cot. A milky beam splashed across the cover.

"Cool!" said Benny. "Look at his face."

Famous Monsters of Film Land, an issue featuring Lon Chaney as the Phantom of the Opera. He had hardly any hair parted down the middle and the worst set of rotting teeth you ever saw.

"I'll trade," I said.

"No," objected Benny, "I will. Gil asked me."

"Gil asked us both, Benny. I said it first."

"That's a good lesson for you, kid. Take what you want."

I firmly held *Jimmy Olsen* between the pinch of my right hand's thumb and forefinger until my left felt Gil loosen his grip on *Famous Monsters.*

"Wait," Gil told Benny, "I got something for you, too." His hand slithered back into his duffle bag. He grunted with the effort of further exploration. "Yeah, here, it is."

He trained the flashlight on his open hand. Stretched across his palm was a long skin-colored balloon with a puffy tip at the end, like a rocket ship.

"You know what this is, right?"

"Yeah."

"What?"

Benny's voice dropped to a whisper. "A Trojan."

"That's right. Your sister tell you about them?"

"*No.* I just know."

"Gimme *Betty and Veronica.*"

Benny handed them over.

"Wash it out before you use it. If you know how to use it."

I wanted to get out of there, but Benny was already at the door. He cracked it open and the light pressed hard against our eyeballs. I grabbed Augustus by the collar and dragged him to his feet.

"And hey, kid," said Gil, settling back down on the cot to read at his leisure Jimmy Olsen's adventures as Elastic Lad. "Your dog stinks."

"He does not," shot back Benny. Benny always stood up for dogs, but he especially respected Augustus. Augustus was huge.

"Smells like a barn in here," said Gil.

Benny straddled Augustus's haunches, hunched over his big head, and sniffed. "He smells good," he reported. "It stinks in here 'cause of you, Gil."

Gil didn't even hear him.

"And hey," he said from behind the comic book, "you tell your sister I want her to come by and visit me sometime, okay?"

✦ ✦ ✦

I longed for super powers.

Usually, they descended upon an ordinary but virtuous mortal by accident. An unduplicable error in the student chemistry lab. A lightning strike at just the right angle. A bite from a radioactive insect.

In comic books, only the villains plotted to acquire the powers of flight or invisibility or blinding speed, and then they invariably paid a great price. Banishment to the Phantom Zone. Being hurtled to the furthest reaches of the universe by a superhero's shove of superhuman strength. Finding themselves reduced to a quarter of an inch so they fit snugly into the municipal jail of Kandor (the former capital of the planet Krypton), which was shrunk many years ago by the green-skinned supervillain, Brainiac, and sealed in a bottle that now safely resides in the North Pole inside Superman's Fortress of Solitude.

In the shower, I watched the water roll off my shoulder to trickle down the naked sleeve of my straightened arm and I wondered what it might take (thunderstorm, earthquake, strange brew radiating from the municipal waterworks?) to transform my molecular makeup so that I was granted the sudden power to shoot streams of water from my fingertips with the concentrated force of a fire hose. Better yet, Yosemite Falls! (Someday we were going there for vacation.) I pictured myself as Shower Lad, blasting villains against brick walls, reducing them to a piteous slosh—a technique I'd seen on the TV news in Birmingham, Alabama. I'd join the Justice League of America, along with Superman, Batman and Robin, Wonder Woman, Flash, and Green Lantern. Together we would battle and bring to justice Brainiac, Bizarro, General Zod, and Mr. Mxyztplk, the imp from the fifth dimension. Almost certainly, I had a vocation.

"When're you gonna clean up after that damn dog?"

I lay on my bed, arms stretched wide and fastened at the wrists, feet strapped to either corner, staring up at the ceiling and into the bald-headed face of evil genius. From a trembling steel cable, Lex Luthor slowly lowered the boulder of kryptonite and I was rendered defenseless into the clutches of the merciless supervillain.

"You hear me? Quit daydreaming and get out there and clean up after that dog or he's going right back where he came from."

Luthor's smooth, pink, evilly hairless skull hovered above, glaring down at me—until I realized that, of course, it was Dad. I bolted upright and slid off the bed and hurried out into the yard.

Next to the compost bin, in the dirt, covered with straw and grass and a conspicuous wide stripe of his own shit smeared across his rump, I found Augustus, sleeping.

One eyelid flapped open, spotted me, slammed shut like a gate.

Augustus was always sleeping.

"Wake up!" I lifted his long black rope of tail by the tip and wagged it for him. "C'mon, boy!" I scratched his head with both hands, drumming my fingertips upon the flat plate of his skull. "Thatta boy, Augustus, good boy!" I slipped my arms around his neck and shoulders, lowered myself onto his back, taking care to avoid the putrid smear at his other end, and I squeezed. His planet head slowly rolled into one shoulder, his features materializing like the man in the moon. A wide ribbon of red tongue washed my mouth. "Good boy, Augustus. Want to go for a walk, boy? Do you?"

Augustus pushed himself up by the front paws, assumed the sitting stance that I tried to teach him, and began to bark.

"Quiet, boy. Quiet."

Augustus kept barking, his pace quickening, the singular yelps now blending into an air raid siren ululation, a hearty yowling with long gummy ropes of saliva dangling from his cavernous maw as he threw back his huge meaty head and gobbled the air for no reason at all.

✦ ✦ ✦

Dad used a licked-clean root beer Popsicle stick to ladle the fresh pollen of a pink cotton-candy hybrid tea called Bewitched onto the stamen of a lavender Lady Banks climber—forever altering the destiny of his roses. Creating something aromatic, beautiful, or peculiar, something *new*—that was the thing! When cross-pollination failed, Dad resorted to simple grafting, placing five varieties of pears on a single rootstock, showing anybody who cared to observe (I watched, but my mother did not) how to execute a whip graft, cutting both the branch and scion at a shallow angle, binding them together, and sealing the joint with candle wax. Nursing along the graft, watching it take, flourish, blossom, fruit. Sometimes Dad sang to his plants, as Luther Burbank had done, coaxing them along with "They Call the Wind Mariah." Something about vital forces, he explained, an instinct surpassing mere cell division.

And yet reminders of the susceptibility of all living things to accident, pillage, and decay also littered his garden. Rust attacked the roses. Gophers raided his staggered rows of peas and carrots, pulling them underground like Morlocks devouring the Eloi. In the side yard, next to a wreath of wound-up hose and nozzle, Dad planted a regiment of snowy freesias. Natives of South Africa, he bragged, tough as nails and sweet as honey to the nostrils. Augustus thought so, too, and one afternoon he devoured a half-dozen aromatic funneled flowers, leaving only the tooth-sawed shoots. My dog foamed along the pink and black folds of his blubber lips and his breath smelled like Dial soap. We staked him out back with enough rope to slink into the shade once the wrathful sun began to cross our yard.

"You come in now," suggested my mother. "You've been out here working all morning."

Dad snapped shut his Army-issue teeth like an angry tortoise. He glowered at Mom as though she had straight out called him a failure.

For whatever refused to thrive, Dad had nobody to blame but himself, and so he always did. But he also bristled and fumed at the positioning of the sun, the stab of a late spring freeze, the stinginess of seeds bought cut-rate and hoarded over too many winters to produce what they had originally promised. Earlier that morning, I had watched him fling a shovel across the yard and then throttle a wilting sunflower, yanking it out of the soil by the throat.

My mother folded her arms across her chest and stared far over my father's shoulders, the corners of her mouth pinned tight. The end of our block was still fenced off with barbed wire warning against hunters on the prowl, and game birds honked overhead every morning: not a town at all, she sometimes grumbled, but an empty place still making itself up. If a snail devoured his shoots of red chard and spinach, it really wasn't her fault.

I sat on the concrete walkway, both arms wrapped around Augustus, his neck as thick as an elephant's foot. I could sense my parents' uneasiness as each gauged some rivalrous absence in the other. The bay breeze fluttered through my dog's matted black fur and I felt frightened and cold.

One Sunday afternoon, I was surprised to see Dad cheered up within the barony of his bushes, fruit, and flowers by a visit from Uncle Win. They stood alongside the trellis of wisteria, its stalks of violet petals sputtering in the breeze like Roman candle fire. Their heads tipped towards one another in concession to the blood tie and neighborliness. I couldn't even smell an argument.

Dad hefted a lightweight black plastic pot off the ground and fit it into Win's clutches. Then he stood back and beamed. They both admired the plant's tangled sunbursts of tiny petals, the centers of the flowers swollen into the shape of raspberries.

"Now you need to plant this fella someplace with plenty of sun, and water him good. You understand?"

My uncle nodded. "Sure, Slick. I'll do it today." He seemed touched by his older brother's tenderness towards the flowerpot.

"Maybe drop by the nursery on your way home and pick up some fertilizer. Feed and water is the secret. You be sure to feed and water this youngster and you'll get results before you know it. Maybe I'll even rustle you up a few more for your backyard."

Win wrestled the pot into a surer grip, resting its edge against his belly. "What's it called?"

"I'll write it down for you." Dad extracted his notepad and pencil stub from his jacket's inside pocket and bore down hard on the page, studying the results as they materialized. "The scientific name is *Nilknarf's Deew*. Think you can remember that?"

"What is that, Latin?"

"Old Norse." Dad tipped back the brim to his cap and ran an open palm over the smooth dome of his skull. "The Vikings brought it to Greenland long before the Spanish and the Portagees even set sail. It took a spell to get to California."

"I appreciate that, big brother."

When my uncle left, we all took a lunch break in the kitchen.

"What did you give Win?" asked Mom. She removed a frosted pitcher of blue Kool-Aid from the fridge and found a glass for me in the cupboard. Then she pivoted to face the stove and stirred a pot of Campbell's SpaghettiOs. The kitchen smelled like boiled catsup, but sweeter. It made me hungry.

"What're we having for dinner?" wondered Dad.

"There's Rice-A-Roni, if you want. Or I can take the Chef Boyardee pizza out of the freezer."

"Pizza!" I had already decided.

Dad sampled a mouthful of SpaghettiOs and issued an extravagant sigh of satisfaction.

"Say, when're you going to make that Tunnel of Fudge cake again? I enjoy a good Tunnel of Fudge."

"What did you give Win, honey?"

Dad pulled his pipe out of his shirt pocket and began stuffing the bowl with a sack of Lucky Strike Half-and-Half. He sparked a match, and I remembered him telling me that years ago they used to sell the strike-anywhere variety under the brand name of Lucifers.

"I offered him a nice little specimen of common ragwort." His false teeth parted in a smoky rictus. "*Nilknarf's Deew*. That's *Franklin's Weed* spelled backwards. It'll be all over his yard by the end of summer."

I laughed. Dad puffed gray clouds over the SpaghettiOs. Mom slammed my glass of Kool-Aid down hard on the Formica table, its blue wave lapping over the rim.

"There is something mean about you," she told him. "Sometimes something mean and small."

I drank my Kool-Aid and they didn't talk. When we finished lunch, Mom joined me in the front yard, down on her hands and knees, rooting out the dandelions with an awkward pull on a foot-long screwdriver that didn't begin to get the job done. I snuck a glance at her face once or twice when she was stooped over on all fours and found that her eyes were as empty and bored and faithless as I feared my own must be.

✦ ✦ ✦

I came home before dinner to walk Augustus, but he was gone. In the backyard, I found paw prints in the radish patch and a large pile of dog doo that turned out to be cold when I prodded it with my index finger, but no sign of my dog. I thought he might be sleeping behind the fireplace out back, but all I found was his muddy hole and a broom handle ravaged with tooth marks. I wondered if somebody had left the side gate open by accident.

Maybe me.

I jogged into the middle of the street and whistled. Augustus never came when I whistled. I called out his name, though I wasn't absolutely positive that he knew it.

I cut a path down Brook Street, crisscrossing at Yale, Harvard, and Princeton. No Augustus sprawled across the hot tar, no dying dog flopping on his side like the goldfish I'd won at St. Bernard's Easter Festival the year before and spilled one afternoon onto our kitchen linoleum.

Of course! He must have headed to the park. Augustus loved to mark his territory, kill squirrels. He would have remembered the park. Augustus was smart, probably.

"*Augustus!*"

I pictured him at the edge of the swimming pool, lapping up refreshment, urinating into the gutter, diving into the deep end with a deafening splash and sinking to the bottom like a boulder wrapped in bear's hide.

I gripped the cyclone fence with two hands, pressed my face into its mesh, rattled the screen.

"*Augustus!*"

No dog in the swimming pool.

Maybe the eucalyptus grove where he chewed the bark off saplings and bayed at the sea gulls.

"Here, boy! Come home, Augustus!"

In the parking lot, beyond the grove, I spotted a familiar car: *Dee Dee Dinah* inscribed in pale ivory above the gas tank. I dashed to the driver's window, breathless and full of hope. My head bobbed at the open window.

"Gil! Did you see my dog? Augustus? He's black and huge."

Gil gripped the steering wheel with both hands. He cocked his head in my direction and squinted as though he couldn't quite place me. His upper lip curled like Elvis's.

"You talking about a nigger?"

Sandy Bingham was crumpled in the corner of the passenger seat. She was crying. She turned her head away, concentrating on the eucalyptus grove.

"Did you see him, Sandy? You know my dog. He's gigantic."

"Go away."

I ran home, two blocks. The front door was open, which meant my mother or father must be there.

Mom stepped into the living room as soon as I shouted for her.

"Mom, Augustus got out. I looked all over for him. But he's disappeared."

She hesitated, shifted her weight from one foot to the other. "Your father," she stated, as though that explained everything. Her eyes scoured the carpet as if it were rippling with grubs and maggots. "Your father brought him back to the pound. You weren't living up to your responsibilities."

"What?"

"He was too big for here, honey. He was a big dog and he needed a place to run."

"He brought him to the pound?"

"This morning. He felt very bad about it. He did. I could tell."

✦ ✦ ✦

The existence of Superman raised questions. Why didn't he go back in time using his super-speed to visit Germany before the Nazis and strangle Hitler in his cradle? Why didn't he squeeze coal into diamonds and pass them out to everybody so everybody could be rich? If he was so powerful and so smart and so good, why didn't he irrigate the Sahara desert somehow—he should have figured out how—and turn it into a place where everything grows with plenty of room for everybody and everything.

Superman did not exist. So you didn't need to worry about it. You didn't need to talk. I didn't say a word for days.

I felt sleepy and restless, blurry, vacant—every part of me down to my fingertips too sensitive to the touch, like my skin had been scoured down to the nerve endings. I didn't cry. My father passed me in the front yard while I was rooting out dandelions—I didn't see him. I refused to see him. I felt sick when

I heard his voice. I stopped listening. I plunged the screwdriver deep into the green belly of the lawn, but I didn't think anymore about Lex Luthor. I dug up that lawn with a thousand puncture wounds, my screwdriver like a dagger to the heart of every innocent dandelion.

I missed Augustus: I must have. I thought about the times I stuck my nose into his collar of fat, wrapping my neck around his neck while he panted his meaty bad breath and I inhaled the loamy odor of dog, my dog. Then I forgot about him for a day. Forgetting made me furious: I squeezed both hands into bloodless white fists when Mom called me for dinner, retreating into the backyard for as long as five minutes. If they were both sitting at the kitchen table, waiting, I might place the heel of my Keds on the tip of a white freesia and mash it into the soil or yank a radish and lob it over the redwood fence into the yard of some stranger.

Dad said maybe someday we'd try another dog and that made me feel like my insides were bleeding, my guts riddled with BBs. I hated him. I told Mom that I hated him. She said that I didn't and offered to help me outside with the rest of my job. We worked together on our hands and knees, not talking. In an hour, there were hundreds of dandelions scattered across the front lawn like tiny corpses in their silly, stupid, yellow-flowered hats.

Phil asked about Augustus and I explained that he was a big dog and needed room to run. Benny never mentioned him, but he stopped coming by our house for nearly a week. At school, on the playground and in the halls, he wouldn't look me in the face.

Then one night, I heard a small fist pounding frantically on our screen door and I knew Benny was back.

The porch light blazed above him, and from behind the grill he looked like he was shattered into a million pieces. Benny was hopping up and down, actually hopping.

"C'mon, hurry! Mr. Bingham's got Gil treed."

I slipped out the front door and we tore across the yard, down the block, and onto the sidewalk in front of the butcher's house.

Gil had climbed to the top of the Binghams' sycamore, perhaps seven feet high, and he was now inching along on both feet across the only branch sturdy enough to bear his weight.

"Daddy, stop!" Sandy rocked back and forth, her hands wrapped around either shoulder like it was impossible to stay warm.

Mr. Bingham stood next to his daughter, directly below the sycamore, arching up on his toes and swiping at Gil's ankles with a meat cleaver.

"Ernie!" shouted Mrs. Bingham from the end of their walkway. "You're not making it any better."

Mr. Bingham took another swing at Gil and barely missed.

Gil crept further out on his limb, balancing on hands and knees. He was talking fast to Mr. Bingham, not looking down at the ground, not making much sense, I thought. Mr. Bingham's white t-shirt was soaked with sweat and his face had turned red and gold.

Gil froze on the far end of his limb.

Mr. Bingham wrapped both hands around the cleaver handle, bending back so far that his spine looked like it might snap, and then threw all his weight forward. The blow severed the branch cleanly, though I could almost swear I saw it freeze in midair for an impossible instant like in the cartoons when the Road Runner screeches over the cliff but doesn't realize it yet—and then it crashed to the ground with a crack and bounced several times across the lawn along with Gil, who rolled over twice and tried to scramble to his feet but fell and was curling himself into a ball when Mr. Bingham got close enough to kick him twice in the stomach, hard.

Lucky for Gil, I suppose, the police were there by now—a pair of squad cars rearing up over the sidewalk with cherry tops flashing, the policemen hustling Gil out of the way of Mr. Bingham's feet, scooping the meat cleaver off the grass, and then placing them in separate backseats. They drove down the street and around the block, and disappeared. Everybody went home after that to get ready for work or school or whatever the next day was going to bring.

✦ ✦ ✦

"What're these?" asked Dad.

He studied his plate. A large heap of greens occupied the center, pooled in oil. To me, they looked familiar, though oddly placed. Dad sucked on his teeth and kept both eyes pointed down at the table.

"Your dinner," said Mom. She ladled two large spoonfuls onto my plate. "*Soffione*. It's a southern Italian specialty."

I scattered them with a fork, searching for yellow blossoms. The light from the overhead milk-glass fixture bore down on us like the sun. "Dandelions?"

"With garlic."

I could smell the garlic. Some people said it stunk, but I never thought so.

"This all we having?" asked Dad.

Mom served herself before answering.

"Yes."

Dad didn't touch his silverware.

"If you don't like what I give you, you can always fix yourself something else. Nobody's helpless around here, are they?"

Dad prodded his mound and fished up a long green stem on the tines of his fork. He studied his dinner. Then he eased it into his mouth, nibbling delicately with his front teeth like a rabbit.

Mom sampled a forkful. She made a little face and patted her mouth with a napkin.

"You're excused," she informed me.

"I'm hungry."

"Make yourself some cereal. There's a box of Trix open."

"I like Frosted Flakes."

"Mind your mother," said Dad. But his blue eyes roved easily in my direction and he vaguely smiled. I found the Trix in the cupboard. Orangey orange, lemony yellow, raspberry red.

"I'm going back to work," announced Mom. "They need a secretary at the elementary school. Somebody with experience."

Dad kept working the dandelions around his plate, concentrating very hard on swabbing the greens into one of the puddles of oil and garlic that had accumulated at the margins. He didn't look up.

I shook out a bowlful of cereal and poured myself a large glass of Hi-C.

"He's old enough." Mom pressed the weight of both elbows onto the table. "He can come home and do his homework. He can watch television if that's what he wants."

My mouth was full, but I spoke up anyway.

"I'm not picking any more dandelions."

"You don't have to," my father conceded, his voice raised to warn off anybody who might think that I did. "You done a good enough job already."

Mom placed her fingertips against the rim of her plate, pushing it to the table's edge. "If you want, I can still be home in time to make dinner." Her voice was trembling. "If that's still what you want."

Dad eased back from the table, chewing his lower lip. He drew a long breath, his chest swelling enormously before it collapsed. Then he remembered me and winked without actually turning his head in my direction. "Long as we don't get too many more nights of these dago greens, right?"

I watched my mother refuse to smile. Her face looked like marble, pretty and cold.

"'Least we're not eating snails like those French people. Right outta the garden, they pop them in their mouths for a little snack. Maybe some parsley and a glass of froggy red to wash 'em down."

I didn't say anything.

Dad forced another forkful into the side of his mouth and ground them with his back molars. "Hey, these are all right." He rose from his seat and scooted over to the stove. "See here—I'm going to help myself to more." He scooped out a generous second serving and set the ladle across his plate. For a moment, he stood at the stove, paralyzed: wondering, I suppose, about that little twitch of unhappiness, where it comes from and how it worms its way into our hearts. What and who, when you came right down to it, was really to blame? He stood there, trying to decide how to return the ladle to its pot while gripping his plate with both hands, knowing that everything now depended on his getting back to the table and finishing dinner without uttering another word.

* * * * *

Walter Cronkite fills the television screen, intoning calmly about this and that, while dinner materializes on the new TV tables—the Swanson's aluminum trays divided into bunkers of mashed potatoes, peaches, a carrot-corn-pea medley, and the succulent stack of chicken flesh and bones. Look up from dinner and a mouthful of gleaming white teeth have taken over the screen. Their lips and tongue advocate for Colgate toothpaste with Gardol and its invisible protective shield.

Then a sultry blonde with a vaguely Swedish accent—or is she French, who can tell?—moistens her lips and sighs. "Take it off," she whispers. "Take it all off..."

When thousands of doctors across the country were asked if they ever recommended Milk of Magnesia, the overwhelming majority said they did.

Ajax is stronger than dirt. The National Cotton Council agrees.

Cheerios has Vitamin B-1 for Go Power!

Mmmm...Boy! Almond Joy! Indescribably delicious.

To wash down the grub, try a glass of Wink, Squirt, Tab, Teem, Tang, Sprite, Spark. Or Coke or Diet Rite or Pepsi or RC Cola. Try Barley's grape, Shasta orange, Dr. Pepper. Get Mom to buy you some Dad's Root Beer or Dr. Brown's or Stewart's or Barq's or A&W or Mug. Make that Mountain Dew, Hawaiian Punch, or plain ginger ale.

Show me a filter cigarette that delivers the taste, and I'll eat my hat.

For dessert, there's Twinkies and Sno Balls and Hostess Chocolate CupCakes (and for a while, orange ones, too), or a Moon Pie or Scooter Pie, or an Eskimo Pie from the freezer, where you might also find a Klondike Bar, Nutty Buddy, ice cream sandwich, or plain ice cream, imitation ice cream, or ice milk.

A brunette with a vaguely Russian accent—or is she merely German, who cares?—sits in the passenger seat of a silver Jaguar driven by a man who is obviously a spy. She tosses her chestnut tresses across her bare shoulders, turns toward the camera, and purrs. "If you don't give him 007—I will..." She's talking about 007, the bold new grooming aids that make any man dangerous. "They've got a license to kill...women."

On the television set, Walter Cronkite speaks calmly, reassuring the nation in drab, cozy tones about the arrival of US Marines on the shores of the Dominican Republic, our forces dispatched to quell the latest turmoil among people who can barely govern themselves.

* * * * *

FIVE

Escape from Frog Island

Every Wednesday evening, right after dinner, Boy Scout Troop 623 devoted a full half-hour to drills and maneuvers.

Inside the empty, echoing, barracks-green lunchroom of Ulysses S. Grant Junior High School with its thirty-foot ceiling, we ran wind sprints over and over and over again under the pale, milky glow of halogen light until we dropped to our knees and wheezed.

We slapped above our heads our soft and flabby hands that had seldom held a rake or hammer, never mind a map, compass, or rifle, dispatching a barrage of manic, slapdash jumping jacks.

We recited Scout oaths in allegiance to the Antelope, Bobcat, Moose, and Indian Patrols with the whooping rhythm of Parris Island Marine recruits—preparing ourselves to someday parachute behind enemy lines as fledgling agents of the OSS. Then crisp orders barked out from the back of our formation and we hoisted the American flag up a ten-foot pinewood pole, transporting our nation's colors endlessly back and forth, back and forth across a generous expanse of high-gloss, crud-brown, hard-waxed linoleum. The scent of floor polish, boys' sweat, and the janitor's vodka-perfumed pipe tobacco filled the room.

The exercises, which followed the drills, offered myriad opportunities for distinction. In the center of the floor, match-slender Nicky LeRoux executed a half-dozen one-armed push-ups while the rest of us gathered around to scrutinize the throb of his knotty triceps. Rotund and round-bottomed James Thuggleborn proved the ideal anchor for a merciless game of tug-of-war. The temperature climbed and the lunchroom grew clammy and rank. We panted and we gasped. My own uniform sprouted soggy half-moons at the armpits while warm rivulets trailed down my back. I chanced a furtive glance at the fat eye of the wall clock: 7:20. The worst was yet to come. Finally, Lloyd Barnes, our scoutmaster, hollered for us to halt. Time for inspection.

We lined up by patrols. I stared up at the ceiling. The acoustic tiling was riddled with a million holes the size of BBs. I silently ticked off their number, imagining that the scope and ambition of my project would render me less susceptible, but Mr. Barnes found me anyway.

"Scout, your neckerchief is crooked."

"Yes, sir."

"What are you going to do about that, Scout?"

"Straighten it?"

"You certainly will."

Mr. Barnes moved down the line. His Florsheims glistened like anthracite. I released my breath.

"Scout, your shoes are shined."

Nicky LeRoux gazed down at his feet.

"I guess."

"That's an outstanding shine."

"Uh, thanks, Mr. Barnes."

"Outstanding."

And next.

"Scout—*what's this?*" Our scoutmaster's eyeballs spooled, aghast at the travesty set before him. His jutted his chin out fiercely and nodded at each of our four patrol leaders, cuing their attention. "Scout, I am very, *very* disappointed in you."

"Why Dad?"

"Give me twenty! Boy, your left breast pocket is unbuttoned."

Phil Barnes swatted his khaki shirt and grimaced. Then he dropped to the floor and began to push up and down like a piston. A batten of stage lights cast his bloated shadow on the far wall. In gloomy silhouette, Phil looked as powerful and duplicitous as Clark Kent.

"That sound about right, Ed?" blustered Mr. Barnes, pivoting on his heels to address Mr. Ortiz, our assistant scoutmaster. Mr. Ortiz sat in his folding chair at the rear of the auditorium, staring into space, bored out of his mind.

"I don't care, Barnes. If you gotta."

"He should be setting an example for the other boys, shouldn't he, Ed? *Mister*," said Mr. Barnes, folding himself at the waist to peer into Phil's crimson face and bark orders. "You better grasp that if you plan on becoming an Eagle Scout, you don't walk around with your shirt pocket unbuttoned. Do you understand me?"

"He's doing fine," said Mr. Ortiz, shaking himself to attention. "Can't you ever leave the kid alone?"

Endless inspections would have driven all of us out of the troop, except for the promise of overnights. Every other month, we camped out in the desert, at the shore, or in the foothills close to home. Mr. Ortiz usually came along, sometimes my father, too. The men relished the time spent talking around the flickering light of the campfire about growing up close to the woods, the trout they always brought home as boys for Sunday dinners, the stags and wild turkeys that got away. Dad got on well with Mr. Ortiz, who was not drawn to scouting for the drills and discipline—even less for pitting the Moose Patrol against the Indian Patrol in a contest of fern identification, or worse yet, for inducing the Bobcat to collaborate with the Antelope to produce a campfire banquet of Spam and foraged miner's lettuce. Mr. Ortiz preferred to shoot ducks, sleep under the stars. He had served at Guadalcanal; he didn't want to talk about it. Lloyd Barnes idolized this reticence, but he could not emulate it.

Our patrols disintegrated and one by one we looped into a large circle, bowing our heads in preparation for the closing prayer. But first, Mr. Barnes had an announcement. Two new Tenderfeet would be joining us for the overnight. Girlish chatter rippled around the circle and we temporarily broke ranks, even our patrol leaders snickering like third graders over the evil-genius initiation rites to which we would subject the newcomers on Frog Island. Then Mr. Barnes nodded to Mr. Ortiz, who opened the auditorium side door and whispered into the hall.

"Don't be shy, boys," Mr. Barnes called out vigorously. "Come meet your new friends."

Two teenagers slouched across the threshold. They were ridiculously old to be Tenderfeet, perhaps sixteen or seventeen. The tall one wore crumpled blue jeans and a white t-shirt with the front pocket stretched into the shape of a pack of Camels. His sallow complexion and caved-in chest indicated poor nutrition, bad hygiene, and a pitiless indifference. The other kid was bull-necked, smirking, clad in a white ruffled dress shirt, his blue jeans split six inches up the cuff with the seams extruding red velour. A towering blonde wave rose from the crown of his skull like a petrified tsunami.

"Boys, introduce yourself to the troop."

The two teenagers glanced at each other, and then the scrawny weasel boy stepped forward, clicked his heels, and elevated his right arm in the Nazi salute.

"I am Rommel of the Desert, Herr Commandant. *General* Rommel."

The other one slugged his shoulder. "Don't lie, man."

"Hell, no!" whooped weasel boy. "I'm Henry Eagle!"

"No, *I'm* Henry Eagle."

"No, I'm—"

"Young man," Mr. Barnes informed him patiently, "your name is Ralph. Ralph Studge."

"Oh, that's right. I'm Ralph Studge. Don't nobody laugh. And *this here* is Henry Eagle. Maybe you heard of him. Say hello to the nice boys, Henry."

Ralph Studge had not fooled me. Although I was merely a freshman, I had personal knowledge of Henry Eagle, our high school's leading delinquent, a second-try junior, a boy shaped like a refrigerator and inclined to felonious assault.

I had met Henry in first-period General Math, where we shared a desk on those irregular occasions when he was not residing at Juvenile Hall. Since Henry shouldered the responsibility for maintaining our school's high standard of statutory offense, he did not always have the leisure to complete his homework or even vaguely acquaint himself with the general direction of his own education. Fortunately, he was willing to accept my answers to every exam, and on Monday mornings, as a reward, he summarized for me his weekend activities.

"I got arrested again."

"Ah, that's too bad."

"I don't mind. I hit a cop. See?" He thrust a freckled fist under my eyes, displaying the teeth pocks. His thumb and forefinger were yellowed from nicotine. He smelled years older than the rest of us. "You ever been arrested?"

"Ah, no. Not really."

"You're young still. You got time. Gimme your homework."

Now Henry Eagle stood at the front of the lunchroom in Ulysses S. Grant Junior High School, and as the overhead halogens rained down a flood of insipid pale beams, he bowed at the waist in mock surrender to Troop 623. He held the bow for several moments too long and I wondered if perhaps he had gotten stuck. My eyes shifted around the room to our four patrol leaders. Nobody volunteered to help.

"Right," said Henry, gradually rising vertebra by vertebra to meet our incredulous stares with a nasty little scowl. "That's right, I know who everybody is now. And hey, we're really glad to meet all you Boy Scouts."

+ + +

My father had just finished reading a biography of Millard Fillmore and was moving on to the life of Rutherford B. Hayes. As a young lawyer, Hayes had concocted on behalf of a deranged murderess an elaborate insanity defense, one of the nation's first. Citizens regarded the tactic as ingenious, but despicable. Ninety years later, my father sat in his green Naugahyde La-Z-Boy recliner in the corner of our living room and complained in a complementary vein that our neighbors knew so little of the Republic's foundations that they could not distinguish Rutherford B. Hayes from James Garfield, or Garfield from the craven and corruptible Chester A. Arthur.

"Hayes is the one with the beard," I told my father.

"What kind of beard? I want to remind you that Garfield's got a beard. Grant, too, of course."

"The whiskers come down to the top of his chest."

Dad settled volume H of the *World Book Encyclopedia* in his lap. He was making the best of Sunday evening following an argument over something that had driven Mom out to tend the backyard clothesline. I sprawled across the carpet, soaking up his undivided attention. On the other side of the living room's picture window, the patio fountain splashed and burbled. Mountain lions or vultures or more probably our neighbor's cat had recently been scooping out and devouring our pond's Rexall goldfish.

"What color?" demanded Dad, flipping to the relevant page.

"They only had black-and-white photographs back then."

Dad stared darkly at the photos, sizing-up their sorry limitations.

"What shade?"

"God, I don't know. Gray."

"Then what does that tell you?"

"That Rutherford B. Hayes was the president with the long gray beard. Not those stupid white sideburns. Those stupid sideburns belonged to Chester A. Arthur. They named my elementary school after him."

"Chet Arthur, who kissed Roscoe Conkling's ass—that's correct."

Dad flipped shut the encyclopedia. "All right, then." He reared back in his La–Z-Boy. "Here's one for you, smart guy. Mr. Teddy Roosevelt!"

"The only president to have shot an elephant."

Dad nodded appreciatively. He extracted his pipe from his front shirt pocket, stuffed it with pouch tobacco, and fired the bowl with a single match. "Your turn."

I thought hard for a moment.

"Buchanan!"

"He never married," said Dad firmly, "and the man had no family. Not to mention he pretty much instigated our Civil War. What about Polk?"

"He fought the Mexicans."

"I guarantee you," replied my father, leisurely puffing on his pipe, "that he didn't do any of the fighting or the bleeding or the dying. Half a point." Then a beat later: "Lincoln!"

"Had a big black beard, but no moustache."

"Every Tom, Dick, and Harry can see that."

"Freed the slaves."

"Oh, good Lord!"

"His kids were dead and his wife was crazy."

"All right," said Dad, settling back into the curve of his recliner, relishing his authority and adjusting his bifocals before immersing himself in Rutherford B. Hayes. "I guess we can agree about that for now."

What was worth knowing? This question confused me lately. Was it more important for a young man to know how to swing an axe and navigate by the stars—or be able to name each member of FDR's Brain Trust under the direction of Rex Tugwell? I could only hazard a series of estimations, moving from one to another of the puzzles Dad routinely set before me.

When the doorbell rang, I sprang to my feet, first by a mile.

"Well, say hey there, Little Slick!"

Win flicked the screen door handle like a pinball lever and eased himself inside. He grinned at me with that moon-in-his-mouth smile, wiping his feet cautiously on the throw rug and then examining Dad to see if he had appreciated the effort. He had not. Win smelled of Old Spice and a recently extinguished cigar. I figured there was probably some trouble again between him and Aunt Tina. I couldn't count the number of Sunday evenings when Win had arrived at our house with time on his hands. He slapped me on the back like we were old pals, which I believe we were.

"Hello, Win." My mother drifted in from the back bedroom, her hands encircling the girth of a yellow plastic laundry barrel. "Is everything all right?"

"Whatcha all watching?" Win nodded at the television set. The screen was blank. Dad held up his presidential biography, snorted, and returned to the page.

"*Bonanza*'s at eight," said Win. "Should I turn it on?"

"Sure," I answered.

"No," said Dad.

"I'm going to call Tina," offered Mom.

"Aw, she'll be fine, Sis. Just give her a chance to cool off."

"Stay out of it," ordered my father. "Let him clean up his own mess."

"Nothing to worry about," muttered Win. He crouched at the foot of the TV console, bashed the power button, twirled the channels. The camera panned the Ponderosa—Ben Cartwright's endless spread of priceless ranch land just over the border in Nevada.

"Don't you got homework?"

I dashed into my bedroom. Returned with a library book. Settled down to study and watch *Bonanza*. The puzzled face of Hoss Cartwright hove into view, occupying the entire screen. When Little Joe appeared, Mom joined us on the tufted sofa chair positioned within shouting distance of my father. I set my book between my knees and flipped a few pages.

"What are you reading, dear?"

Win turned up the volume so we could all hear now.

"Mom, you wouldn't be interested."

"I might."

I was fourteen years old. Already confirmed by the Catholic Church as a Soldier of Christ. In three years I could buy cigarettes—even join the Army if I wanted (as long as I had my parents' written permission, according to Nicky LeRoux). What I read, as Dad would say, was my own business.

"Tell your mother!" said Dad.

"It's about history."

"Show me the cover, dear."

I slid my library book across the end table. It was a lap-sized survey of ancient Crete borrowed from school. The ancient civilization of Crete was a subject that intensely interested me these days because, as was evident in the highly detailed color illustrations in the first few pages, the women all walked around naked from the waist up.

Win snickered into his hand and leaned across the couch to clap me between the shoulder blades. He was himself a devoted reader of *Stag*. I had borrowed the latest issue to read about the Lustful Leopard Girls of Burma.

"Ancient civilizations," I explained cagily. "It's what we're studying now."

"He's studying naked ladies in school," corrected Win, addressing Hoss Cartwright on the TV screen. "Slick, ain't times changed?"

Dad regarded the book jacket's feeble promise: *Crete: A History*. "I'm going to turn off the squawk box right now," he said, "so we can all read in peace." He tossed a copy of *Life* at Win's feet. The cover featured Cassius Clay beating the brains out of Sonny Liston.

"What about you?" Dad demanded, glaring at me as he clicked off the television. "You got any real homework?"

"I want to watch *Bonanza* with Uncle Win."

"No, you don't."

"Study your Scout book," suggested Mom, "and you can earn some more merit badges."

"I'm quitting Boy Scouts."

"Wrong," explained Dad. "You're not."

"Scouts can teach you your way around the woods," said Win, sinking into the sofa folds. He peered thoughtfully out the picture window at our burbling fountain and the shoulder-high hedge of golden junipers, their sentinel bulk arrayed in the increasing darkness like a detachment of Praetorian Guard. Eventually he would have to return home and face the music, but there was no sense rushing it. When my father settled back into his chair, Win figured he had earned another half-hour's stay. "Your grandfather knew his way around the woods," Win told me. "Didn't he, Slick?"

Dad grunted assent.

"You remember the ol' man?" asked Win.

"He died when I was just a baby."

"Hell, I remember the ol' man. What a son of a bitch."

"Win," cautioned Mom from behind *The Saturday Evening Post*.

"I wouldn't tell a lie, Sis."

"Read," ordered Dad.

"I'm too old to be a Boy Scout!"

"Well, if you want, you can bleach out those oil stains covering the garage floor."

"I don't even like to hike!"

"Isn't your friend Philip still a Boy Scout?"

"Mom, Phil's a leper."

It was true. But for now, he was still my best friend.

"Leopard?"

"And I've still got about two hundred nuts and bolts under my workbench that need sorting."

"All we ever do is march around. It's like the Army."

"You could always do the ironing for your mother so she doesn't have so much tomorrow."

My eyes flipped back and forth between Dad and Win,

spotting no sympathy or assistance from either quarter. "I'm going to read about merit badges," I announced. The notion really did seem to originate from my own bright and lively imagination. I rooted through the stack of newspapers in the wire reading rack at Dad's side and eventually found my *Boy Scout Handbook* at the bottom.

When you are a Scout, I read silently to myself from the first chapter, *forests and fields, rivers and lakes, are your playground. You are completely at home in God's great outdoors...*

✦ ✦ ✦

I dreamt of Alma Ardilla. Her flat face and bulging white teeth flitting past like an Aztec war mask. Her sable tresses tied in a bun and coiled at the top of her skull like a bird's nest. Alma's wobbly spindle-brown legs, her webbed fat feet squeezed into too-small red peep Confirmation pumps. Her thin, slack shoulders wrapped in the same kind of front-buttoned short-sleeved Sear's white dress shirt that she and her brother Teo had been wearing every day since elementary school. In my dream, Alma bared her teeth, raised her chin, and sniffed at my face, no longer the shy, sad, mute little girl I had known since First Communion class. Her brown eyes pooled, her black pupils swelled and pulsed. In my dream, Alma clipped her fingers at the corner ends of either collar, slowly drew her hands six inches apart, and button-by-button plucked open her flimsy white shirt from the throat to her brown belly—astonishing.

That's always when it happened: me bucking and flexing beneath the sheets, waking with a gasp, my eyelids collapsing in a ruthless desire to catch one last glimpse of Alma's bare plain of copper skin, the spectacle of her tiny nipples more guiltily imagined than seen—and then the soppy, warm, sticky realization that whatever had transpired down there at the erupting hot crook of my imagination, the mess was already coating my thighs and saturating the sheets.

Phil and I ardently discussed the theoretical pleasures of

young women. How Merrie Banderas bobbled her hips in the hallway, unconscious of the devastation wrought among us. The bulbous, bouncing riches contained within Karol Kowalski's stingy blue cotton sweater. The way Mademoiselle Derain's small pink tongue darted out to moisten her lower lip when either of us dared an imperfect verb conjugation at the front of her classroom, then pursed her mouth in mock disapproval and formed a perfect wet red circle that hinted at expert French joys for her husband.

Yet Phil and I never talked about what was actually happening in our ordinary lives of failure among the girls we actually knew. How I had longed to ask Gretel Pell to slow dance with me on Friday nights when the last tune before the lights came up was always Gene Pitney's "Town without Pity." How finally I had traipsed across the Death Valley of our school's multipurpose room floor, asked her, and then, when she refused, turned around to retrace my steps across a much vaster Sahara and take my rightful place next to Phil, a leper, who patted my back and advised me to forget her.

How Phil stammered in the company of any girl he liked. How sometimes in their vicinity he excreted an odor reminiscent of smoldering nylon. How last year he had stood at the front of our eighth grade Social Studies class after volunteering to be the first to recite the mandatory preamble to the Constitution, only to discover as Angela Bonaire whinnied and neighed in the front row that his barn door was wide open.

As manhood loomed, new challenges had arisen and the talents I once prized in my closest friend—his facility with his Gilbert chemistry set's Bunsen burner and Pyrex beakers, his knowledge of all the names of the Luftwaffe high command (*Oberkommando der Luftwaffe*, Phil corrected pedantically)—would not help us to prevail. My boyhood best friend was becoming a liability.

His impetigo blossomed, trimming his lower lip and drooping across his chin like a scrofulous ruby goatee. He wore his Boy

Scout uniform to school, deaf to the ironic queries of sophomore girls who recalled their own childhood stints as Bluebirds. Phil would plead with me to wait for him after school, even though I negotiated the most roundabout route home to avoid our new classmates' scrutiny—a maneuver that Phil wretchedly believed was intended to prolong our time together. And once—no, more than once—when Phil and I were joined on the way home by Nicky LeRoux or Benny Chang or even the Chestnut brothers, who were wildly unpopular due to their Tennessee drawls and their identical bad complexions of ten thousand blackheads, we all conspired to ditch my old friend at Porter's Market when he dipped inside to purchase a sack of Brach's candy corn. As we hurried around the corner, I saw Phil standing there, switching his head back and forth like Burgess Meredith in that episode of *The Twilight Zone* when, having been locked inside an underground bank vault during an atomic war, he finally stumbles outside to find himself excruciatingly alone. *Where'd everybody go?*

✦ ✦ ✦

By 6:30 a.m., most of the troop had assembled in the parking lot and squeezed into Mr. Ortiz's Oldsmobile and Mr. Heilborn's Buick. Mr. Ortiz took off first, hammering out a farewell shivaree with alternating fists on his car horn and gassing it hard so that all eight cylinders snarled and spat as he rumbled down the block. Mr. Heilborn followed closely behind, permitting several Scouts to snake their worm-boy torsos out the passenger seat windows and bay pointlessly at a remaining sliver of pearl moon. I stood in the parking lot with Phil and Mr. Barnes, waiting for our two new Tenderfeet. A heavy lid of kettle-gray sky settled upon the rows of peaked rooftops. High above, a few stars still flickered. Still, it felt like an adventure to be up and out in the world so early. It felt full of promise about the things men do on their own.

For the next fifteen minutes, Mr. Barnes paced silently back and forth in front of his Rambler. Phil fixed his dead eyes on the blank wall of the nearest classroom. I stared at the toes of my black high-top Keds, sensing that we were all supposed to be in mourning about something or other. Finally, I glanced up and spotted Henry and Ralph dragging themselves into view—each cupping a cigarette in his retracted talons, passing back and forth the brown-bagged dregs of a twelve-ounce can of Olde English 800. Henry had confided to me more than once in General Math that he was a morning drinker.

Mr. Barnes bawled them out, employing copious references to letting down the whole troop, chains only being as strong as their weakest links, the mortal necessity of unit cohesion under enemy fire. The Tenderfeet looked baffled. Following our scoutmaster's orders, they shouldered up the Army surplus backpacks borrowed for them earlier in the week and staggered for an instant under their heft. Mr. Barnes looked pleased.

We fit all our packs in the back of the Rambler station wagon, climbed in, and hit the road. I balanced on the backseat hump between Henry and Ralph. Phil rode shotgun. Mr. Barnes switched on the AM radio to catch the weather forecast, followed by the farm report, both of which seemed to cheer him up. Scouts, he explained, should strive to acquire precisely this kind of information. Henry and Ralph glanced at each other, perplexed.

"Are we really going to sleep outdoors?" Ralph asked as we sailed down the greased-clean empty freeway. It felt like we were explorers at the edge of the known world.

"Of course, son."

"Haven't you ever been camping before?" wondered Phil.

"No."

"Me neither," admitted Henry.

"You'll like it," I offered.

Ralph popped his balled-up fist into my solar plexus. I gasped for breath.

"What about animals?" demanded Henry. "Bears and shit. We taking along a shotgun to protect ourselves?"

Mr. Barnes laughed like he thought he was supposed to do in

order to establish *esprit de corps*. "There're no bears where we're going. And remember, son: Scouts don't swear."

"Christ, where *are* we going?"

"Or blaspheme," clarified Mr. Barnes. "We're heading to a little place on the Delta called Frog Island. There'll be swimming and races and you boys'll definitely get a chance to do some map and compass work."

We approached the Carquinez Strait. The Rambler rattled across the bridge and passed quickly through the tollbooth. Nobody was on the road weekends.

Ralph grabbed my skull in a headlock and squeezed hard, pulling my head down into his lap.

"*Hey!*"

"Faggot! Quit trying to bite me!" Ralph thwapped my skull with the flat of his hand. "You see what this faggot did?"

"Boys!" erupted Mr. Barnes, whipping around for a perilous instant to peer into the backseat. "Last warning. No roughhousing 'til we reach the woods. Then if you still have a disagreement, we can put on the boxing gloves and solve it like men."

"When we reach the woods," Ralph whispered into my ear, "I'm going to pop your head like a pimple."

"Why?"

Ralph smiled and shrugged good-naturedly. "Dunno."

Several miles rolled by all too quickly. I kept my eyes straight on the road. Mr. Barnes turned up the radio and hummed along with Percy Faith's "Theme from *A Summer Place*."

"Hey, Henry," I asked, hazarding a glance at my occasional classmate, aiming to renew our alliance and gain a measure of protection from Ralph Studge. "Did you go to the football game Friday?"

"Nah, we was in Juvy. Who won?"

"They did," I had to reply, but that wasn't really my point. Warren G. Harding High School never won. Winning wasn't something our team got involved in. But we had tried hard. Maybe that was my point.

It had been an exhibition game at the very beginning of the season, with Harding playing a small private school from somewhere in the Oakland hills near Piedmont. The private school was full of the sons and daughters of doctors and lawyers, dentists and architects.

Before the kick-off, our marching band had wandered onto the playing field, the trumpets breaking into pig squeals on the high notes, the cymbals crashing persistently off the beat, the clarinets squeaking and striding into the end zone like the lost and the blind and the deaf. People in the grandstands were laughing through "The Star-Spangled Banner."

Yet by some miracle, our football team, renowned for its unbroken losing streak extending across five consecutive seasons, inexplicably found itself ahead at halftime by a single field goal. The crowd on our side of the stands was delirious; we could smell victory, so sweet and rare. Then the rich kids' cheerleaders ordered the crowd on their side of the bleachers to rise, which they all did with quiet, disciplined unit cohesion, and the song girls led them in an impromptu cheer that we had never faced before.

They cheered:

"HEY, HEY,
THAT'S OKAY,
YOU'RE GOING TO WORK
FOR US
SOMEDAY!"

Then their team ran all over us throughout the second half.

"Actually, it wasn't a very good game, anyway," I suddenly remembered.

Ralph drove his knuckles into the soft spot right above my kneecap. Hard.

As "Theme from *A Summer Place*" concluded, Mr. Barnes mercifully stopped humming and nudged Phil several times until he finally swiveled around to face the two new Tenderfeet.

"So," Phil asked without a flicker of genuine curiosity. "How did you get interested in scouting, Henry?"

Henry sat picking his teeth with a long, filthy thumbnail.

"The judge," said Ralph.

"How's that?" I asked.

Henry honored me with a cursory glare.

"The judge said we could join the Boy Scouts or go to California Youth Authority. We flipped a coin, and you guys won."

Mr. Barnes struggled with himself not to say anything. He lost.

"Boys, both Henry and Ralph have been remanded to the Scouts by the juvenile court. The judge thinks maybe we can make men out of them. Young braves. Teach them the meaning of responsibility."

"What'd you guys do?" I asked.

"Stole a car."

"Murdered my brother. And also my mother and father."

"Don't get smart, boys."

"*Smoked* them motherfuckers!"

"Boys!"

A pause. Ralph Studge sighed and stared out the window. We passed the refineries, the naval base, the new suburbs chewing up the flaxen-haired hills. The world was the most boring place imaginable.

"We didn't do none of that stuff," he confessed.

"Nope, we're innocent as hell."

"Going to be Boy Scouts," sighed Ralph.

"We'll make a regular Lewis and Clark out of you two," Mr. Barnes assured them.

Ralph's poxy complexion brightened. "The dude's named Louis? Sounds like a faggot."

"Two men, boys. Young Bill Clark and his companion Meriwether Lewis. Our national Corps of Discovery."

"*Meriwether*!"

"Two faggots!"

Mr. Barnes glanced into the rearview mirror and forced

himself to smile. He was not positive that he liked what he saw.

"Dot-*dah*, dot-*dah*, dot-*dah*," said Mr. Barnes. "*Dah, dah, dah*!" He droned on in a nasal, electrified hum. "Who wants to practice their Morse code?"

• • •

What made the popular kids popular?

Football players were obvious recruits for the in crowd. At least, the backfield. A tackle or guard had to insinuate himself by other means. Say, a '59 flat-black Ford jacked up three feet high on hydraulics with an eight-track booming "Sugar Shack" by Jimmy Gilmer and the Fireballs as his calling card. That worked for Elbert Graff, a gobbling oaf who once pantsed Benny Chang as he innocently stood on his number out on the P.E. blacktop in the middle of winter. (This automotive strategy could work to cross purposes, too—as with Ted Parina, a doleful senior with a pepperoni complexion, no achievements, and an A-*uuuga* car horn signaling his arrival that only drew attention to the fact that nobody cared.)

Cheerleaders clearly belonged. They even did their own sorting, making room for Panda Quilby, an otherwise unsuitable, too-tiny, figureless, dishwater brunette who bumbled, pitched, and toppled to the ground every time our marching band launched into its up-tempo and off-key rendition of "Semper Fidelis." The squad stubbornly deemed her "cute," and who could argue with them?

Hard cases fell into a subspecies. Henry Eagle strutting late into Auto Shop, his Juvenile Hall t-shirt yellowed at the armpits, his two-day stubble looking all the more sickening for being soft and blond like the bristles of a shaving brush. This was not the face of budding in-crowd insouciance and poise. Still, they granted him recognition as an object of alarm, best tolerated until the bell tolled and Henry's time, too, came for the Army, prison, or death by helmetless motorcycle mishap.

The in crowd was blessed with superb timing.

Bottom kids were easy to identify. Everybody knew who they were, though *they* sometimes, amazingly, did not. Oblong, freckled, clumsy, nearsighted—and let's face it—stupid Allan Allwater ensnared himself in perpetual ridicule one day in art class by plummily singing to himself:

"Don't play
with me
'cause you're playing with fire..."

Randy Motram's mother washed his gym clothes with a scarlet towel, dyeing Randy's jockstrap pink: branded forever. Arnold Hines was thirty pounds too fat, so some hard cases stripped off his sweatshirt when he wrestled the equivalently porcine Bobby Degas, their bellies rippling and rolling, crashing into one another in bucketing waves of nauseating gristle and lard. Unforgiveable. Guaranteed to be beaten, belittled, tripped in the hallway, dunked in the boys' bathroom toilet, backhanded and headbutted on the perilous trek home, labeled spaz, retard, maggot, faggot, creep, leper, goon, dip, dork: the uncoordinated, the unconfident, the ridiculously small or farcically tall, the ever-studious and blatantly dumb, bed wetters, crybabies, anybody donning a leather jacket and sunglasses without sufficient aggression and indifference to pull it off. Anybody whom anybody else, regardless of their status, could successfully label a spaz, etc., without bloodshed or other consequence.

I prayed to Jesus, pleaded with God, beseeched the Holy Spirit to never let me wander into this category of the damned.

Certainly not to keep Phil company.

Girls were another matter when it came to separating the winners from the losers. Girls operated according to a pattern imperceptible to boys, even the popular ones. Girls made you wonder what the rules were really all about.

In junior high, when Debbie Hamsun's parents took the stage on Talent Night to play electric guitar and sing "Matchbox"—just released on the Beatles' *Something New*—the prospects for lasting dishonor appeared staggering. Yet for reasons indecipherable to all but the inner circle of in-crowd females, the event was judged a triumph and Debbie began to walk home from school with Karen Benavides, Stacey Pastor, and Katrina Rodriquez—our school's flat-chested, hair-ratted arbiters of deportment and style.

Taking the kind of risk that Debbie Hamsun had allowed her parents to assume on her behalf was reckless, foolish, unthinkable, stagey, sly, brilliant, successful.

Not to be repeated.

Yet overnight—certainly, over the summer—new members of the in crowd were stealthily coined. Though only a lowly freshman, Mickey Dupree ran with a pack of older cousins who taught him to smoke, drink, flirt, fight, and (or so he claimed, though Phil and I both told him to his face that we very seriously doubted it) feel up Stacey Pastor in her own living room when her parents went out on Friday night to roller derby. Mickey stayed up late to study *The Steve Allen Show* and at the lunch table where he sat with upperclassmen Danny Rivera, Ralph Studge, Charlie Rivers, and other marginal in-crowd soldiers and hard cases, he mimicked his master, Steverino, by intermittently and inexplicably screeching: *Smock! Smock!* The fourth-period bell chimed portentously. "*Smock! Smock!*" shot back Mickey. I just smiled and kept my mouth shut.

To the countless spies and infiltrators, the in crowd divulged nothing.

Yet already, in science class, we were learning how the wolf detects her mate, how the ant locates the path winding intricately back home to the nest. Discrete, minute chemical secretions. Pheromones—which are nature's way of saying who's ripe for reproduction, whose body knows more than his head. You can't fake it. It's ready or not. We all get a whiff of each other and learn the truth.

+ + +

"We're lost, aren't we?"

Mr. Barnes ignored the question. He sat on a small boulder shaped like a medicine ball, unfolded the map, and studied our prospects. His official Boy Scout compass roved over the squiggle of topography allegedly delineating our position. When the compass did not produce the expected results, he thrust it in the air and shook it wildly like some figure from the Old Testament berating Jehovah.

"A Scout is never lost!" he explained, exerting himself violently in an effort to calm himself down. We circled around our scoutmaster. For nearly two hours, we had beavered through the tall grass in a vain effort to catch up with the rest of Troop 623. A vindictive sun blazed above. The wind slapped our faces and stung our eyes. Now we sat cross-legged alongside Mr. Barnes's boulder on the dusty patch of ditch-grass and poison oak that he had mistaken for the main trail across Frog Island. The exhausted air smelled of ragweed and buzzed with flies.

"It's just like your Scout handbook explains," Mr. Barnes ventured tentatively, and we all perked up in expectation of a way home. "Ralph, have you purchased your Scout handbook yet?"

"Course not."

"Henry, what about you?"

"No way."

"Well," continued Mr. Barnes, "it's just like your Scout handbook informs us. Somebody once asked Daniel Boone if he were ever lost, and the great woodsman replied, 'I *ain't* never been lost'"—Mr. Barnes's stress on the crude folksiness of "ain't" signaled his own recognition of the faulty grammar, and this distinction seemed to momentarily cheer him up—"'but I have been a might bewildered for a day or two.'"

"You saying we might not get out of here for a couple of days?"

Henry's bulgy biceps twitched and he demonstrated his disapproval by kicking up a suffocating cloud of dust.

"Rule number one," replied Mr. Barnes, quoting directly from the Scout handbook. "Stay calm."

"Fuck this shit," said Ralph. "Man, we should've just done six months at Youth Authority."

Mr. Barnes waved his hand in the air, trying to settle the dust and whisk away the aroma of fear and hostility rising off the two Tenderfeet.

"Phil," I asked, "where do you think we are?"

"Yeah, Boy Scout," said Henry, full of sudden hope and indignation. "Where are we?"

Phil studied the map, stood up, surveyed the skyline, and raised his thumb to his eye to take the measure of a lone tall tree on the horizon, and then he pivoted a half-circle, calculating Lord knows what. Over the past year, Phil had earned merit badges in Camping, Pioneering, Forestry, and Wilderness Survival, along with less immediately useful achievements in Astronomy and Book Binding.

"Can't tell," he concluded.

Henry smacked the back of Phil's skull, tumbling his cap into the dust.

"Don't fuck with me," he advised.

"Scouts!"

"The rest of the troop wouldn't have left without us," Phil reminded everybody, "if these two guys hadn't been late."

Phil shook the dust off his cap, resettled it on his head, and crouched close to the map. "Look, here's where we want to go. And it seems like we can cut across here"—he indicated more unintelligible squiggling—"and maybe pick up the trail on the other side of the creek."

"Thanks, Phil. Henry, you be nice to Phil because he's going to show us the way to get the fuck out of this place."

"We're just a might bewildered," suggested Mr. Barnes, raising one hand over his eyes to reconnoiter the fields of yellow lupine and the towers of yarrow gone to seed and spouting like crowns of broccoli.

"If anybody says one more word about how they know their way around the goddamn great outdoors," promised Henry, "I'm going to kick their teeth down their throat."

"You boys just don't understand the woods yet," explained Mr. Barnes, deaf to sound advice. "Experience. That's what Scouts is going to teach you."

Frog Island wasn't actually the woods and that was the problem. Frog Island was a marsh pitted with bogs, punctuated by swamp, enclosed by fen. Tule grass, toad rush, picket-fence alignments of cattails and what looked to me like waist-high relatives of the basic backyard dandelion sprouted from the shoreline like patches of wild hairs on an otherwise balding, scraped-raw, dust-laden, stamped-over scalp. The few trees left standing were stumps filled with evil gray spiders and large, frisky, biting black ants. (Ralph had already found that out while removing a stone from his shoe and plopping his butt on top of their colony.) Poison oak prevailed. The pollen made everybody's eyes water. You could detect the faint odor of skunk nearby. I didn't understand why we had come there. It might have been an agreeable place to spend the afternoon for a cloud of mosquitoes, but not for two dozen Boy Scouts from the suburbs.

"Be cool, my man," Ralph cautioned Henry.

Mr. Barnes caught up and resumed command.

"Boys," he declaimed passionately, "we're going to reason our way out of here!"

Lacking an alternative, we paid attention.

"I think Phil has pointed out the sensible route to locate the rest of our troop. From the map, I'd say it's going to run us"—he consulted the map again and frowned judiciously—"what do you think, Phil, maybe a half-hour?"

"Four hours."

"Between a half-hour and four hours," confirmed Mr. Barnes. "Depending on our pace."

"Then get your ass moving!" said Henry. "Christ, you're like a bunch of old ladies."

We slogged along the marsh banks. Ducks skittered down in the distance, vanishing behind a fortress of water plantain and cattails. Our scoutmaster encouraged us to keep our eyes open for edible plants. I raked an open palm across my forehead to swab away the grime. Ralph kept prizing off my tennis shoes at the heels. The leaden air gained another ten pounds with every hundred yards we stumbled. Henry whispered into Phil's ear what he was going to do to him if we didn't find the troop campsite by dinnertime.

"Who wants to sing?" shouted Mr. Barnes from the rear. "*Sound off*! Left. Right. Left, right, left. I don't know, but I been told..."

Nobody picked up the cadence. We hit a dry patch on a gradual rise that blossomed into a wider grubby trail leading nowhere and bracketed by blackberry vines. Everybody broke ranks to sample the berries and let Mr. Barnes catch up.

"Hey," Ralph asked, "you like pie?"

I glanced over either shoulder. Nobody there.

"Yeah, I'm talking to you. You like pie, buddy?"

I nodded. The sudden camaraderie made me wary, but I appreciated the way Ralph didn't punctuate his question with a slug to my guts.

"What kind?"

I shrugged. "Pumpkin?"

Ralph shook his head. "No, not pumpkin. What about berry?"

"Sure, I like berry."

"Then have a big slice!" He placed two open palms on my chest and shoved. I fell over Henry, who was crouching on all fours behind me, and tumbled into the blackberry bramble.

Mr. Barnes finally caught up.

"Scout," he ordered, as I thrashed about and further entangled myself in the web of thorns and bristles, "get out of there right now before you stain your uniform."

In a half-hour, we reached a small stream. Our two Tenderfeet plopped down at the edge of the sand spit, plashing handfuls of cold water into their pink sun-flushed faces. Phil detached his canteen from its belt pack, sipped moderately. I followed his example, but Ralph grabbed my canteen and finished it off. Phil motioned for us all to fall in around the map. He fingered our probable location and indicated a shortcut to the main trail. We would ford the stream for about twenty yards and then head due east over the hills.

We stripped off our packs and pressed them up above our heads as we waded across. Phil eased into the water first, balancing delicately with each step. Twice he almost slipped, skating over the smooth surface of polished stones, swishing into a deep muddy patch.

"Toss your packs to the shore," Phil hollered once he had reached the other side. "It'll be easier that way."

Mr. Barnes raised his pack to his chest and pushed with all his might, launching the load high into the air—but the weight of our troop's frying pans and cast-iron pots sucked the pack directly into the channel, where it sank below the water line about two feet from shore.

"Too heavy," reported Mr. Barnes. His voice strained to remain pleasantly informative. Ralph sniggered. Henry cursed. Phil dragged the pack out of the water and our scoutmaster waded across without further incident.

Henry, Ralph, and I carried our equipment across the channel. Ralph shoved me out of the way, lifted his pack over his head, and carefully retraced Mr. Barnes's steps. I followed Ralph. Henry followed me, but somewhere in the middle his legs skipped a foot or so ahead of his shoulders, and he jackknifed to the muddy bottom. His head bobbed at the water line. He cursed the Boy Scouts of America. Finally, Henry stood and dragged his pack to shore, stirring the swill.

"Gimme a towel!"

"My dad was carrying all the towels in his pack," explained Phil, "and they're soaked."

Henry focused his eyes into rays of loathing.

We spent the next twenty minutes tramping across an expansive field of burrs and stinging nettles. Henry tripped, disappeared for a moment amid the towering sedge, and rose with an elaborate and blasphemous execration. He was flocked in the style of a miserable Christmas tree with hundreds of cottony tufts that seemed in the sudden breeze to flit directly up his nostrils. He snorted, coughed, cursed. With a groan he stretched out his open palms to reveal a plastering of prickly spines.

"You okay, Henry?" asked Phil. His voice sounded as smooth and sweet as cough syrup.

"I'm going to reach down your throat and pull out your appendix!"

"'Cause why I'm asking," said Phil, shading his eyes as he monitored the sun's progress, sagely nodding to himself over the probable nearness of our next calamity, "is I'm hoping you didn't pick up anything bad for you in that water."

"What do you mean, 'pick up' something? Like what?"

"Oh, nothing. Don't worry about it."

Henry shook off his burrs. He fell into line behind Ralph and we swished into a mud patch and then back through the nettles.

"What are you talking about, squirrel-brain? Tell me."

Phil suddenly halted. I bumped into Ralph and he punched me in the stomach. Mr. Barnes marched slowly, bringing up the rear.

"You don't smell anything funny, do you? I mean on your own body."

Henry sniffed his wrist, worked his way up his arm.

"I just fell into a fucking swamp, butt-breath. What do you think I smell like?"

"I'm sure you're right. No reason to worry. Let's keep marching, men."

"No, wait a minute. We're not going anywhere until you tell me what's in that water."

Phil fixed his gaze on Henry. His lower lip protruded in an earnest expression of dread and compassion for a fellow Scout. "As long as you didn't swallow any, like even a *droplet*, Henry—then they can't usually hurt you."

Henry promised to gouge out Phil's eyeballs with his own thumbs.

"Ever hear of snipe fever?"
"No."
"I think maybe I have," admitted Ralph.
"Well," said Phil, "the way you pick up snipe fever is if you fall into a muddy channel, like the one we just crossed. But it has to be the late spring—which it is now, actually—in frog egg-laying territory, which I suppose would be Frog Island. Anyway, you still have to get some water in your mouth. Well, just a little. Just a drop barely touching your lips, actually." Phil locked eyes with Henry. "Because they're microscopic."
"They're real small," Ralph explained.
"Fuck you."
"Exactly," said Phil.
"And so?"
"So most of the time, no big deal. You make it to camp, towel off, and the next day you don't even remember it happened. Most of the time," emphasized Phil. "But if you do get some water in your mouth, even the ittiest, bittiest droplet, and then you find yourself starting to smell kind of…funny…Well, you should probably get to a doctor immediately."
"Why?"
"Of course, there are no doctors on Frog Island. And anyway, we're lost."
"Why, you gimpy four-eyed Boy Scout rat-fucker?"
"Because with snipe fever, these microscopic worms—the snipe, which normally feed off the frog eggs, particularly the northern leopard frog, which we got tons of here on Frog Island—they travel down your stomach and start nibbling on your intestines and then they come out the other end, all fat and juicy and still wiggling—"
"*Eeeuuuw!*" Ralph shrieked like a little girl.
"And brother," finished Phil, "is it ever painful!"
"Ah, he's putting you on, man. There's no such thing as snipe fever."
"You just said there was."

"What do I know, man?"

"You don't itch, do you, Henry? 'Cause itching's the first signal."

Henry clawed his stomach, scratched at his damp scalp like somebody rubbing out head lice.

"Look!" cried Ralph. "He's got 'em!"

"No, I mean the other end. No offense, Henry, but does your butt kinda itch? Because if it does, that means you got snipe. You got them bad. *Bad*! And the only thing to do is to get up there and root 'em out. Every one of them."

Henry ripped open his blue jeans at the fly, peeled them down to his knees. He slipped one leg behind the other and curtsied into a crouch, his rear end gingerly thrust forward, his hand slipping into the back of his shorts. As his index finger prodded and drilled, his face made a lemon-eating expression and his hips swayed right to left in a series of jagged thrusts as though he were attempting to corkscrew himself into the dirt. I stared, my eyes popping like flashbulbs. The mighty Henry Eagle.

"What're you looking at, you freak?"

I closed my mouth but kept gawking. It suddenly occurred to me that Phil was a genius.

"Or even worse, Henry, they go straight to your brain. And they start chewing away at the gray matter. And that makes you so dumb that it takes you five or six years to graduate from high school, and you'll believe anything anybody tells you, even about getting sick from microscopic animals that don't even exist, as any moron ought to—"

Henry stumbled over his jeans as he lurched and flew at Phil's throat. "You little maggot!" he cried, tumbling into the ragweed. "There's no such thing as snipe fever. You were putting me on."

"Tenderfoot initiation," Phil explained warmly. "You don't know nothing about the woods."

"I'm going to pull out your front teeth with my own hands and stab them into your forehead."

"Son," said Mr. Barnes, "I've heard just about enough of those kind of promises."

"Man, he had you going," laughed Ralph, "you really believed him." Ralph mocked Henry with childlike exuberance. "Snipe fever!"

"Shut up! I'm going to tear off your arm," Henry told Phil as he yanked his pants back up, "and use it to pry open your rib cage so I can eat your heart raw while it's still pumping."

"Congratulations, son," said Mr. Barnes. "You're now an official member of Troop 623. The only question now is whether you join the Moose or the Indian Patrol."

For the next two hours, we marched in silence—except for Mr. Barnes, who spoke at length about how we could survive for days if we had to on wild strawberries and the raw meat of salamanders. Being lost had for him grown into an achievement, reminiscent of his entirely imaginary adventures behind the lines with Tito and the Yugoslav partisans. When the sun grew intolerable—a huge pulsing grapefruit looming unbearably close to our dank and dismal little island—we all stripped off our shirts and tied them to our waists, which cooled us down pretty well until around four o'clock, when the mosquitoes descended, enveloping us all in whining billows of stinging black clouds. Henry swatted his face and shoulders while enumerating all the unpleasant things he would do to the insects sometime in the unspecified future. We pulled our sweaty shirts back on and ploughed ahead.

Maybe ten minutes later, Ralph threw down his pack and collapsed upon a dry hillock at the side of the trail.

"Time for a motherfucking break."

We joined him, flattening down a patch of spear grass and sedge. Ralph fished a pack of Camels from his pack, thumped the bottom until an unfiltered end peeked out, and inserted the cigarette into the corner of his mouth. "Who wants a smoke?"

"Son, put those away this minute!"

"Boy Scouts?"

Phil and I declined.

"Hey, c'mon! Sure you do!" Henry thumped two cigarettes

from the pack. "It's time you Boy Scouts earned your Smoking merit badge." He cackled cretinously and dipped into his pack for a can of lighter fluid, which he spurted generously across Phil's trousers. An acrid *ping* lodged at the ceiling of my throat. When Henry struck the match a waft of sulfur slipped up my nose, and when he tossed it at Phil—and missed—I watched the flame latch onto several stalks of tall grass, explode amid a thick, dry patch like an incendiary bomb, and sprint across the field.

Phil and I popped onto our feet and furiously kicked dirt into the fire. Mr. Barnes stomped an ineffectual tarantella in the middle of the flames. Henry and Ralph rolled in circles, whooping and crowing. "Boy Scouts!" hollered Henry. "Boy Scouts!" The fire rushed up the hill and widened at either side. Phil poured his canteen onto the blaze. Henry emptied his can of lighter fluid and watched the flames dance across the tall grass to erect an impregnable wall barring the trail.

"*Run*!" cried Ralph.

We tore off in the opposite direction, abandoning our packs and our equipment.

Phil took the lead, his legs pumping like mad. I paced directly behind him, my eyes fastened to his heels. I could hear Henry and Ralph wheezing behind us.

Smokers.

Mr. Barnes hollered, "Slow down!"

All I saw were Phil's two feet switching in front of me. He puddled through swamp, scrambled into bogs, sloshed his way over a crisscross of squelchy trails and parched thicket. The air congealed, growing murky with smoke and the sickly scent of burning sweet grass and charcoal. Henry yelled for us to slow down. Phil sped up. I stopped for a moment to gag and rasp. My lungs felt like shredded cheese. Mr. Barnes hollered at Phil to slow down. He sped up. I followed at his heels, struggling to stick with Phil as he kicked like an Olympian into his last lap, my eyes glued now to his back as it receded in the distance, as my brave and brilliant friend disappeared into a throng of bulrushes.

I tripped and fell over a cross-hatch snare of lasso roots and traveling vines. For a moment, I was perfectly alone, no sign of Phil in front or the others in back. All that mattered was the percussive thump of my own heart nailing itself into the mud. I rose into a crouch and wiped the sweat from my eyes. I knew exactly where I was.

I jogged out of the high grass and tottered into the parking lot, panting and coughing and gulping down all the air I could get. Other members of the lost patrol soon burrowed out from the greenery behind me—everybody folded over at the waist and gasping, pointing at everybody else, howling who's to blame. An orange glow scored the horizon. The rest of Troop 623 was heaving their backpacks and sleeping bags into the trunks of Mr. Ortiz's Oldsmobile and Mr. Heilborn's Buick.

I took my place at Phil's side and waited for whatever was coming next. Mr. Ortiz was shaking him by both shoulders, demanding an explanation. Phil lowered his head and confessed in a near-whisper that he just wanted to make new guys bitch and moan and blister their feet. He had always known where we were heading. In the distance, tule grass spouted gray clouds like smokestacks.

"Tenderfoot initiation," he explained. Then he bent over, gagged, and splattered the blacktop with vomit.

"I want to know who set the goddamn island on fire!"

My legs wobbled. I felt scared that I might start laughing. I pictured Henry squatting over the field of ragweed.

"They're bullies," I peeped up staunchly. "They deserved it." I patted Phil's back and he convulsed once more.

"Barnes!" shouted Mr. Ortiz. "What the hell happened out there?"

Mr. Barnes roused himself from the rear bumper of his Rambler, where he sat crumpled, exhausted, struggling for air. "Those two," he huffed. "They'll never get beyond Tenderfoot. They don't take scouting seriously!"

"Not us," Phil explained, still humped over and rasping. "The other two."

Mr. Ortiz slammed shut his Oldsmobile's trunk and glared over one shoulder at our scoutmaster. It is extraordinary how much exasperation and dislike can be conveyed with a single shake of the head.

Mr. Barnes scanned the parking lot. He found all of Troop 623 now inspecting his blackened elbows, the grime scuffed into the knees of his trousers. His shirt was torn at the shoulder stitches, his hands and face were filthy. He started to speak but reconsidered. He daubed one cheek with a grubby palm, applying a faint pancake of charcoal.

"Tell them, Dad."

Mr. Barnes switched around to face Phil, raised one hand to his shoulder, and then hit him across the mouth with the back of his hand. Phil spit up blood in a burp of astonishment, tattooing the pavement. Mr. Barnes had everybody's attention now. Even Henry and Ralph's. Certainly Mr. Ortiz, which I suppose was the point. But our scoutmaster just stared at his shoes with nothing else to declare. The soot on his chin gave the rest of his complexion a sickly pallor.

The smoke and ash billowed back into our faces. The air stung from cinders. Fire engines squealed a path in our direction, pealing their alarm, and Phil was wailing so loud in his hurt and fury that I could barely hear the approaching roar of flames as the world of our fathers and their fathers before them receded further and further from our comprehension and grasp.

* * * * *

Squeezed up against the big city borders, the suburbs feel themselves most alive in panicky opposition. True, no blacks have yet crossed over to establish residence. None. But listen: you get one in here, and the next thing, you have five and then ten, and after that...Well, make way for Boogieville. Basically, you got them taking over.

So the border holds, and the suburbs double, then triple, then never really stop. The developers scoop out a wealth of topsoil, excavate millions of tons of bayside silt, fill in the mudflats. You can glance out your window where the shoreline used to lie, where the farmlands were scraped clean like the scalded hide of some unnecessary beast, and find the past paved over. What you have worth defending boils down to this: one boxy house, a tree, a patch of green—the thumping monotony nobody even imagined fifteen years ago, but whose threat of interruption now makes white folks fretful and mean.

Citizens of suburbia cannot stop thinking about the spades, the spooks, all those jungle bunnies running wild right next door.

Home from swing shift, the working man plucks a Hamm's from the top shelf of the fridge, eases into the folds of his scratchy broadcloth recliner, plops his feet up on the ottoman, and switches on the late-night network news. Stokely Carmichael, his eggshell eyes scanning from a coal black face, his head sixteen inches tall and filling the screen, invades the living room from the depths of lonesome Mississippi, where he taunts all those poor, dumb, club-wielding crackers. Stokely shouting, "We want black power!"

"They want black power!" mimics the working man, scratching his belly with a grunt, his long arms dangling as he strolls across the carpet in his best swaggering imitation of an ape until his wife orders him back into his chair, where he should just shut up now, be quiet and shut up. He feels foolish, ashamed. "Some of them are good people," he will later admit. "Certainly, there are some very fine colored people," he will proclaim like a true democrat, "and many of them work damn hard and take care of their children, and each and every weekend they mow their front lawn, if they have one. But these jigaboos, these spear-chucking Mau Maus with their fat-bastard preachers driving brand-new Cadillacs that nobody can afford...What do they want? Why can't they stick with their own kind?"

* * * * *

SIX

Jungle Music

Our silver jackets flickered in the spotlight. Our lime-green slacks shimmered. Our sheer white nylon pimp socks peeked out from our alabaster imitation alligator Italian pumps and glowed in the dark. We were iridescent.

Pico plunked the opening bass line and the rest of us started moving—the guitars taking a giant step forward and then gliding back into formation at stage right; the horns following along on the left—the five of us stationed in front of the drums and organ now, and working together on the Temptations routine: spin, slide, and a genuflection to the audience as overhead spots rained down a flood of milky light.

At the center of the stage, Teddy rotated a full circle, dropped to the floor with his two skinny legs scissored into the splits, popped back up, and held himself perfectly still. He grasped the microphone stand with both hands, breathing hard and already sweating. He pressed the cold metal against his heart, closed his eyes, and opened his shovel mouth of pearly teeth and metal fillings to rasp and holler and growl.

All aboard

The horns climbing three sharp steps...

for the Night Train!

A two-tap punctuation on high hat cymbals and then the horns started chugging along...

Every Saturday night, we opened with an up-tempo version of "Night Train," our signature tune borrowed from James Brown's *Live at the Apollo, Volume I*. Pico slapping the bass with his meaty palm. Danny thudding his tom-tom and spitting out rim shots on the snare. Teddy skating across the stage on the side of one foot, plunging his microphone into the brass bell of my Selmer Mark VI so I could noodle through a half-dozen choruses of spit-and-snarl tenor sax riffs lifted note-for-note from Maceo Parker.

Miami, Flor-da

Bodies crowded the foot of the bandstand—everybody dancing the Fly, the Funky Chicken, the Boogaloo. Teddy tossed his microphone to Frankie and started to Camel Walk, his shoulders loping side to side, his head dipping and dunking. "Give the drummer some!" shouted some kid pressed up against the lip of the stage. "Give the drummer some!" And everybody else picked up the call.

Dee-troit, Mish-gan. Philly-dell-feeyah

Tapps elevated his trumpet bell shoulder-high, ripping it down to one knee, and suddenly we stopped playing—Danny Andretti's cymbals and tom-toms immediately filling in time. Danny's eyes rolled up to the ceiling, like he'd just died but couldn't stop his hands—his jaw locked in a rapturous grin, his cheeks flushed to the shade of strawberries, beads of sweat rolling off his forehead and into his eyes as he worked through some tricky maneuver to implicate the snare drum and pound the bass pedal on the offbeats.

And don't forget Jefferson Manor—'cuz it's got so much soul

In the middle of the first tune, somebody took a swing at somebody else down on the floor over the fact that this guy was standing there, blocking the view with his too-tall turd-brown Stetson; or because he was just standing there, period. The Manor Lords considered themselves connoisseurs of soul, but they mainly came to guzzle Coors in the parking lot and then fight all night on the dance floor. One evening, I counted: nineteen scuffles, prompting the lights to rise and the security guards to clear the combatants eleven times. The Lost Souls was a brawling band.

Fortunately, Teddy could cool things down when the occasion demanded. He'd call a slow number—say, "God Bless Our Love" by the Ballads. At the edge of the stage, Teddy would sing directly to Lucy Sylvestre, his girl, slender as a microphone stand, with pencil arms folded across her flat chest. Lucy had strategically positioned herself in the center of the crowd, as she did every Saturday night, to wail like a three-hundred-pound diva from some lost masterpiece by Verdi because she and Teddy had just broken up for the twenty-fifth time and now, in front of the entire world, he was making it up, pledging his love, bleeding his guts across the floor for her alone. Every drunken young thug would melt into the arms of every eyebrow-plucked, ratted-haired damsel with a switchblade hidden in her beehive, and the world would pause for a moment in unrealistic peace, life harmonious and in tune. And then Teddy would raise his prayerful head, slowly surveying the crowd of five hundred kids or more, our fans and minions, our brothers and sisters, and flash his big grin full of gratitude and disbelief that it should be him—*us*—up there on stage.

Are you ready?

Boom-bah!

Are you ready?

Crash-crack!

Are you ready for the Night...

Nothing but silence.

...Train!

We played soul music exclusively. Elongated bar-band covers of the three-minute masterpieces issued by Motown, Chess, Stax, Volt, and Atlantic. Seven suburban white and brown boys performing the black man's urban rhythm and blues. We learned all our best moves from the TV appearances of Wilson Pickett, Sam and Dave, Otis Redding, and Little Stevie Wonder on *Shindig*, *Hullabaloo*, and *American Bandstand*. Most of all, we bowed down to our savior, the Hardest Working Man in Show Business, Mr. TNT, the Godfather of Soul, Mr. Please, Please, Please, the singer who introduced us most extravagantly to the world beyond Jefferson Manor: James Brown. We played "Try Me," "Out of Sight," "You Got the Power," and "It's a Man's, Man's, Man's World" with Teddy falling to his knees and Frankie covering him up with a floor-length red velour cape his mom made. We played "Papa's Got a Brand New Bag," parts I and II. We played "Don't Be a Dropout" (without an education, might as well be dead) and for a brief time, until the obvious made everybody uncomfortable during a gig at Castlemont High in East Oakland, "Say It Loud (I'm Black and I'm Proud!)."

We were a blue-eyed soul band—though come to think of it, none of us had blue eyes. Frankie played lead guitar, and his family way back was English, Irish, Scots, German, and French—your basic backyard mutt. Tapps's grandparents came from Belgium, though he thought it also could have been Luxembourg. Pico Rosario, our bass player, had been born in Guam, so everybody called him Cannibal. Vincent Chestnut, our organ player, claimed he was "all-American," but in truth, Vince had never met his dad. I was a square head and penguin dick on my dad's Scandinavian side; and from Mom's, a dago, guinea, greaseball, and wop. (Danny Andretti, my paisano, called himself Benito and reminisced about Italy's slender victory over Abyssinia: "Tanks versus spears," he cackled, "and we still nearly lost.") Teddy Chavez's family came from Mexico and so we called him Pancho, Zorro, Frito Bandito—but never to his face.

By our junior year in high school, the Lost Souls were gigging two and three nights every weekend, lining our pockets with twenty-dollar bills. We planned to stick together until we all turned eighteen, and then who knew what might happen? Probably it was off to the Army, the factory, an apprentice slot wangled by an uncle with union connections—but maybe not, too.

We all knew what the Righteous Brothers had accomplished. Mitch Ryder and the Detroit Wheels. Felix Cavaliere and the Italian soul brothers from Jersey and South Philadelphia. Just because you came from nowhere didn't mean you weren't going places.

✦ ✦ ✦

Frankie and I were passing the hour in Woodshop when the word first came down. Some bullet-headed no-neck from the football team yanked open the shop door, hurled himself inside, and blared, "The Black Panthers just invaded Sacramento, and they got guns! So now all the spades from Castlemont are coming to riot! So you men follow me!"

I glanced at Frankie, who shrugged and returned to the drill press, where he was using a sixteen-inch bit to perforate the cover of his social studies textbook and spell out:

THE

LOST

SOULS

"I want every member of the football team," shouted the no-neck, "to follow me!"

A couple of young Neanderthals rose from the workbenches, nodding to one another—willing to sacrifice fifty minutes otherwise devoted to the construction of a perfect miter box to defend the rest of us from Nat Turner's rebellion. This was old news. The day before, the Black Panthers had left Oakland to pile into the State Assembly building in Sacramento, bearing arms and preaching about their constitutional rights. I'd watched it on television before dinner. Mom made pot roast.

"C'mon, men! What's stopping you?"

Danny Andretti was sitting in the back row, sealing his geometry textbook in a pot of glue. When our shop teacher, Mr. Hodge, nearly three hundred pounds—we called him Mr.

Huge—lumbered up from his chair to address the football players, Andretti lobbed a pound of nails over his shoulder and the pack exploded at their feet, scattering across the tile floor with a metallic chime.

"All right, all right," wheezed Mr. Hodge, "everybody back to their seats. Andretti, you clean up that mess."

"How'd you know—"

"You're a moron, I ever tell you that? The rest of you help your good friend with the housekeeping or I'm going to inform coach about the grades you really deserve. Dimwits. My god, really. Dumbbells, every one of you. How come I got to spend my life with you cretins?"

"*Busted*!" sang out Frankie. He tossed a drill bit at Andretti but missed.

Me, I didn't believe the black kids from Castlemont High School were coming for us. The Lost Souls had played there just last month. Once Teddy started dancing to "Twine Time," they even seemed to appreciate us. Unlike the no-necks, I knew the territory. Fact of life: spades didn't own cars. And from what I could figure out from the news, nobody got on the 1A bus to ride the ten miles across Oakland, transfer twice, and then riot in the suburbs.

Still, what did any of us know? Jefferson Manor was a white wilderness—that's what Frankie said.

Yet white wasn't all we were.

We were Limeys and Krauts, Japs and Chinks, Hunkies, Kikes, Bog-Trotters, Beaners, and Frogs. We were Portagees, Polacks, Pope-kissers, Christ-killers, and snake-handling Bible-thumping sister-*shtupping* redneck crackers.

We were white only in opposition to whatever wasn't white, and only when the occasion proved convenient.

Consider my pal Frankie—son of an Okie by way of the Cherokee nation. Frankie spoke frequently of his family's tribulations: how his grandparents lashed their mattress to the roof a Ford sedan to pursue jobs then ripening in the fields of the

Central Valley; then on to the canneries and factories in Stockton and Oakland; then a return to farm labor after somebody's daddy slipped back into the bottle or joined the Air Force or went to prison, or simply wandered away. Frankie always bragging: "My cousin on the other side of Jefferson Manor keeps his refrigerator propped up against the fence in his backyard like he was planning to plug it into a tree. On his damn lawn—like he never left Oklahoma!" On Frankie's mother's side, they were Arkies mixed with Choctaws and bore long records of larceny and sloth. Frankie's cousin Jimmy Steven was congenitally unemployable and too fond of Thunderbird and Mad Dog 20/20. His aunt Maytheen kept a cockroach in her pocketbook to defray charges at the Woolworth's lunch counter, placing the dead bug under a leaf of iceberg lettuce after finishing her grilled cheese sandwich and then demanding a strawberry milkshake on the house. "Don't look for a pretty girl," advised Maytheen's husband, Uncle Elmer. He had clearly heeded his own advice: Frankie's aunt bore a long, spindly nose like a twisted stick and chafed pink skin the shade of cows' udders. "Get yourself a girl with a trick or two up her sleeve. Get one with a steady job, if you can."

We were American mongrels, and we loved black music. Every one of us. Even those lumpy football players who stumbled around the dance floor like they were still wearing their cleats. *Everybody* loved soul music—but especially the greasers and cholos, the hoodlum element, our own Manor Lords.

Take Henry Eagle, their maximum leader and still the baddest ass in the Manor. Henry would swear up and down that James Brown was the most righteous singer in America, hands-down the best dancer in the world. Henry would crawl across a sea of busted beer bottles to kiss the eight-inch heels of James Brown's blue suede sneakers. But off the dance floor, it was nigger-this and nigger-that, Henry's face turning crimson and his eyes falling dead whenever he thought about them. It would get worse once he started railing about how they were taking over. Henry was as white as they came, like everybody else; though in reality, "white" never came up.

I poked Frankie. I needed his opinion. This matter of race relations, current events, and so on...It could get complicated.

The truth: I was worried.

I feared that ABC's father would not let his beloved and beautiful daughter go with me to the Lost Souls' Friday night gig if the citizens of Jefferson Manor thought Black Panthers were lurking in the juniper hedges and crouched behind every mailbox.

ABC was my—well, what was ABC? She was not precisely my girlfriend. I wanted her for my girlfriend. I wanted her. Smoldering briquette eyes, raven hair flipped at her shoulders, a swivel of hips as she stepped down the street in her red plaid parochial school skirt to catch the bus to St. Elizabeth's in Oakland, along with her eight brothers and sisters. Her full name was Antoinette Bettina Crikvenic. For the first two months we dated, I figured she was Irish or Mexican or Italian like everybody else. Her family attended Mass every Sunday at St. Bernard's, her mother looked exhausted, her father was mired in perpetual rage, and there were all those kids milling around the house. It took Frankie to open my eyes to the possibilities of a larger world and finally explain to me that her family came from someplace called Croatia. Croatian girls, explained Frankie, could not get enough.

I couldn't say, one way or the other. But I had to concede that ABC's lips did form a perpetual open-mouthed kiss. Her breasts bulged the buttons running down the front of her regulation white cotton blouse whenever she swelled her chest to take another long, deep, revelatory breath. ABC was a continent of desire, but to my knowledge, entirely unexplored.

Frankie was the expert on matters of the heart and so forth. After the Lost Souls played an afternoon gig at the Alameda County Fair on the plywood bandstand directly across from an agricultural exhibit celebrating the world's most intelligent rooster (he could add, subtract, and peck out answers to long division on the dirt floor of his cage), Frankie met a Hayward girl who took him behind the bleachers and let him slip his hand up her skirt. Frankie reported to the rest of the band as we were packing up our speakers that what he found down there felt like fish gills and smelled like the ocean. Then, following our gig at the Boys' Club, Frankie got even luckier in the parking lot of Pring's.

It tastes, he was telling me after the no-neck departed from Woodshop, like a combination of tuna fish and honey.

"Tastes?" I objected, putting together the picture. "Man, you never did."

"I'm just preparing you."

"Disgusting," I muttered to myself, blinking back the forthcoming rush of life's realness.

Me: I knew nothing. *Tastes?* I let it ride and went back to my miter box.

* * *

I remember my first heartache tune. I was in second grade, and she was pretty, with a straw-blond ponytail and a mouthful of teeth.

For Christmas, my parents had presented me with a handheld portable AM transistor radio the size and shape of a small kitchen sponge. I carried it to bed each night, my ear fastened to its minute speaker for the mighty signal of KEWB. As the records spun, I thought about Pamela Ashbury.

They were playing "Stand by Me" by Ben E. King, "Quarter to Three" by Gary U.S. Bonds, and "The Wanderer" by Del Shannon. When I listened to "Daddy's Home" by Shep and the Limelighters, the tremulous swooping two-part harmony cut in rapid three-quarters time, I could picture my dream girl's bony shoulders tottering into the clutch of my own broomstick boy's arms and we'd baby-step back and forth on the dance floor, the world fading to mottled twilight. The six-to-midnight disc jockey spun another round of "Runaround Sue" by Dion and the Belmonts, and I glimpsed love's inconstancy, knowing that there would long be a world of hurt and worry tied up in the tangle of throbs that I had discovered to be my heart.

As I got older, the tunes became more complicated. Big Mama Thornton singing the original "Hound Dog." The Kingsmen's version of "Louie, Louie" with the unintelligible dirty verse. Then, once I traded in my elementary school clarinet for a Conn alto sax in junior high, there was the stuff I knew nobody else was listening to—Dave Brubeck's "Take Five," with the extra beat you had to work hard not to fumble, and "Blue Rondo à la Turk," written in 9/8 time.

On my uncle Win's advice, I tried listening to Hank Williams and Ernest Tubbs, and I even liked them, sort of. Hank definitely had something going on, especially in that hiccuppy yelp at the top of his voice. I'd drop by Win's house on Saturday afternoon—sometimes he let me borrow his car if I made a big deal about how pretty the girl was going to be that evening—and in the living room, I'd find him downing Scotch on the rocks and spinning a Merle Haggard record with the turntable arm reared back, so "The Fightin' Side of Me" kept repeating until Aunt Tina finally stormed into the room and yanked the plug. Johnny Horton, Johnny Cash, Bobby Bare, Conway Twitty. Win called it "real American music." With the exception of Hank and E.T. and maybe Bob Wills and His Texas Playboys performing "San Antonio Rose," I couldn't stand the stuff.

"Open your ears," my uncle pleaded. "Try listening to something besides that damn jungle music." He didn't mean it as a compliment, but I didn't mind. Country music, Win declared, told the truth—about lost love and faded love, about getting screwed and getting even. Country music was full of cheating songs, leaving songs, songs about popping your boss straight in the nose and walking off the job with your head held high—about looking for another job that might never come. Country music was about being lonesome. About almost giving up. About going on just the same.

I'd nod as Win waxed on, calculating how many more sides of Ferlin Husky I'd have to endure before bringing up the subject of borrowing his car keys. Country was music for old men. And I was just getting started.

✦ ✦ ✦

When I arrived to pick up ABC on Friday night, her little brother Andrzej kept me standing at the front door in the rain.

I waited patiently for a minute. Then two.

"Andy?"

Then five. We were wearing our sparkly silver jackets for the gig, along with the lime-green fake silk pants and grey suede boots. My outfit was sopping.

"Who is that person still standing out there in the rain?"

Mr. Crikvenic's voice rose with the belligerence of a small dust storm from his encampment of newspapers and dinner plates in the living room. Andrzej had disappeared, folding himself into the roaming brood of Crikvenic siblings.

"It's *me*!" I cried out, immediately spotting the lameness of my claim. "ABC's, uh, friend. Ah, Antoinette's..."

From the stamp of his footsteps, I reasoned that Mr. Crikvenic was enraged, which was pretty much a safe bet. He was a serious, compact man, prone to outbursts like a snappish terrier. I made a show of wiping my feet on the doormat in preparation for his hospitality. Through the screen door, I could make out the silhouettes of ABC's eight brothers and sisters swarming across the living room, wandering half-dressed down the hallway, wiping the walls with their jelly sandwiches, screeching and mewling and crying and shrieking.

No wonder...

The screen door clicked open. I cleaned my feet for a second time and then rushed to follow Mr. Crikvenic's furious padding back into the living room. For the next few minutes, the two of us concentrated on the television set, discreetly not speaking. I noticed my pants making a soggy imprint on the couch. Finally, it came to my attention that the news program we were watching had the sound turned off. I leaned forward, my head in one hand, my elbow fixed upon my wet knee. I furrowed my brow, narrowed my eyes, concentrated on the picture.

"So you," said Mr. Crikvenic. "You understand, do you?"

Martin Luther King filled the screen, surrounded by a crowd

of angry white men in t-shirts. Some waved baseball bats. You could tell they were cursing even without the sound.

"*Crnaca*," said Mr. Crikvenic, translating the national convulsion into a single word. I batted my eyelids blankly.

"The blacks."

I nodded enthusiastically, and then diplomatically.

"They want to live in Cicero, Illinois." He thumped his ample belly with knitted fingertips. "Now what do you think of that?"

I considered repeating the rumor about Castlemont spades invading our high school two weeks before. I knew it was a terrible idea, but I couldn't think of anything else to say. So I concentrated on the screen. I grinned my simple idiotic appreciation.

Mr. Crikvenic cocked his head, encouraging me to say more.

"We might play the new James Brown tune tonight."

He regarded me for a long uncomfortable moment and then suddenly snapped off the television.

"My wife's sister," he informed me sternly. "She works at the cannery this year on the fruit cocktail."

I brightened. This overture on the part of my almost-girlfriend's strict Croatian father suggested a potential alliance between our families. I boasted: "My uncle just made foreman there."

"Yes," answered Mr. Crikvenic grimly. "I know all about him."

I considered that possibility. I hoped he did not. Did Mr. Crikvenic know, for example, that Aunt Tina had sent Uncle Win to live in the garage last summer during tomato season? Something about a young picker, and her husband showing up with a baseball bat, and the line boss warning Win that this was positively the last time. Probably Mr. Crikvenic knew more than I did. I got the news from Mom, who got it from Aunt Tina, who said that she was leaving this time, but none of us ever believed that.

ABC materialized in the doorway separating the bedrooms from the living room. She wore a shiny blue dress that swished down to her kneecaps, her shoulders bared as a provocative compromise. She raised her arms and twirled at the foot of her father's chair. I felt his wrath momentarily subside. Then he noticed that I was sitting next to him in a small puddle on his sofa, also admiring his daughter. He looked me up and down, crinkling his nose.

"Why are you dressed like that?"

"It's his band uniform, Daddy. I told you. We're going to a dance. He's playing. He gets paid to. We won't be late."

"You look like a pimp," he told me.

"Thank you."

ABC swaddled her arms around her father's shoulders, embossing both cheeks with kisses, blinding him with affection and radiance, which is how we made our escape.

"I don't think your dad likes me," I told ABC as we hurried down the hallway.

"Not very much," she agreed brightly.

* * *

At sixteen, I was deep, deep into jazz—the only teenager in Jefferson Manor to mail twelve dollars to New York City in order to secure a biweekly subscription to *Down Beat* magazine. I scanned every issue for news of the most romantic world imaginable: the world of Birdland, the Five Spot, and the Blue Note, where John Coltrane and Johnny Griffin and Johnny Hodges all held court on the saxophone while zip young men in silk suits and pink shirts donned cheap sunglasses long past sundown and clinked chilled tumblers of Scotch and soda with slinky young women wearing their thick black hair slashed to the shoulders and carrying in their purses the keys to their own studio apartments. I imagined myself someday attached to one of these creatures of my imagination. Formidable listeners who from the first sibilant utterance of the tenor saxophone could distinguish the obsidian tone of Rahsaan Roland Kirk's overheated post-bop antic blues from Stan Getz's breathy West Coast cool. Who had twenty reasons why she preferred the cymbals technique of Tony Williams over that of Roy Haynes, or vice versa. Who passed each day for the moment when she could return home to her stereo sound system and bask in the aural bubble bath of *Miles at Newport* or *Sonny Rollins at the Village Vanguard*.

In other words, I knew nothing.

Still, Frankie kept asking about me and ABC.

"Get anything yet?" he demanded.

I shook my head.

"No lip?"

"Sure. Lip."

"Tongue?"

"Yeah," I admitted. "Sometimes." ABC's darting tongue felt about the size of a large sardine, salty and warm.

"Move slow and steady, my brother," advised Frankie. "Stay just as cool as you really are."

But I wasn't in the least bit cool. ABC made me spasm and twitch. ABC tangled up my thoughts and caused my throat to close, and I just stood around looking deaf and dumb. But I couldn't keep my mind off ABC.

"You get anything on top?" Frankie kept pestering me.

I didn't want to talk about it.

"Sly," said Frankie, nodding to himself and winking in my direction like I was Billy Eckstine, the ruby-throated balladeer who fronted for Count Basie's band on the covers of Frankie's dad's hi-fi records. "You keep every detail to yourself, selfish bastard."

In fact, I did have a secret that I was holding back from Frankie—and that was unusual for us at this point in our lives. Frankie and I swapped secrets and discoveries like we were brothers. Which as members of the Lost Souls, we certainly were. He'd tell me about a band he had heard on Saturday night in Oakland with the assistance of his fake ID, and how their tenor player had blown off the high harmonics with a stratospheric sonic squeal in the style of King Curtis on the 45 rpm version of "Soul Serenade," and then later that week I'd coax him over to my house after school to study the new album by Charles Mingus.

I had recently got my hands on Mingus's *The Black Saint and the Sinner Lady*. The liner notes, jointly written by the composer and his psychologist, suggested that Mingus regarded the album as a kind of love song. I was intrigued by the possibility that the sound of love might reside in the snort and gargle of the baritone sax and the trumpets bleating like duck calls and the trombones churning slightly above the low end of their register.

But Frankie said it wasn't love we were listening to at all. What we were listening to was the sound of sex.

We flipped the album back over to side one, and we listened to the entire recording once again. There were lush ensemble passages that sounded as though Duke Ellington had suddenly taken command—but they were punctuated by Mingus's hog calls of encouragement as each member of the orchestra stepped up to solo. The sharp little spurts of ecstasy when Booker Ervin rolled out lines of West Texas blues on tenor or Jaki Byard hammered fistfuls of jagged piano chords. Mingus thrumming, poking, plunking, and finally caressing his bass like a man with three hands and twenty fingers. The reeds and brass blending together in a tissue of cries and tiny percussive sighs of satisfaction. Frankie certainly had a point about the meaning of this music. How could I argue with a man of the world like Frankie?

But something else was going on, too. I could hear it. Something at the bottom of the music. Sounds full of signifying, though they made no sense at all when reduced to words. The flamenco guitar bursting into flames and the alto saxophone squealing. The ochre bash of cymbals and earth-brown bass lines charred to black. There was nothing in this music that spoke in the least to my own pale and limited experience. Except what lay beneath the sound. That deep well of undeniable desire.

Frankie swung the needle back to the record's initial groove and we prepared for a third playing. I imagined what it might feel like to be listening to Mingus in the company of a girl who also loved the music and perhaps was somewhat sweet on me, too. But even then, I was able to admit to myself that this girl was not ABC.

ABC preferred the Monkees. Herman's Hermits. Pop music lightly spun with the consistency and nutritional value of pink cotton candy. I had once persuaded ABC to sit through all thirteen minutes and forty-one seconds of John Coltrane's "My Favorite Things." She called it "noise." What about ecstasy? What about passion and craving and heartbreak? Coltrane and Mingus and Rahsaan Roland Kirk and Stan Getz, too—they were all about everything I didn't know how to say to her or myself.

Nevertheless, I did have a secret.

I wasn't telling Frankie. Not Frankie or anybody else.

I had a secret that I was keeping entirely for myself.

So this is my secret: I had seen ABC naked.

We were pretending to study in her bedroom, the door propped open as her Croatian mother required, the AM radio squeaking out KEWB's Top 40 amid a shit storm of static. Then ABC rose from her desk and turned the radio up loud enough to cover any peep of excitement that might escape from my trembling lips. She asked, "Want to see something?" Before I could stammer or speak, ABC nudged her bedroom door shut with one knee and then, with a suppleness and speed borne of instinct rather than experience, she unfolded herself out of her everyday rumple of gray sweatshirt and blue jeans—removing, as if in a single gesture, the hide of ordinary existence to display for an instant her beautiful naked white body.

How long did I get to stare at her? It couldn't have lasted five seconds. We both heard feet on the stairs, ABC's older sister Belinda groaning her name. "Get out!" hissed the naked girl, pushing and tumbling me back into the hallway as Belinda rounded the corner.

"She's dressing," I explained with a gasp, fighting to catch my breath, staring down at my feet. Belinda looked at me with pity, and with the demeaning acuity of an older woman who knew that I would never get past that hollow pine bedroom door to gaze upon her sister's beauty.

But I had.

I had seen ABC, inexpressibly gorgeous. I had absorbed as rapidly as possible that hint of pink nipples, her bush of black hair, lighter than I would have expected.

It was a distinction of the highest order, the revelation of a lifetime.

But this is what really slays me.

As ABC hurriedly undressed, the AM radio was blasting "Tijuana Taxi" by Herb Alpert and the Tijuana Brass. A tune like fly paper; far worse than cotton candy. One of the most moronic melodies ever conceived. Instantaneously, the song was branded into my mind, seared into the limbic system: "Tijuana Taxi" would be forever associated with my first vision of a beautiful, naked young woman. It was a travesty, irreparable and unmusical.

• • •

"Now look, listen, and learn, little Slick."

Uncle Win dropped the needle and it plunked to the record with a screech and a bounce. Aunt Tina set her Ballantine's on the sports page covering their end table. Satchmo was scatting and singing his way through some standards.

"Ol' Louie," said Aunt Tina wistfully. "He was one of the good ones."

I preferred Miles or Diz, but Armstrong was certainly an improvement on the hillbilly ballads.

"Now, there's some music you listen to," Win informed me, "just for the enjoyment of the thing." He extended his big paw to Tina, and she rose from the sofa, gingerly clasping two fingers. Joe Louis, my uncle's elderly and arthritic dachshund, staggered to his feet with a huff and a moan and then scrambled for cover behind the overstuffed La-Z-Boy. "Some songs, you can't sit still. So you shouldn't."

Tina stuck out her cheek and Win fastened his onto hers. They straightened one arm, their fingers laced together, their eyes shooting darts towards the far wall of the dining room. As they marched in time to the music, Win clasped Tina tighter, massaging her back with three fingers, and her hips started twitching.

Man, I thought I was going to be sick.

"*Another season,*" sang my poor old uncle, dragging his wife across the imaginary dance floor of their sad little living room, "*another reason, for makin' whoopee...*"

✦ ✦ ✦

"I am not getting in the trunk."

"Come on, Vincent. Be a prince."

"I got in last time and you guys didn't let me out until the first feature was half over."

Saturday night at the Stadium Drive-In, the line of cars already beginning to form alongside the vast empty parking lot of the Bayfair shopping center. One guy in the trunk meant a savings of 25 percent. It was just sound economics.

"You didn't miss much."

"We did you a favor, Vince."

"*Blood Feast,*" remembered Frankie. "About this Egyptian caterer who was actually a cannibal." He inserted his key into the trunk's lock, flicked his wrist, and the lid opened slowly like a crypt. "Vince, it was awful bloody."

"Why do I always got to be the one in the trunk?"

"Oh, Lord!" sang out ABC. "Don't be such babies." A thirty-foot pole light rising above the drive-in's exterior wall cast her features in a fluorescent shimmer I couldn't help admiring. "I'll get in the damn trunk if it's going to save somebody two bucks."

I suddenly felt my face redden and swell. That was my two bucks she was talking about. The shame. And a bad start. Frankie had confided that he thought tonight might be my night.

"Vince, I thought you was chivalrous?"

"Can't you talk like a white man, Frankie?"

"I'm saying do you want to be the guy who makes the girl, especially one as pretty as this"—he fluttered his hound's eyes at

ABC like I wasn't even there—"climb into the trunk with all the spiders and shit?"

"See, that's what I'm talking about!"

"Vince." I clapped a heavy palm across his shoulder the way Frankie sometimes did when I needed persuading. "I'll pay for your popcorn."

It took him about a second to decide.

"Okay. Plus a giant root beer."

"Christ, you drive a hard bargain," acknowledged Frankie, grinning all the time at ABC.

Vince ducked his head under the lip of the trunk of Frankie's sister's boyfriend's crummy borrowed Rambler and squeezed in next to the spare, waving good-bye to the three of us like an astronaut about to take leave of this earth forever. I slammed down the lid and Frankie jerked his thumb in the direction of our concealed cargo and silently made a face that said it all: *Sucker*. I opened the rear door on the passenger's side for ABC. The cars were already lining up at the entrance for the first feature. It was always best to sneak in with the crowd, when the attendant didn't have the luxury of inspecting every vehicle that sagged from the rear.

"No way," objected Frankie. "What do you think, I'm your chauffeur? You two ride up front with me."

"Two guys and a girl? They'll suspect something."

"Then you better join Vincent."

"I don't mind," said ABC. Her head tilted onto one shoulder and she melted me with a wink. "I'll sit between."

"Of course you will."

I started to argue, but ABC was already sliding in front next to Frankie. The line snaked around the outside wall of the Stadium Drive-In for almost two blocks. We drove in silence, Frankie nursing the squishy brakes and making them squeal. I considered holding ABC's hand but reconsidered as we drew closer to the gate. Everybody had to stay as calm as possible. At the gate, Frankie forked over enough for three admissions exactly. The ticket seller was this skinny Mexican kid I'd seen hanging around Pring's late at night once the Strip shut down, but he didn't seem to notice me or Frankie, although he gave ABC a big grin and blew her a kiss as we drove away.

"You know that guy?"

"No! Why does everybody always say that?"

"Say what?"

"That I know a million guys."

People said that? This was news to me. The news made Frankie cackle.

"Just find us a good place to watch the movie, okay?" Sometimes Frankie made a very big deal over how much he knew about the world. "Pay attention to what you're doing."

"Sure, chief. You're the boss. Don't you think he's the boss?"

ABC concentrated on staring out the windshield, reserving comment.

We passed by a long line of familiar rides in the middle section staking out the best view of the giant white screen. A T-Bird blasted to bare metal and primered gray with ghost flames stenciled across the hood. You saw it on the Strip late Friday and Saturday nights after the dances ended at Carpenter's Hall. Frankie said it belonged to the trumpet player from the Post Raisin Band. Somebody's '56 Chevy floating on hydraulics six inches off the ground with frenched headlights, fender skirts, Laker pipes, rolled pans, magenta custom paint job—lowered, nosed, decked, shaved, and louvered. It got driven around by this kid at school who never said a word to anybody, but whose brother loaned him the car while he was in the service with the understanding that he'd wash and polish it every weekend. Under the pole light alongside the snack bar, we cruised past the flat-black Ford pickup with a 472 on the big block, belonging to Elbert Graff—Elbert, who had dropped out of Russell Continuation High and was practically a professional criminal now—with a Hurst on the floor, Cobra heads, Holley carburetor, dual glass packs with tips.

Once Frankie pulled up to a speaker along the outer rim and killed the engine, we could hear Vincent banging at us from inside the trunk.

"We got time for the snack bar?" I asked.

Frankie consulted his watch. "Maybe five minutes before the first movie. You want I should go?"

"I thank you, my brother."

Frankie flashed me an indecent smile, his eyes instantly angling in the direction of the backseat. "My brother, don't get *too* comfortable."

"What about your friend?" asked ABC.

Vince kept banging away inside the trunk.

I allowed my hand to crawl across the top of the Rambler's front seat like a tarantula and come to rest on ABC's shoulder. She did not object. I wondered what was playing for the first feature. I thought she smelled soft.

Vince kept banging.

I clutched ABC's hand and we studied the advertisements on the big screen featuring a cartoon volcano spurting buttered popcorn and an ocean of Pepsi surrounded by a forest of Fudgesicles and boulders made of Big Hunks, Tootsie Rolls, Clark Bars, Goobers, and Kit Kats. I couldn't think of anything to say.

Frankie returned, slipped into the driver's seat, and passed out the corn dogs.

"You get anything for Vince?"

Frankie's mouth was already full of corn dog.

"Who?"

Vince started kicking both feet against the trunk lid, making the Rambler buck suspiciously from the rear, so we decided to let him out as soon as he got tired and calmed down. The pole lights fizzled to a lucent blush and the trailers for coming attractions splashed across the screen.

Frankie and I opened our doors and slid around back towards the trunk. Frankie opened it. Vince sort of dribbled out face-first onto the tarmac.

"You pricks!" He stared death rays up at us from the littered ground.

"Hey, watch your language. There's a lady present."

Vince pulled himself onto two feet, dusting the sand and gravel from his jeans.

"You can both bite me."

"Is something the matter, Vincent?"

"*Hard!*"

"Vince, you should've said something if you wanted out. Next time for sure."

ABC surrendered her seat to Vince, who insisted on riding shotgun even though we weren't going anyplace for the next couple of hours. I moved as close as I could, but the driveshaft formed a hump down the middle of the backseat, a barrier I wasn't positive I should breach. ABC smelled like roses, or honey, or I couldn't tell what.

"You guys can lick my ass, both of you."

"Vince, the movie's starting."

"I apologize for Vincent," I told ABC. "He's usually a gentleman."

"Dick breath."

"In or out of his tuxedo," said Frankie, "the guy shows nothing but class."

"You can eat my donkey dong."

"Around school, he's often mistaken for David Niven."

ABC sighed. "You *guys*..." Her sweet puckered pink lips shriveled into a small sour oval. My hand lurched across her shoulder and perched there. I imagined that everything underneath would feel softer and warmer than anything I'd ever touched.

"Hey, Vince," asked Frankie, his voice warming to an approximation of apology. "You see the Chevy parked in back?"

Vince craned his neck around and peered into the darkness. "I don't think the Chevy's so bad."

"Badder than you, Vincent."

"You wish."

"I know."

"You blow."

"You wish."

"God!" cried ABC. "It's like babysitting my little brothers." She shook her shoulder out of my grasp.

The film turned out to be another masterpiece by Herschell Gordon Lewis, this one about a small town in the South called Pleasant Valley, where all the residents had been massacred by the Union army during the Civil War and now came back every hundred years to slaughter the Yankee tourists who accidentally stumbled into their midst. Something like the musical *Brigadoon* that my father liked so much, but instead of Gene Kelly and Cyd Charisse, you had two thousand bloodthirsty maniacs.

"Oh, *man*!" squealed Frankie, thwapping both palms on the steering wheel and rattling the chassis. "That is gross."

The maniacs were holding down one of the Yankee girls on their kitchen table while one big rube chopped her arm off with an axe. She shrieked long and loud, causing ABC to muffle her ears with both palms. Then they roasted the Yankee girl in a barbecue pit.

"Hey, Vince. Your family's from the South, right?"

"Take a big deep breath of my butt, Frankie."

"Oh, sick!"

"He started it," protested Vince. "Talking about my family."

"No, on the screen, stupid. Pay attention."

The maniacs were stuffing one of the Yankee men into a barrel embedded with six-inch nails. Then they rolled him down a long and bumpy hill. When the barrel came to a stop, the camera tracked close in to show the damage.

"Oh, man! Oh, Jesus."

"You hillbillies are vicious, Vincent."

"Yeah, you remember that next time you lock me in the trunk."

"Should've never let you out. You're a maniac."

"I'm a maniac!" shrieked Vince. He grabbed Frankie around the neck, pretending to throttle him. They wrestled in the front seat for a good thirty seconds, and that broke me up.

"I can't see!" protested ABC.

Vince and Frankie slunk back to their corners.

Soon, on the screen, the maniacs were tying one of the guys' legs and arms to four horses that took off in opposing directions. All that was left of him was the stump and what came pouring out of its empty sockets. It didn't look the least bit real—the blood was way too red, like ketchup or spaghetti sauce. Still, it was pretty sick.

"You know what's really scary about this movie?" Frankie turned around in the front seat to address me and ABC. He looked me in the eyes and then switched to ABC, lingering there.

"The stump is scary."

"The fucking music. That goddamn banjo those rednecks keep strumming."

Vince clapped his palms over either ear. "It's driving me crazy!" He shook his crazy head and the Rambler rocked in rhythm. "It's making me a maniac."

"Hey, Vincent," said Frankie. "You know what the definition of perfect pitch is?"

"Is this a real question?"

"It's when you're driving by the junkyard and you heave your sister's accordion out the side window and it lands right on top of the pile of busted banjos."

"Two thousand banjo players! Save me, Jesus!"

ABC pressed her back into her side of the car and rested her feet in my lap.

"This is stupid. Let's leave. Let's get some beer."

"Interesting proposal," said Frankie. He had the phony ID and he knew that we all knew he did, which made him feel even more important.

"Turn down the speaker, Frankie. I don't want to hear no more Flatt and Shruggs."

Frankie switched off the sound, fished an eight-track off the floor, held it up for our approval. Gladys Knight and the Pips, *I Heard It through the Grapevine*. I nodded. Vince, too.

The music pulsed from the dashboard and our heads began bobbing. Up on the screen, a great number of maniacs thrashed around in a silent bloody blur.

"So how'd we sound last night, Annie?"

"That's not her name, Vinnie."

"So her name's a bunch of initials?"

"What he's asking," clarified Frankie, "is did you think the Lost Souls sounded great last night at the Boys' Club, or merely spectacular? Were we suitable for you teenagers having a good time dancing and such?"

"I sat through you guys playing, 'Cold Sweat' for thirty minutes."

"Hey, girl. We were damn hot last night."

"We was cookin'!" agreed Vince.

"Did you think we sounded okay?" I pictured ABC in her bedroom, the sound of "Tijuana Taxi." I scooted closer.

"Everything except 'Twine Time,'" said Frankie, basting his lips with a snaky tongue. "'Cause Vincent here kept losing the beat."

"Hey, you can lose your beat in my meat."

"You can eat my meat."

"Chew it."

"Gum it."

"Swallow it."

"Fart it back out your butt and breathe it in deep, Frankie."

"I want to apologize for my friends," I told ABC.

"Oh, God," she lamented, staring straight ahead at the big silent screen and continuing hillbilly mayhem, "I can't wait to grow up."

"Numb nuts!"

"Pencil wiener!"

"Butt boy!"

"Dog molester!"

"Fish fucker!"

"Clam sucker!"

"Amoeba licker!"

For a moment, nobody said anything. Gladys Knight and the Pips kept pipping. ABC spoke first.

"What's that supposed to mean?"

She sounded genuinely curious.

"Better ask Vincent," said Frankie.

Vince shrugged. "How do I know? I'm not a scientist."

The two of them grinned into the big-screen glare of way too many maniacs wielding axes and strumming banjos—a pair of happy little kids at the drive-in picture show. Frankie turned around to beam his best careless, bright smile at ABC.

"We're *rascals*!"

I felt like I might start bawling. There was such a gap between what any of us felt and how we managed to explain it. We didn't have the right words, or the exact order, or the proper emphasis. I couldn't really say what the problem was, except that must have been part of the problem, too. Sometimes up on stage, in the middle of a tune like "Turn on Your Love Light" by Bobby Blue Bland—a classic, we'd played it a million times—I'd feel something so strong and certain that it just seemed obvious and impossible to argue about. Then Teddy would spin around on the last chorus at the foot of the stage, look every one of us in the eye—somehow all at once—and we'd be off in another direction entirely. The horns and guitars and organ would cut out altogether to leave the drums working the backbeat, while Teddy started double-clapping on time. Then the rest of the band would start clapping too, and a minute later, everybody in the hall was clapping, and Teddy would be grinning into the blinding light and we'd all be looking into each other's faces, knowing that *this is it*. Something truer and purer than anything any of us have ever felt or are ever going to feel again. Three hundred, maybe four hundred pairs of hands clapping double-time on the dance floor at Carpenter's Hall with nothing but the drums playing, and for a short time that seemed like it was going to last forever: we were standing at the center of the only thing that mattered. We couldn't say why or how we got there or what we might do the next night to get back to the same place, because we never could get back there by planning it. Afterwards, we'd say, "Hey, 'Love Light' was *bad* tonight—Christ, yeah, it was bad as could be." Then, a minute later, we couldn't begin to explain what had happened. We couldn't talk about it, or anything else that mattered...

"Okie dip shit."

"Limey dick chewer."

"Sheep-humping squaw man."

"Ofay honkey cracker mother-fucking leprechaun-licking kilts-wearing *Captain-Kangaroo-looking loser*!"

ABC sagged into my shoulder, deflated. "*Boys...*" she breathed into my ear, and I got goose bumps everywhere. "Can we see about the beer?"

Frankie gunned the Rambler as we skittered past Elbert Graff, pulled out of the Stadium Drive-In and into the darkness, and headed for the MacArthur freeway. Vince punched the radio button and twisted the dial, searching for KSOL. Two gorgeous voices filled the cabin of the car, Marvin Gaye and Tammi Terrell singing "Ain't No Mountain High Enough." Our ears perked up. Our heads were bobbing. The Lost Souls were always studying.

"Marvin's *bad*," said Frankie with a grave note of approval.

"Tammi, too."

"Yeah, but Marvin wrote the song."

"No, it was Tammi. She wrote it for the Supremes, but they passed." Vince snorted. "Gordy Berry must've been *drunk*!"

"You're drunk."

"You're a punk."

"That why you keep grabbing my ass?"

"Too fat an' ugly your ol' pimply white—"

"You're both wrong," I blurted out from the backseat. "Marvin didn't write it. Neither did Tammi. It was Ashford and Simpson."

Vincent and Frankie locked eyes. They turned toward the backseat in unison and addressed me forthrightly.

"Fuck you!"

We drove to a liquor store at the Oakland border, up in the hills near Oak Knoll Naval Hospital.

"There's usually a Chinese guy behind the counter," Frankie explained to ABC. The Chinese were well known for being incapable of distinguishing the ages of cunning white teenagers. Plus, Frankie had his fake ID.

We parked at the far end of the lot, away from the pole lights. Frankie thought of everything. We all scrambled out of the Rambler with Vince walking point. As the door swung open, the overhead bell clanged twice to alert the clerk to potential customers and I felt a sudden need to urinate. Instead, I feigned interest in a wire rack display of Twinkies and Hostess Cup-Cakes. ABC nodded towards the freezer full of Olde English 800, her lips moist and slightly parted, the tip of her pink tongue trilling. But Frankie preferred a fine wine tonight and Frankie was buying. He selected a bottle of Lancer's from the chilled stock case. The clerk turned out not to be Chinese at all, but an old white guy with hair sprouting from either ear like two bottle brushes. Frankie slid his ID across the counter. The clerk just wagged his head.

"That's hilarious."

"Whaddya mean? I'm twenty-one."

"Go away, you kids."

"No, really. I'm shipping out for Nam next week."

"Son, you make it back, I'll buy you one."

"We'll pay double," offered Vince.

"No, we won't, you idiot."

"Just get out of here, you kids."

"Hey, this is not cool, man."

"C'mon," said ABC, swelling her chest and then licking her lips, but almost immediately deciding better. She took a baby step backwards and whispered, "Who's it going to hurt?"

"I swear on the Bible I'm twenty-one. You got a Bible back there?"

"Little girl, if you were my daughter, you wouldn't be leaving the house until you really were grown up."

"Oh, kiss my ass," spat back ABC.

"Tramp."

"Hey!" I objected. I figured everybody must be expecting something from me.

"Get outta here before you got trouble. There's a cop comes in here every night."

"Sure there is," said Vince. "I'm so scared."

"We ain't going anywhere without purchasing our merchandise." Frankie lifted the bottle off the counter by its neck and cradled it with one arm.

That's when the cop walked in. Then suddenly, he was on top of us, pinching Frankie's ID from the counter with the tweezers of his extended huge black thumb and finger. He stood about seven and a half feet tall, his face a luminous, coal-colored, unsmiling planet. Frankie dropped the Lancer's and it shattered at our feet.

"Hey, we're all cool here," said Frankie. "Aren't we, brother?"

Vince strolled towards the door, but the cop now had a gun in his hand and he pointed it at Vince's heart. He barked something in my direction, but exactly what didn't register. I know he didn't call me "brother."

I did urinate just a little.

"Don't worry," Frankie assured ABC, his arm flopping across the length of her shoulders. He gave her a sympathetic squeeze and she started to cry.

The four of us barely fit in the patrol car's backseat. There were no handles on the inside. The doors locked with a click. After the cop called the stationhouse, all we could hear on the radio was static.

+ + +

If you leave me, sang Teddy.

Drumroll…

If you leave me
Staccato punctuation by the horns...
If you leave me
Nothing but silence across the dance floor...
I'LL GO CRAZY

We played the chorus, the beat slow and pulled back, with Danny bashing the high hat each time Teddy sang:

cuz I love YOU
love YOU
OH...yes, I do

...and then Pico started thudding his bass, picking up the rhythm like a locomotive—*chug-chug-chug*, but just a bit faster with every beat—and then the horns were swinging left to right, instruments held as high in the air as we could manage while blaring *ba-BAH-Da! ba-BAH-Da!* The opening to "There Was a Time" by James Brown. Just three notes over and over—*ba-BAH-Da!*—but nobody minds, because Teddy is dancing now. He's sliding across the stage on the side of one foot, and then he's dropping to the floor, popping back up, freezing, and staring straight into space. Our man flashes a smile down at the crowd, our people, covering the dance floor—there must have been six or seven hundred of them. Then he's doing the Camel Walk, he's doing the Mashed Potatoes just for a laugh, the Hully Gully and the Fly and the Swim, and finally Teddy launches into the Boogaloo, which he grinds out not so much like the Godfather of Soul, but like Teddy Chavez himself.

I stared past the spotlights, the sea of dancing bodies, tucking my sax under my shoulder as the horns kept swinging back and forth. Up close to the stage, football players were baying along with the music, falling over their own feet. At the side of the auditorium, Henry Eagle punched a tall skinny basketball player wearing a letterman's sweater from Arroyo High, our rival—Henry the Patriot—and when the kid hit the ground, bounced, and didn't get up, the rest of the Manor Lords lapped up around him like waves, making him disappear, and that was that.

And that kid down front, screaming up to Teddy, "Give the drummer *some*!"—Andretti going crazy now on tom-tom and cymbals.

I didn't expect to see ABC. The police had called our parents to take Frankie, Vince, and me home. Our fathers showed up sometime past three a.m., sleepy and pissed off but unsurprised, because at our age they'd all been in trouble themselves—at least, that's what Frankie tried to tell us while we were sitting in the cell. Sometimes Frankie didn't know shit. ABC they drove home with a stern warning. I didn't imagine her father was pleased. I phoned her house for days, but each time I got Andrzej, who hung up once I started speaking.

No matter. I could live without ABC if she could live without me. I still had the band, my brothers, this night up on the stage...

We picked up the beat and launched into "Night Train."

Anyway, I had discovered a new piece of music, which gave me plenty to think about all week. On stage, we stepped back and forth, right to left, blocking out a simple box pattern while Teddy danced—and I thought about one tune in particular.

I had purchased the album, *The Bill Evans Trio, Live at the Village Vanguard*. Evans on piano, Paul Motian on drums, and Scott LaFaro on bass. Ten days after completing the recording, LaFaro died in a car accident on his way home from a gig. Spooky. You couldn't help thinking about it while listening to "I Loves You, Porgy," which everybody knew was the best cut on the album. It was about just two things. Desire and death. That's what I told Frankie and he agreed.

In the final ninety seconds, Bill Evans hit the main line of the melody, while LaFaro paused at each beat and Motion scratched at his snare drum with brushes. And in the background, you could hear the muttering of a girl in the audience, her voice pitched above the roar of the bar and the clink of glasses—and she laughed. Here she was, missing this amazing performance, three great artists at their peak. Yet after you listened to the song twenty times or so, it didn't seem like an interruption. The girl's careless, giddy, snockered giggle fixed to the moment, and then she was indispensable, too—practically a member of the band.

Dee-troit, Mish-gan. Philly-dell-feeyah...

We kept swinging our horns back and forth, blaring the high notes until they almost bent out of tune.

I liked to think about how someday the girl on the record would play that cut for her boyfriend or husband or her own kids even, and they wouldn't believe it was her chattering away ten or fifteen or thirty years before, until they recognized that laugh.

I imagined something else, too.

No, I knew.

I saw myself, someday, playing "I Loves You, Porgy" for some girl I hadn't met yet. We'd be lying together in bed, done with whatever it was that people do, and it'd be raining outside, but warm where we were still touching. Near the bed there would be a bottle of something, probably Lancer's. We'd be trading sips from the same glass and listening, bobbing our heads in time to the swish of the drummer's brushes. And she would get it. Every note. Definitely. So would I.

On stage, I had to shut my eyes tight against the piercing light of the overhead spot. Frankie's guitar switched chords and the Lost Souls eased into "Ain't That a Groove."

I couldn't picture what she'd look like. I just knew that she would be so fine.

* * * * *

During the summer, the heat drives them into the kitchen, where they cover the counters, the floor, any dish you might leave out until morning that still contains a few crumbs of graham cracker and a smidge of Knott's Berry Farm boysenberry preserves. Then comes winter, and the rains push them into the cupboards to infest the jumbo sack of Purina Puppy Chow. Or they swarm across the sink's ceramic tiling, nibbling the grout and digging trenches.

What do they want, these invaders, these staggering columns of pitiless marauders who stream through your home like hordes of tiny six-legged Mongols?

Outside, where they really belong, the ants tramp up and down your forty-foot willow, partaking in what you must now admit to be a kind of majestic symbiosis—ants protecting plants, plants sheltering ants, plants feeding ants, ants feeding plants: ants dispersing seeds, pollinating flowers, pruning and weeding the vegetable patch. In the compost bin, beneath the black tarp you've draped across the plywood walls, the workers from another colony transport particles of vegetable and animal remains, whip their aphid slaves into action, supercharge the soil with doses of carbon, nitrogen, and phosphorus.

Everybody has his place in the world, his work to do. Our responsibilities are unmitigated by time or desire. Monday through Friday, you shear the sheets of stainless steel that some other Joe will cart across country. There, another half-dozen guys test for torque and resistance. They bend and press the metal into grip-sized strips with four prongs at the tip—so that you or somebody almost just like you can wolf down the bacon and eggs the wife cooks to get everybody up and out of the house and ready for another day's work.

Scatter that line of ants with a stick, kick dirt over a hundred of them, pour gasoline on their nest and burn them out for good—they'll be right back. They come back for more because they're just like you: they have no choice. They've got work to do. We've all got work to do, and necessarily we do it together. One labor fits into the contours of another in a grand design that nobody in the world could plan if they had all the time that ever existed or ever will.

That's what your kids need to understand. Everybody does their bit. Liking it or not doesn't figure into the equation. Every little one of us, shoulder to shoulder, oblivious mostly to one another's feats and valor, losses, failures, wasted efforts—though nothing's ever really wasted, is it? Tote that barge, lift that bale. Count those widgets, gimme a glazed old-fashioned with my cup of coffee—black!—and make it hot as it comes. It's all part of the mix. It's what we call civilization.

An ant alone is an ant in trouble.

SEVEN

Labor Day

A shrill toot from the factory whistle called starting time. I clocked in for the graveyard shift and hurried across the catwalk through the guts of the place—a tangle of steel pipes twisted into pretzels, storage bins the size of city dumpsters, the cooking vats shaped like Doughboy swimming pools, the dials on their pitted gauges obscured in clouds of chalky steam. Past the factory floor, the air cleared and the roar subsided—just the steady hum of conveyor belts remained, hauling cardboard ketchup crates one story overhead, and the hard-rubber scrape of forklift tires screaming their stop-and-start along the concrete.

The warehouse was a better place to spend the shift, no question. You didn't feel the heat rising off the pressure cookers all night or catch a blast in the face from the steam vents when you weren't paying attention. I gazed up at the hole in the ceiling, a backflap the size of a garage door opening to a patch of inky sky. My uncle had advised me to steal a glance whenever I could.

Win had pulled strings to get me into the warehouse. I didn't turn eighteen for another four months. "Just don't say nothing stupid," he counseled.

I fit my lunch bucket under a link of conveyor line and

reported for work. The night had barely begun and already I felt like I was drowning.

"Hey, kid."

The box stacker from swing shift dropped his last crate of ketchup bottles onto the pallet, then shrugged off the evening with a mournful roll of his shoulders. He dead-stared the concrete wall and smiled at nothing as I stepped into his place.

"'Night, kid."

The crates first crept into view fifty yards up the conveyor line, discharged from a small breach in the wall; then fifty more were rolling down the twisting rack of metal casters, picking up speed and emitting a piercing whine as they headed in my direction.

I grabbed my first crate of the evening with both hands, jerked it waist-high, pivoted on one foot, and tossed the load onto the pallet, bending my knees as I had been told to do. Every ten seconds a new crate spurted into the warehouse, each arrival spaced eighteen inches from the last. I set the next two crates lengthwise, sitting side by side with the first. Then I laid down another line adjacent to the first; then four more positioned sideways. When I finished the bottom row, I started a second level by fitting the first four crates sideways on top of the lengthwise row. Then another level reversing the pattern. In less than ten minutes, the pallet rose five levels high. The forklift driver squealed up short, needling his prongs into the catch of the pallet, and drove off into the dim light of the loading docks.

I moved to the next pallet and began building a new stack.

A couple of hours into the shift, our first breakdown occurred. Something had happened up the line, but you could never tell what at the warehouse end. The conveyor belt squealed and stuttered to a halt and boxes shifted into one another, erasing the two feet of daylight between them. I glanced up and down the line to see what the other stackers were doing. Two guys sprawled across their pallets, studying the ceiling. I upturned a crate bleeding ketchup from the corners and sat. The sweat streamed down my back. My heart's drumbeat began to slow. I thought about nothing at all.

No, that's not true. I thought what I thought every night.

Please, God—let me go, get me out of here...

Half a minute later, the conveyor started up and we all flew at the line double-speed, plucking off boxes as fast as we could so that they didn't jam and tumble to the floor. A few casualties jolted off the line. They hit the concrete, shattering like wind chimes.

The line ran steady until lunch. At 2:30 a.m., my replacement tapped my shoulder. I nodded and he stepped forward. Before I could mutter thanks or good luck or whatever you were supposed to say, he was snatching boxes off the conveyor belt.

I climbed the catwalk and snaked back through the factory's steel intestines until I reached the lunchroom. A clock on the wall told me that I'd spent five minutes of my lunch break just walking the length of the factory floor, but the constant dull glow of overhead neon rails made it impossible to feel the time. The screech of conveyor belts persisted in the distance, their racket swamping the room whenever somebody walked in or out the door. An old man in blue coveralls occupied a stool in the corner, spooning down warm diced tomatoes from the can.

I grabbed the sports page, sat on the bench, and read about Sal Bando's triple. The A's had just relocated to Oakland and already they were doing better than they had in the previous sixteen seasons in Kansas City. Catfish, Reggie, Bando—looked like we were going to have a ball club.

Sal Bando: I longed to talk to somebody about Bando. They had him playing third base these days, which seemed perfect. He'd found his spot, he was hitting fine. But there was nobody in the lunchroom ripe for conversation except the old man in his blue coveralls, and I'd upchuck for certain if I had to watch him swallow another spoonful of warm tomatoes.

So I ate the ham sandwich my mom had packed, downed a quartered orange from our backyard. Ten minutes later, the whistle blew. Sometimes, I thought, it helps to be just a little bit dead.

I climbed back up the catwalk and walked slowly to the warehouse. On the floor, I tapped my replacement on the shoulder as he fit his last crate onto the pallet.

"Thanks, man."

"Later."

The line screeched, jerked, and halted. Thirty seconds passed. Then a minute. I listened to the thrum of the immobilized conveyor belt, pinning all my hopes on failure far up the line—the kind of all-systems breakdown that could result in fifteen or twenty minutes of uninterrupted idleness. But a few seconds later a fresh discharge of crates shot through the wall trap and began hurtling our way. I craned my back over the conveyor, bent my knees, reached for a crate, and began building my first pallet of the shift's second half. The forklift driver scooted up too close this time, just missing my ankle with the prong. I did a little dance to show him I noticed.

Friday nights were the worst, Win said. People drunk by the first break, some of them lethal before the shift ended.

The line halted. This time one of the stackers slipped behind a tower of empty pallets. Guys sometimes napped after lunch, waiting for the line to jam, the music of two hundred bottles tumbling to the floor sounding the alarm.

I built a little throne for myself—the pallet's back row stacked three levels high, the floor left empty, and a crate on either side to rest my arms.

"Take every second," Win said. "They're yours and you should take them. Otherwise, it's like you're never off work because the boxes sail down the line at you even in your dreams. They just keep coming at you, just keep coming."

Win had been working at the cannery for thirty years. That thought made me catch my breath and I tried to think of something else. I tried thinking about the shift's end at 6:30 with the sun rising just above the factory gate and the salt air breezing across the tarmac—but the line suddenly started up and instantly jammed, and several crates toppled from the second story. One of the stackers dashed out from behind the pallets and began ripping crates off the conveyor, clearing the line in a fury. One after another, he raised the crates above his head and hurled them to the floor. Another stacker joined him. Soon we were all ripping crates from the line and heaving them to the concrete with all our might. In two or three minutes, we had cleared the line and could return to a steady pace. At our feet lay a red carpet of ketchup and splintered glass. The crates kept coming at us, they just kept coming.

We all had the rhythm now, pumped up for the remainder of the shift. I began slinging my crates onto the pallet, my heart banging away, the sweat running down my forehead, soaking my shirt. Sometimes I smacked the crate down too hard and the corner sagged—a blot of ruby goo oozed to the floor. I switched the bleeding end inside to hide the damage. Then I sped up to catch up, everybody keeping pace now, nobody talking, all of us relishing the exertion, feeling a sense of accomplishment for an hour or so until fatigue and noise and heat and boredom whittled down everything once again to plain old work.

The forklift driver fit his prongs into the pallet, screeched forward, lifted, rode away.

I started a new one.

Time just kind of melted...I could hear the plop of crates and the shattering of glass, the peal of rubber tires. I heard the heavy breath of the other stackers.

I finished another pallet. The forklift screeched up close, too close this time, and for an elastic second, I watched its wheel roll up over the back of my work boot and then thud down upon the concrete—and before I could give a name to the pain jolting up from the numbness of my heel, I discovered that I was screaming, hopping on one foot like a ridiculous person, cursing and screaming.

The other stackers gathered around, watching me dance. The

forklift vanished into the stacks. I twisted full-circles on one foot, the faces all a blur.

Somebody bundled me up the catwalk ladder and into the factory. I inched along the top-story walkway, past the guts and steam and crashing of machinery to the far side of the lunchroom—I leaned against the railing for support and watched my injured foot trailing behind. I knew that it must hurt—it had to—but I couldn't feel a thing.

Thank God, I thought. *Thank you God for getting me out of this place.*

At the nurse's station a man in a white lab coat waved me inside, pointing to the single folding chair in the corner. I could feel the blood drained from my face, my cheeks clammy and cool. I explained what had happened and he eased off my work boots, peeled away my socks. He jiggled my ankle, squeezed. I gasped. He told me to wiggle my toes and I could.

"You're fine. You can go back to work."

I was standing now on my one good foot, corkscrewing in his direction, maybe trying to get my hands on him, I don't know.

"*Motherfuckingsonofabitchcocksuckingmotherfucker—*"

When the foreman arrived, he told me that I should cool down, take a rest if I needed. For the better part of the next hour, I sat by myself in the lunchroom under the dusty glow of neon rail lights. My foot didn't hurt that bad anymore, nothing broken or torn—not that I knew about. It had felt good to curse out the guy in the white coat. Like I'd accomplished something. I'd tell Win about it and he'd laugh for sure. When the foreman came back to reassign me to the pit—quality control down in the basement—I trailed along behind him and didn't really mind.

The pit was the drainage area, the last stop for damaged crates and bottles. Working the pit was easy money. No boxes coming at you, nothing to stack or load. It was quiet down there, cool. Like everyone said, easy money.

I followed the foreman down the stairwell, bracing myself between the handrails, careful to keep the weight off my sore foot. It was dark and cold and you could smell the thick stench of tomatoes cooking three stories above.

I shook hands with my shift partner, a young guy with long greasy hair and waffled red cheeks. I held his gaze just a second too long and his eyes cinched up tight.

Please, God—I don't want to be here.

A dozen pallets pressed up against the near wall, each piled five levels high with crates of ketchup. The foreman told us to inspect each crate for broken bottles, then drain the bad ones, toss the glass, insert unbroken bottles in their slots, reseal the crates, and load them onto another set of pallets at the opposite wall. Come the end of the night, everything got hauled up to the loading dock.

Easy money.

We unsealed and opened the crates. Neither of us talked. We lifted each of the twenty-four bottles from their slots, checked for damage, dropped each back into its place, resealed the crate, and then humped it over to the new pallet. Now and then, we'd find a broken bottle and replace it with a fresh one from the feeder crate. In twenty minutes, we finished off three pallets.

"We're being chumps," explained my partner. His eyes roved from wall to wall, though there was nothing to look at but concrete.

"What do you mean?"

"The corners." He spoke with a taut, jittered voice, higher than I would have supposed. His eyes darted everyplace but my direction. "They're the only ones that show if they get busted. The middle don't matter 'cuz you can't see 'em."

I nodded okay and we opened a few crates, inspecting the corners only. If a bottle had broken and started to seep, we traded it for another in the middle, daubed off the gunk, slapped the glue back on the cardboard flaps, and called it done.

We filled a couple of pallets.

"What do you think?" I asked. "Think they'd notice?"

He looked suspicious at first, like I'd been sent down there to spy for quality control.

I slipped the flat of my hand under the sealed flaps and eased them open, taking care not to rip the cardboard. Then I reached for the glue brush and immediately resealed the flaps. I let some glue slop over the side to prove that we'd made an effort. My partner's pitted red cheeks swelled with a big grin. We dispatched a half-dozen crates awfully quick.

After that, neither of us could see the point in even pretending…

We humped each of the damaged crates from the old pallets to the new pallets, dispensing with the inspection altogether. It saved lots of time.

Afterwards, we sprawled across the floor. I rested with my eyes closed and my partner smoked. The bare concrete felt like an iced-over pond and it was too cold to get comfortable.

"Easy money."

"Yeah."

I wished I still had the sports page. I could study the box scores, commit some stats to memory. I could figure out something. I looked at my watch. Still another hour and a half until the shift ended. I prodded my injured foot with the steel tip of my other boot. Mostly, it felt numb. I cradled my hands in my lap. They looked soft and filthy.

I felt dead.

I pulled myself off the floor.

"I'll be back soon."

"You watch out for the foreman," ordered my partner. Like he still didn't trust me. Like somehow he knew.

I hobbled up the stairs, along the catwalk, and towards the business office on the third floor. I inhaled a lungful of cannery stink and thought I might vomit. I pushed open the door.

The foreman was standing over his desk, flipping through a stack of papers fastened to his clipboard. He glanced in my direction, offered me a little nod, and went back to his job.

"I'm not eighteen," I told him. He pulled the clipboard away from his chest, reared back his head, and inspected me closely to see if I was crazy. "I'm just seventeen." He just stood there. Then he asked my name, all quiet and soft-spoken like he was afraid I might not tell him now. I spelled it out slowly, last name first, and then he snatched the receiver off the wall and whispered something hoarsely to somebody, I couldn't tell what or who. Hiking up his trousers by the belt loops, he ordered me to get the hell out of there right now and don't tell nobody I ever worked there, ever. I limped out of his office and down the catwalk, and I heard him call after me, "Kid, you come back next year!"

I had lasted ten nights on the job.

✦ ✦ ✦

Out in the garage, under the hood, one hand waggling up towards the rafters in pursuit of a socket wrench as the engine to our Chevy Impala screeched and grumbled and spat, my father sang out as loud as he could manage: "You gotta be something!"

I slipped the wrench into his palm.

"I know that, Dad."

His hand disappeared. He ratcheted, bumped his head, and blasphemed vigorously.

"Then what are you planning to be?" He emerged from the Chevy's chassis, rubbing the sore spot on his skull.

I shrugged miserably, wiping the grease off my hands and onto my coveralls.

"How about nothing?" he said, "Because that's what you'll end up if you don't start taking life seriously. Maybe you'd rather be digging ditches your whole life."

"I'm not going to dig ditches my whole life."

"I know you won't, because you got to be willing to work hard and sweat like a son of a bitch. You aren't interested in sweating all day, every day, fifty-two weeks a year, are you?" He returned to his hideout beneath the muffled steel hood. "Only a stupid son of a bitch sweats his life away in some damn ditch!"

Dad extended his open palm from behind and batted the sky like a spastic.

"Hand me the screwdriver."

"What kind?"

"The kind that's sitting on the workbench right in front of you."

"I mean straight-edge or Phillips?"

Dad and I had spent countless hours in the garage, with me fumbling my way through the most elementary procedures. Wrenches and hammers got entwined in my fingers, hardware was sucked to the floor by lumpish gravity. I drove nails into my thumbs. Probably, he figured, I was unteachable.

"Use your eyes."

Of course, Dad didn't win any prizes as a teacher. When we broke out the power tools with their heavy lariat hanks of yellow extension cord, relics from the golden days of home repair, my father's edginess hinted that we would soon be maiming each other with trilling blades and steel bits otherwise designed to pulverize wood and puncture metal. He foresaw our mutual electrocution.

Extracting himself from beneath the hood, my father set his palms on either hip. His mouth gathered into a fierce little pucker and his blue eyes peered inwards. Already he perceived numerous opportunities that would arise for me to live off the sweat and blood of the people who did the real work in this country, the ordinary folks from places like Jefferson Manor who made life hum along for everybody else: the ditch diggers, for example.

"You must think we're rich."

"I know we're not rich."

"You must think so."

The rich—those mythical creatures. In the hills above our town lived dentists, city planners, and the managers of discount carpet store chains; but certainly not the rich. What did anybody in Jefferson Manor know about the rich? The rich, as my father finally had to concede (having studied the corrupt administrations of Presidents Buchanan, Hayes, and Harding), were men without genuine jobs, pushers of paper; "financiers," he stipulated, which was another way of saying plain crooks. The rich were purely theoretical.

"Well, you're not sitting on your ass all summer like you was Nelson Rockefeller." Dad ducked back under the hood. "We wouldn't even be having this conversation if you'd've kept the job your uncle got you."

"Look, Dad. I was underage to join the union. Is that my fault?"

I held my breath, waiting for him to intuit and then bark back the truth.

"Your uncle went to some bother to land you a spot. He could've got in trouble, too, I suppose."

I exhaled. Relieved to see my sorry lie standing—sorry for my old man that he couldn't spot it.

"I know."

"Win did it for you! You understand that?"

"Yeah. No sweat."

"*No sweat?*"

"Yes. What can I say? I understand, I do." I sighed and watched my breath take shape in the cold air of the garage. "I'm too young, so sue me."

"See, that's what I'm talking about."

With the job completed, we moved to the garage's washbasin, dipping our hands into a tin of lanolin soap. We rubbed hand over hand over hand as black suds filled the basin and splashed across the concrete floor. I wondered what either of them would say if they ever found out.

"Dad. You see Mr. Barnes's car?"

"Why are we talking about Barnes and his automobile?"

"He put a sticker for Nixon and Agnew on the bumper."

Dad rolled his tongue over his upper teeth, clearing out the bad taste. "Well, the man drives a Chrysler, doesn't he?"

"Who you voting for?" I filled my voice with innocent curiosity.

"That's for me to decide in the sanctity of the voting booth."

"But you wouldn't vote for Nixon, would you?"

Dad shrugged and sucked on his cheeks, making a pretense of serious rumination before he said, "The man's a good Quaker."

"Bullshit."

"Language like that is the sign of somebody who can't express himself. You're displaying your ignorance."

"You said worse just a couple of minutes ago."

Dad sniffed at the proposition. "Sure," he said, amiably wiping the sweat from his face and smearing his forehead with grease. "But I bumped my head."

✦ ✦ ✦

After quitting high school, my uncle Win set out to see the world as a fruit tramp. He followed the harvest up and down the coast. Work started at five each morning and wound down just before sunset when the men were paid for their day's labor according to their barrel tally. The prevailing wage for a day's work ran about forty-five cents. At night, Win sometimes added to the bundle at blackjack.

Many men new to the fields didn't last their first shift. Stoop labor was excruciating, but Win didn't mind working hard; he could work as hard as anybody when he wanted. With a long reach and a fighter's fast hands, he adapted quickly to the job, relying on his balance and agility to ripple down the rows, plucking out the ripe cukes from their tangle of foliage, never even sneaking a glance at the man ahead of him. Over the weeks, Win acquired speed; his barrel rate climbed and topped out at eighty cents per day. But then he started losing at cards. Perhaps he felt too tired from the extra effort in the fields. In any case, he didn't play smart. Work added up to a wash and Win decided to move on.

For over a year, he traveled courtesy of Southern Pacific's boxcars, crisscrossing the Northwest, stopping off in Spokane, Boise, Vancouver, Seattle, Portland, Coos Bay, Fortuna. He unloaded trucks, cleaned up kitchens, painted houses, swept out barns, and cleared storefronts. The work lasted two weeks, a week, a day. Win picked up his bag and followed his nose, figuring that almost anywhere something to eat and a place to sleep were waiting for him. He was just a kid, still in his teens. Win loved this time on the road, his days of labor and nights to himself, the world in his pocket. The Great Depression—they sure got that right. Win always said that it was the best time in his life.

Down in California—it was May in Redding, the temperature already hitting 105—the sheriff arrested Win and two other young guys straight out of the railroad yard. After convicting them of vagrancy, the judge put them to work for two weeks tarring public roads and laying down back-acre sod on properties belonging to the mayor, district attorney, and other good citizens of the town. Win told himself that work was work, and now he had seen Redding. He didn't owe nobody nothing, he didn't have a care.

Retired from stoop labor, he pictured himself in San Francisco. Maybe high up in the air painting those pretty bridges or working on a cable car. Wearing a smart uniform and creased cap. Clanging the silver bell like a lunatic referee at the end of a twelve-round prizefight. All those girls and a few drinks and their nights off strolling along the beach without the compromising light of the moon, and nobody to tell him what to do until the next job rolled around.

* * *

Dad put me to work on the roof.

It'd been seventeen years: we needed a new one.

So we started with the inspection.

My father fit a twelve-rung wooden stepladder against a flank of rain gutter and clambered to the top of our house. I followed behind, not looking down.

"For beginners," he instructed, "you better check the flashings."

"What are flashings?"

A glance of astonished disbelief.

"C'mere." He hunched his way towards the peak line, legs spread in an overturned U, his balance holding like it was second nature, and then he crouched in front of the chimney, tapping at a sheet of metal wrapped around the four corners of brick with the edges filtered beneath the asphalt shingles. "These here are flashings. You see any damage where the edges meet the shingles? Rot, rust, wear?"

"I guess not."

"Don't guess. See any discoloration that might point to water damage or seepage? Seepage is hell's own bitch to deal with."

I crouched at the chimney, laying my hands on the flashings like some miracle worker.

"No seepage."

Dad rolled back on his haunches, his butt pressed up against the roof's slant. He rubbed the edge of one shingle with his big thumb.

"You look here. The asphalt should feel something like fine gravel. It should scratch your fingertips like one of your mother's emery boards. You don't want it smooth, like this son of a bitch. Now look down in that rain gutter. What do you see?"

"Looks like sand."

"What's that tell you?"

"You mind if I bring my radio up here while I'm working?"

"Christ almighty! Prove to me you're paying attention."

"The sand isn't sand, it's gravel, or whatever that stuff is from the shingles. So the shingles are wearing out and I got to replace them."

"Bingo," he said. "I already been up here scouting around and I found at least a third of these are scraped clean as a baby's ass. Now what does that tell you?"

"That I'm going to spend the rest of the summer on this roof."

Dad chewed at the side of his cheek like it was a plug of tobacco, the taste satisfactory. "I don't want to hear your jungle music blasting out our neighbors. You use some common sense. And whatever you do, don't fall off the goddamn roof or your mother will never let me hear the end of it."

Dad hurried down the ladder to begin his own projects in the kitchen. He had the week off and he planned to install a new stove that Mom wanted and then paint the kitchen, replace the molding along the baseboards, maybe rewire a living room lamp he'd made back in the Pleistocene Epoch of his own teenage years. I didn't mind placing a layer of roof between us.

So I humped my first load of shingles up the stepladder, each paper-wrapped stack weighing in at fifty pounds or so. At the top rung, I rolled the bundle off my right shoulder and then climbed onto the roof and dragged the sons of a bitch to the far corner. Once I got a dozen stacks on top, I flaked away the old shingles' frayed edges, tossing the composite chunks off the roof and into the wheelbarrow below. Whenever I nicked the barrow's lip, it rang out with a satisfying *ping*! I balanced the portable Zenith borrowed from our kitchen counter on top of the chimney grill, its big bad speaker broadcasting KSOL's Top Soul Forty for the benefit of all of Jefferson Manor's rooftop dwellers.

I peeled off my t-shirt, took a little break. Junior Walker and the All Stars wailing on "Cleo's Back." The sun hit the bare shingles, warming the rooftop like sand. So I sprawled across its slant, pretending for a minute to be James Bond tanning himself on the French Riviera just a few moments before Pussy Galore slides up next to him on the beach blanket and splashes a cocktail onto his hairy chest and then commences to licking…

"Hey, what're you doing!"

My chin nodded into my chest: I saw my old man's face peeking over the rain gutters like a surfacing shark.

"Just taking a rest."

"From what?"

I sat up. Slighted. Wronged. I gestured at the dozen packs of shingles scattered along the roof.

"For Christ's sakes," barked Dad, "this can't wait 'til Christmas."

I held up one hand to assure him, but he'd already submerged.

Sooner or later, you got to start hammering. I ripped open the nearest sack of shingles and buckled down to work. The new shingles had to be installed on top of the surviving layer with the tabs facing down towards the eaves. Each shingle took four nails. To prevent warping, you had to fix the edges flat and even, eyeballing the lines straight. The joints between the tabs had to be staggered. It was going to take forever. The sun made me sweat. I liked listening to the radio—Aretha singing "Ain't No Way." I studied the rake of the slope, the roof already brighter and coarser in several spots, and figured I had all summer.

"Hey, my man..."

The familiar lazy slur of my main man. A blonde bump of hairsprayed razor cut peeked above the roofline—a slow, unsteady wobble with each step up the ladder as his face rose above the horizon of aluminum gutter.

"Frankie!" I swaggered over to the edge like I was comfortable up there and extended an open hand to the civilian. "What's going on, my brother?" Frankie ignored my offer and scaled the roof on his own. He stood up straight and held very still for a moment, making certain that he wouldn't blow away in the breeze. We slapped skin, worked our way through the complicated handshake of the moment.

"You drop by for some pointers?"

He loogied a big one over the side and watched it splatter. "No, man. I'm not into high places. I'm more of a down-to-earth kind of dude."

"Ah, you'll get used to it. You never been on your roof before?" I didn't give him time to answer. "It's cool. Hey, check out the view."

We both baby-stepped to the edge facing the street. I inched up a bit closer than Frankie.

"It's the Manor, man." Frankie wagged his head in admiration.

"Yeah."

Eighteen hundred serried rooftops peaked and crested and then rolled on forever—an elevated seascape of worn wood shakes and tarred shingles demarcated by red brick chimneys and TV antennas, the power lines crisscrossing the sky to emphasize the frantic sameness of everything in view. In the distance, I could spot the canopies of sycamore, elm, and eucalyptus blossoming above a carpet of Merion bluegrass two blocks away at the park. Overhead, vast squadrons of Canada geese skitted past on their way to anywhere else.

"Your ol' man making you roof this whole motherfucker?"

"No big deal. I might help him wire up the new stove and stuff when I get done. Maybe paint the house if there's time. You got to have skills, man."

"Yeah, maybe."

Frankie extracted a pack of Camels from his jeans back pocket. He whacked the closed end and two cigarettes poked magically out the top. Frankie grinned. We sat and smoked and observed our town from the heights.

"You imagine doing this bullshit for a living?" I asked Frankie. "I mean, up here every day, eight hours a day, for forty years or some such?"

"Curse of Adam, my brother." He leaned back against the roof slant and puffed expansive gray clouds into the sky. "Myself, I'd rather be back in the Garden of Eden, drinking palm wine and now and then copping a feel off Eve."

"You blasphemous prick."

"What can I say? Anyway, where did working ever get anybody?"

"Do it one day, and then you just got to get up and do it all over again."

Still, there was something about perching on the roof, watching the rest of Jefferson Manor, and nobody even knowing we were up there. It was like we owned the place, which wasn't exactly what we wanted either.

We snuffed out our cigarettes against the shingles and flicked the butts next door into the Heilborns' yard.

"Hey! I dig that tune."

KSOL was blasting "Tighten Up" by Archie Bell and the Drells.

"Be my guest, my man."

Frankie edged up to the roof peak and fiddled with the

volume. Then he stripped off his t-shirt, talked extensively about how great the sun felt on his bare skin while he flexed his pecs and biceps, and launched into a little dance, wiggling his butt and making his stomach muscles ripple and roll, tossing his head in a wide arc with one hand holding onto the chimney's edge. I laughed along with him, the goon.

"Check it out." Frankie raised one arm stiffly and pointed south like a weather vane. "From here, you can see the cannery stinking up the whole damn town."

I could make out the belching towers where the line of rooftops folded into brown summer hills, the sky kindled with gray and white smoke. They worked three shifts around the clock until September. Some of the guys in my father's carpool timed their vacations to moonlight.

"My uncle says that's the stink of good money."

"Doesn't mean I want it up my nose."

Beyond the cannery, the factories and warehouses of the East Bay slathered the skies with Kodachrome effluence, the low-lying fog of manufacture and transport signifying a future of steady work, a life you could bet on. Hunt's, Del Monte, Continental Can, the Ford assembly plant, General Motors, Caterpillar, the Coca Cola bottlers and Brockway glass, the steel mills at the edge of the bay that turned the adjacent sand spits the color of rust, the Trojan Powder Works and the Ortho garden spray center—the prosperous, arsenical base of heavy industry and future wages.

Frankie lit two more Camels, passed one to me. "It's money, my man. That's the name of the game. Nobody likes what they do."

I drew a deep drag and exhaled with several little puffs. "That's fucked up."

Frankie slugged me in the shoulder, hard, and pulled his shirt back on. "Sure enough."

I stared at the skyline, wanting to feel something. Anything would have been fine. Maybe if you made a little piece of yourself dead, just to get by, and then you weren't careful, other parts started dying, too.

"So you up here for the remainder of the day?"

"Remainder of the summer."

"Then I will catch you in the fall."

I sighed. My life was tragic. Better than the cannery, but still terrible. Boring. Pointless. Who wants to work? I took another long drag. "Yeah, you be cool."

Frankie grinned at me as he disappeared down the ladder, calling out, "I'm always cool, Mister Fix-It."

I went back to hammering. Talking with Frankie had thrown me off rhythm and everything seemed to take more time. The sun was starting to sink behind the most distant houses. I turned up the radio. Some tune by somebody who thought he was Smokey Robinson and the Miracles, but definitely was not. I yawned. I stood up and looked around, searching for who knows what. Nobody was watching, and what did it matter, anyway. I sat down on the slat, sprawled out my legs, and gave myself permission to take a nap.

I don't know how long I'd been sleeping when I first heard the sirens. I rolled over and crawled to the peak, scanning in all directions. I didn't see any smoke. I pulled myself to my feet, struggling for balance. The blare grew louder and soon it was drowning out KSOL. I crept over to the edge, curling my toes, scanning up and down the streets. At the far end of our block, I spotted a huge red fire engine careening around the corner, heading in our direction. I didn't see any smoke. Maybe somebody at the picnic tables in the park was choking on his chicken salad sandwich. The fire engine drew closer, its siren wailing. Whatever was happening, it seemed nearby. The fire engine pulled up in front of our house and stopped. I watched two firemen leap from the cab, clap on their helmets, reel out the hoses, and charge through our garage door and into the kitchen.

Our house was on fire.

I was standing on the roof.

♦ ♦ ♦

Win hitched to San Francisco in July. He hadn't heard one word about what was happening along the waterfront. Later, he told me, he thought it amazing how ignorant a young man could be.

Five days after the Fourth of July, on a Monday, the city still appeared to be shut down for the holiday. No trolleys operating along Market Street. No car horns, no screech of industry. Just the barren black asphalt, an unbroken white divider stripe running down to the Ferry Building, and thousands of people lining either side of the street, standing silently, just waiting. Five days after the Fourth of July, 1934, and the citizens of San Francisco were still waiting for a parade. The men were in their Sunday coats, the women in bonnets and scarves, and Win did not understand.

"Here they come!"

People stood on their toes, heads craning over their neighbors' shoulders to get a better view. Several blocks above the Embarcadero, the trucks bled onto Market. As the first vehicle drew closer, Win spotted the black crepe. A crowd streamed out from the side street, following the trucks. They marched ten and twelve abreast, swarming in formation, running onto the sidewalk. You never saw so many people in one place. They kept pouring into the street…

Win touched the shoulder of a man standing in front of him, not knowing what else to do.

"What's going on here?" he whispered.

He was a big man, great-shouldered, uncomfortable in his Sunday clothes. He searched Win up and down.

"Where the hell've you been?"

Win grinned his ingratiating best.

"Let me see your hands," the man ordered.

Win placed his satchel at his feet and buckled his legs around its corners. He extended both hands and the man inspected Win's calluses.

"You're a working man. Why the hell don't you pay attention to what's going on in the world?"

Out on the street, there was a pair of coffins passing on flatbed trucks. Flowers several feet deep surrounded them. As the trucks rolled slowly past, Win felt as though everybody around him was simultaneously drawing their breath and then refusing to exhale until the bodies had moved on. Win's heart beat wildly. Two shining sedans followed the trucks. Women and children, families of the deceased, rode in silence, their eyes fixed to the road. Two dozen men, shoehorned into blue serge coats, wore brassards on their sleeves indicating allegiance to various fraternities of the First World War. Their standard bearer waved the American flag. You could hear the scrape of the marchers' shoes on the pavement, the solemn swishing of their step as hands brushed against fresh-starched pants.

"Hey, buddy. Tell me, won't you please? Who's in those coffins?"

The man hesitated, made his estimate of Win: his satchel locked between his legs, his thin brown face and muscled forearms.

The man stepped uncomfortably close to Win, breathing into his face.

"They shot them both dead," the man explained. "The police did. Strikers, from the Longshoremen's union. For two months, the longshoremen and the seamen's unions shut down the waterfront. What they wanted is what everybody wants." He looked at Win to see if Win wanted it, too—figured he did. "Keep the companies out of the hiring hall, pay a fair wage. But the day after the Fourth—I was there, in front of the strike headquarters on Steuart—there must have been five thousand of us, yes, that at least, waiting to see what was going to happen next." Win stepped back to accommodate the man, the words pouring out of him now. "The companies shipped in scabs with police protection. Scab truck drivers at twenty dollars a day, plus meals and a place to sleep, four times what a union man makes. We fought them all day, everywhere. So finally, the police charge us, and two guys step out of a car, no uniforms, but they pull out their guns and they shoot into the crowd. Three good men go down. They killed two of them. Died some hours later."

The man peered into Win's face, trying to see if he understood anything at all.

"I'm not a longshoreman," said the man. "I'm just a pipe fitter. But if there's a General Strike, I'm going out with the rest of them."

Win found himself in the street, folded into the midst of the procession. A brass marching band rounded the corner. Trumpets blared a dirge as the bass drums beat ponderous time. Win was walking alongside the longshoremen as they strode eight abreast, clad in black Frisco jeans and white caps. Men from the other unions filed by in rank and column. Boilermakers. Machinists. Teamsters. Laborers. Members of the sailors' union, the marine firemen, ship clerks, masters, mates, pilots. No banners or signs, no slogans shouted out loud. Only monumental silence.

Win walked five blocks in formation, unconcerned about his destination. He felt swell, he told me. Nobody in the street except working people. He'd never seen such a thing in his life, never imagined it possible. He grinned at the big buildings, the banks closed for the day, the figures lining the sidewalk. He soaked it all up. He would fight anybody in the world. He'd march straight ahead with his head held high until they arrived at wherever they were going.

✦ ✦ ✦

We started early Saturday morning, knowing we had the long weekend. Monday was Labor Day. You could feel the end of summer, the bay breeze lapping grass cuttings down the hot tar streets, the last profusion of backyard zucchini and yellow crookneck squash crowding the planter boxes, their skin turned to a thick and bitter hide. The cannery would run full shifts for another three weeks, and then the scent of boiled tomatoes would vanish from the neighborhood for another nine months.

Win spent all morning on the rough carpentry inside the

kitchen and attic. Dad and I hauled a load of shingles up the ladder and pried off the damaged tar paper with a pair of utility knives. Patches of the roof had been burned obsidian smooth, glassy and still warm to the touch. When Win finished inside, he mounted the stepladder and joined us. From the deep pockets of his filthy gray overalls, he produced a bullet-shaped can of Coors and tossed it to my father.

"You want one, Little Slick?"

It must have been 90 degrees on the roof, the sun radiating off the eastern slant, scorching your palms if you had to right yourself on a stumble. Dad took a long pull from his beer and gurgled a sudsy mouthful.

"He does not." Foam stuck to his lips.

"Oh, yeah. I forgot. The kid's not even eighteen yet, is he?" Win produced an old stogie from his overalls' side pocket and sucked at the stub while sparking up the other end with his Zippo. His perfect smoke rings smelled like burning rubbish.

He clapped me on the shoulder. I had to shift the soles of my feet to retain purchase on the slant. When I caught my balance, I shot a glance in my uncle's direction and found his big grizzly bear eyes running me up and down, half amused and half regretful. I threw back my head and studied the clouds.

For the next couple of hours, Win and Dad tore off the damaged patches. I dragged a sack of ridge shingles across the roof and began pounding them in place along a crumbling line of gravel that ran to the chimney. The fire had destroyed several feet of ridge, the rest baked flat and useless by weather and time.

Spontaneous combustion, explained the firemen. They had doused the flames with chemical suppressants and flooded the kitchen floor with their elephant hoses. The fire had started from adhesives and sealants used to install our new stove—construction materials whose treacherous properties Dad had innocently shrugged aside. Up on the roof, you could now see the damage that a little carelessness might cause.

"Slick, you're a lucky so-and-so." Win's voice boomed above the racket of hammers and nails, his back turned against Dad. "Gettin' all this help."

Dad didn't say anything.

The flames had swept up through the kitchen vent, licking the underside of the attic baseboards and scorching the roof frame. Tar paper fused with worn shingles. Our house smelled like dead skunk and burnt tires. Win derived considerable pleasure from these facts but had refrained from further comment after the initial round of mockery and commiseration. Standing in the middle of the kitchen floor full of cinders, he had slapped my father on the back a half-dozen times, insisting there was no harm done, each knowing pat like a hammer blow.

"The Raiders are playing Labor Day!" Win hollered into the wind as he dropped a sack of shingles on the slant. "Exhibition game!" His sunburned head rolled into one shoulder. He was looking straight at me now. "We finish up here, I'm planning to watch in the comfort of my own living room. You two are welcome to join me, if you don't make too much commotion."

"Thank you," said Dad, his eyes focused on the nail, his hammer poised. "I believe I have things to do around here."

"That Stabler is a mean son of a bitch," Win sang out merrily. "Those Raiders play ball like they was in a bar fight. I like that."

"I'll watch with you, Uncle Win."

My uncle bared his teeth in a carnivorous grin, and I could see that he knew everything. Maybe he even forgave me.

"You do that."

Win went back to pounding nails. Dad joined him in a crouch, the two of them working together, one holding down the flaps, securing opposing ends of the composite shingle while the other struck the blows.

Win had quit jobs, plenty of them. At eighteen, just a year older than me, he was picking apples in western Washington, then digging ditches for pipeline just a few months later in Idaho.

He had spent his nineteenth birthday in the Missoula jailhouse. Some disagreement outside a barroom, hard to recall what. In his youth, my uncle had more than once trumpeted his intention to vacate a job by poking the man in charge straight in the nose. They never figured it was coming, even when he had warned them. He told me all about it so that I should understand when my own turn came.

"Hey, you!" shouted my father. "Quit daydreaming."

I yanked another shingle out of a sack, pressed either flap into the peak of the roof, and hammered.

It hadn't been so long ago that Win would take pleasure in teasing me about our life together, his and mine—insinuating that we would always be in league against the rest of the world. "Let's ride up into them hills," he told me, his sly grin dissolving into blameless malice as the bourbon flowed over the bumpy course of family Thanksgiving, which included the requisite after-dinner card game and the inevitable dispute between the brothers. "Kid," said Win, "after I take this next hand from your ol' man, you and me'll rocket up there and pluck out them rich folks by the pointy collars of their starched white shirts. We'll raise them off their fat butts and plop them down here in the real world, where people really work. What do you say? You with me?"

Now I understood that Win would never again flatter me by suggesting that nothing would ever change and that my life might one day be mistaken for his. Whatever happened, I knew that I would not end up ditchdigging, as Dad suspected and feared and perhaps sometimes even secretly hoped. I knew that I wasn't going to spend my life selling men's shoes at Thom McCann's or collecting quarters at the tollbooth on the Richmond bridge or slamming together chassis on the line at General Motors year after year. It wouldn't be my responsibility to keep the conveyor belts oiled, cranked tight, and running steady for swing shift at the cannery, as Win had done for decades.

That was the shame of my life. I had been spared everything. But wasn't that a good thing?

I stood at the edge of the roof, two fingers wrapped around the claw end of my hammer. I just felt so lonely already. All those houses set in parallel lines like crypts, each giving the illusion that inside the lives still being led were identical. And I knew that pretty soon I wouldn't belong anywhere.

* * * * *

After work, men accumulate at the local bar, downing one tall cool Lucky Lager and then perhaps a second before heading home for dinner, and somewhere in between, the conversation starts.

What's happening to this country?

You got politicians in Washington sending their kids to private schools because a woman can't walk down the street two blocks from the White House without getting raped. You got college boys and girls living in the same dorms, smoking the dean's Cuban cigars when they take over his office with their damn feet up on his desk.

And you got to pay for it.

That's right!

You got one damn thing after another.

I heard about some little boy put LSD in the Kool-Aid his mama made for his birthday party. You see the blacks on TV—'cause that's what you got to call them now—they're burning down Detroit. New York, too. Teenage girls traipsing off to the ACLU, buying birth control like it's going out of business. Not my daughter. Not yet, maybe, but you wait. The music they play, it's just noise. You can keep New York, I don't want it. You seen 'em dance? That ain't dancing, it's something else, I don't wanna say what. Listen here. There are just two four-letter words that the hippies don't know nothing about. W-O-R-K and S-O-A-P.

No, no, you guys don't know nothing. I'm going to tell you how it is...

So when Governor George Wallace comes to town, he draws a crowd. On the bandstand, four young men who look like Bear Bryant's defensive line sing a pair of clodhopper songs about their trucks and their mamas, and these days people in the audience know the words—though it wasn't long ago they all listened to Sinatra, Benny Goodman, maybe even Nat King Cole. That's Chill Wills at the microphone—the original voice for Francis, the Talking Mule, now serving as master of ceremonies. He introduces the governor, who pledges to *drive over* any protestor who sits down in front of his *campaign* caravan. He is running for president of the United States because somebody's got to stand up for ordinary folks. Limousine liberals. Pseudo-intellectual elites. Briefcase-carrying government bureaucrats who can't park their bicycles straight. "I was poor growing up. Probably every man in this room was poor. So what did we do about it? We went to work. Tiny Tim, that's the kind of man they're turning out today. Sissy boys who drink tea with their little finger pointing up in the air." (The governor demonstrates, his pinkie erect.) "Some of you fought with

Patton and MacArthur. I served under Admiral Chester Nimitz...Boys with long hair that you can't tell from the girls."

I don't agree with the man about everything, but at least he tells you where he stands.

My son ever come home like that, I'll pull every one of them outta his head.

People from the South, whispers one man guiltlessly, they know...

Your average working person today is getting fucked in the ass, opines one sage. Other men around the bar hold their tongues, roll their eyes. They do not disagree. It's 1968: everything of consequence is happening somewhere else—too far away to be perceived with clarity or forgiveness. Beyond our ken. Let them ridicule George Wallace, call him small and mediocre, unvarnished and greasy, humping all across the country with the scent of hurry-up and hair oil—that's us, too.

But why do the Tom Paines of the local drinking establishment, our independent thinkers, shuffle and mumble and meekly submit whenever they encounter authority? Doctors, the school principal, any guy sitting behind a desk who's got a bit of power to make a small decision that might change their lives. Humbly accepting the verdict. Unwilling to speak up. Fawning. Then raging.

The teachers, they don't teach nothing nowadays. It's the college professors—communists half of them, faggots, marijuana-smoking Tom Fools who figure they know everything 'cause they got a piece of paper says so though they can't even fix their own leaky toilets. It used to be a woman could stay at home and didn't have to work—she had work enough to attend to at home. There was a time when the family all pulled together.

There is a meanness in the world. Remember Navy guys in Hawaii, firing machine guns off the prow, massacring those big turtles, who sank like stones leaking blood in the waves. Think about hitting your kid, slamming the door on your wife, and then driving off to noplace for the next three or four hours. Remember watching your neighbor chase his daughter into the front yard and beat her with his leather belt until the police came.

In France, they almost toppled ol' Charlie de Gaulle.

Soviet tanks rolled through Prague.

On the Italian Riviera, the girls swam topless.

Yet this was history, too—right here: suburbanites recreating the nation.

In August, Mayor Daly grimaced at the camera and screamed at Senator Abraham Ribicoff, "Fuck you, you Jew son of a bitch, you lousy motherfucker, go home!"

* * * * *

EIGHT

O Pioneers!

Buddy Benavides snarled at his reflection in the wraparound wall mirrors, grunted twice, and clanked a pair of forty-pound dumbbells over his head.

Deltoids.

"Hey, Bertie!"

I was spotting Vince while he kicked out twelve reps on the bench press at one hundred and thirty pounds. Frankie leaned against the weight rack, observing Bert and Buddy, the hulking, well-groomed monsters who ran La Touch of Class Men's Styling Salon across the street from the gym. The Benavides brothers wore identical black satin shirts cuffing their twenty-two inch biceps, tan gabardine trousers cinched up like nooses around their thirty-three inch waists.

"You hear me, Bertie?" Buddy continued. "I said I got me a *real* honey last night!"

"Oh, yeah?" Bert pressed two hundred pounds of drooping barbell above his head, locked his elbows, and barked for breath. The sweat rolled down the enormous rift of his satin shoulders.

"She was a sweet little Japanese girl. Hair down to her ass." Buddy fit his dumbbells into their slots on the weight rack and massaged his shoulders with busy piston fingers. "Waist so tiny, I could wrap both hands around her belly and still crack my knuckles."

"Sounds sweet!"

"Sweet? Man, she was a kindygarden teacher. You know what that means."

Bert lowered the barbell to his shoulders, sucked up a chestful of air, and exploded into a second rep, his legs splayed like a colossus. Once he knew we were watching, he flashed a salacious grin at the mirror planks and raised one eyebrow. It fluttered. Frankie laughed.

"Blow jobs," explained Bert. His gaze fixed on the mirror while he flexed his pecs in rapid succession. They spasmed to fascinating effect. "Kindygarden teachers are the grade-A experts."

A thirty-pound dumbbell rolled off the racks where I was sitting and struck the floor with a permanent crack.

"Hey, you kids!" shouted Buddy. "Let us work out in peace! I don't know why Gene allows you in here."

Eugene A'Dair was the proprietor of the Manor Gymnasium, a one-time Mr. Abdominals. These days, Bert and Buddy sculpted a feathery nimbus of coal-black fuzz over the widening gyre of his bald spot, and Gene gave them the keys to open the gym on weekends so they could inflate their upper thighs and chisel their calves.

"We pay him. That's why."

"You getting smart with me, Frankie?"

"What happened to the kindergarten teacher?" I wondered, hungry these days for whatever knowledge might be at hand.

Bert delicately lowered his barbell to the floor. The linoleum buckled slightly. He slipped up behind Buddy and began to massage his brother's posterior deltoids. Frankie, Vince, and I leaned in a little closer.

"Okay," Buddy growled, "so this is what happened. I took her up to my pad, turned the lights down to a shadow, and I put some Oscar Peterson on the hi-fi."

"Mood," Bert explained to us dolts. "Mood is very important."

Buddy scrutinized the three of us, his big thumb jabbing in our direction. "These youngsters nowadays think all they gotta do is pour a couple Lucky Lagers down a honey's throat, whip out their microphone, and she starts singing about the rockets red glare, the bombs bursting in air. It ain't that way, fellas."

"Tell us how it is, Buddy."

"Like I said. I got Oscar Peterson tinkling on the hi-fi. 'Some Enchanted Evening' or some such gar-*bage*. I ask her to sit down and relax on my new sofa. She sinks into the folds about two feet deep, it's so cushy. I just got me a good deal on it from a pal of mine—a massive motherfucker with pecs out to here." Buddy held two hands in front of his own ample chest, approximating the improbable distance of two watermelons. "He works selling furniture at White Front out in jigaboo land. Near the Coliseum. You know where I mean?"

"Go *on*!" Bert spewed into his brother's tiny spaghetti-shell ears.

"I got black satin sheets in my bedroom, too. But I ain't telling her about them—not just yet. From the sofa, she can check out my entire pad. I got my hi-fi, I got my color Magnavox television with the remote control, I got my full-service bar squeezed into the corner with its own refrigerette on metal casters that's stocked up with Bacardi and coconut juice for rum coolers, and from the sofa she can enjoy every inch of it."

"Before she enjoys every inch of you."

"Bingo, Bertie!"

"You got your barber school diploma hanging up so she can see that, too?"

"No. I keep that in the shop."

"Oh, sure. I seen it there."

"Well, where do you keep yours?"

"In the shop. Next to yours."

"Bertie, you're aggravating my story."

"Sorry." He polished a dumbbell with the flat of his hand. "What happened then?"

"So to make a sweet story short, I'm ready to bang her, right?" Buddy pivoted to face Frankie and then waved me and Vince in closer, too. "I got her dress off," Buddy confided hoarsely, "and my pants are tied up around my ankles. A minute later, we're wrestling on the sofa, and we're both just about to sink to the floor, 'cause it's really that cushy, I swear to God. I'm telling her all about what a good buy I got, and how this guy whose hair I been cutting for donkey's years is gonna get me a complete dinette set for wholesale, but she don't want to listen, she's so hot to trot. So finally I get her legs pried apart, and I know she's got ants in her pants ready to dance. It's going to be like Pearl Harbor all over again, except this time 'round I'm the kamikaze pilot in the nip Zero and she's the USS *West Virginia*. I'm telling you, man, it's Tora, Tora, Tora. And then guess what happens?"

"What happened?"

"I can't remember her name."

"What do you mean?" demanded Frankie. "Why's that matter?"

"Explain to him, will ya?"

"It's only polite," clarified Bert. "What with you banging her and all."

"Plus," said Buddy, "she knows. See, I'm about to insert myself, if you get my meaning, but she stops me dead and tells me straight out, 'I don't even think you know my name.' And I don't."

"So what'd you do?"

Buddy raised both fists over his shoulders, faced the mirror, and pumped his biceps like Superman. "Now, you fellas know me, right?"

I glanced at Vince, who was studying Frankie, who was shaking his head.

"Oh, God," moaned Frankie, "he's going to say it."

"You fellas know how I like my honeys..."

"Not again, Buddy. Please."

"I happen to be a man who likes his honeys just like he likes his coffee..."

"Black, cold, and bitter," said Vince.

"I like my coffee and I like my honeys white, hot, and sweet, right? And she's Japanese, right? And I'm a little embarrassed to say so"—Buddy's chest expanded defensively—"but I ain't never had any Japanese honeys before. Practically everything else, sure. Kraut honeys, dago honeys. Even Hawaiian honeys."

"When I was in the Air Force," reflected Bert, "I was stationed in Greenland. They said they got some sweet Eskimo honeys there."

"Yeah, but expand your horizons, Bertie. Look East, young man. You see what I'm talking about?"

"Not really."

"Me neither," I admitted.

Buddy ground his teeth in my direction and caressed an inflated tricep.

"What kind of name does a Japanese honey have? If she was German, I'd figure her for a Helga or a Hilda or some such burgermeister bullshit. But Japanese? Fellas, I didn't have clue one."

"So what'd you do?"

Buddy peered around either shoulder, checking the weight room for spies. "I just told her the truth."

Nobody spoke.

"Whaddaya mean?" asked Bert finally.

"I told her exactly what I was thinking. I said, 'Honey, you are the most gorgeous thing I have ever gawked at in my entire life and I mean every word of what I'm telling you, honey.'"

"That worked?"

"Course not. But it turned out that was her name."

"What was?"

"Honey. Her name was Honey Toyota or something. It didn't matter after that. I mean, she didn't ask me to recite her Social Security number or nothing."

I still couldn't speak.

"You was lucky," Bertie said finally.

"I was lucky. And you fellas know why?" He couldn't wait for an answer. "'Cause I believe in my heart that they're all honeys when you get right down to it."

Buddy beamed at himself in the mirror, proud of the guidance he could provide.

"You guys going to use the incline bench?" wondered Vince.

"Let that be a lesson to you," concluded the barber. "Nah, go ahead. We're working our pecs tomorrow."

The three of us returned to bench-pressing, this time on the slant. I had to take fifteen pounds off the barbell and I was still struggling on the final rep, arms trembling. Vince and Frankie stood over me ready to snatch the bar if it collapsed on my chest, hollering "*Push push push*!" as I squeezed and grunted and finally straightened both arms with a gasp of astonishment. My guys cheered. By next Christmas, said Frankie, I'd be bench-pressing my own weight.

For the next thirty minutes, we worked our biceps and triceps. Then we hit the steam room.

"Hey, look!" called out Bert, though it might have been Buddy. In the mist, it was hard at first to distinguish one huge bulk of a Benavides from the other. "Here comes the Three Stooges."

"Yeah, all three of 'em."

Frankie spoke up for us. "Hey, you big musclemen."

We took our places on the high bench. It was much steamier up there—hard to last more than ten or fifteen minutes. Buddy turned up the classical station on the speaker wired back to the weight room, a bunch of violins sawing away softly in the fog.

"Hey, Vince," said Bert. "You're getting pretty shaggy."

"You need a haircut," agreed Buddy. "How come you don't come by no more?"

Since the start of cannery season, Vince had been letting his hair grow. I checked him out and saw they were right. Black curls trailed down his neck without the benefit of hairspray, practically drooping to his shoulders.

"I'm busy," said Vince. "Besides working, I'm going to college."

"Oh, yeah?" Bert sounded suspicious. "Where you going?"

"UCLA."

"No foolin'!"

I explained. "The Underrated Campus of Lower Alameda."

Bert and Buddy didn't understand.

"It's a joke," said Vince. "I'm just going to the JC. Chabot Junior College."

"That's a good school," said one barber in the mist.

"They got some good teachers and shit there," the other explained.

"It's all right."

Practically everybody from our high school enrolled at Chabot following graduation, even if they worked tomatoes and peaches for the summer like Vince. At the very least, you got a semester of smoking dope in the parking lot and sleeping with the girls heading for beauty school by year's end.

"College keeps your ass out of the Army, don't it?" The steam had cleared and I could see that it was definitely Buddy talking.

"I'm 4-F," said Vince.

"You find 'em," explained Bert, "you feel 'em, you—"

"I got asthma," said Vince. "I got to stay out of hot, steamy places. Like Viet Nam."

The Benavideses both rolled their shoulders, readjusted their haunches on the lower bench.

"So what about you two?"

"I'm still in high school," I explained.

"Maybe. But you won't be next year, will you? You understand what I'm saying?"

Frankie was fiddling with the water hose, cooling himself off and then spraying the coals to amp up the steam.

"I'll take my chances with the lottery," he said. "If my number comes up, I might join the Marines."

"The Marines don't take pussies."

Frankie squirted the floor to wash our sweat down the drain. Then he accidentally squirted the barbers.

"Hey, you little shit!"

"Oh, *sorry*..."

The steam rose quickly and soon we couldn't even see ourselves. For another couple of minutes, everybody sat quietly and sweated even harder.

"You know, we already served."

"Yeah, Buddy did a hitch in the Coast Guard, while I was in the Air Force in Greenland. They got some—"

"Yeah, I heard they do," answered Vince. "Lucky for the Cong you two monsters already did your bit."

Bert and Buddy reared back in the fog and basked in the recognition of their monstrosity.

"But would you go if you could, Vincent? That's what I'm asking. Or are you turning into one of them protestors?"

"Yeah, you protesting at college, Vince?"

"You look like a goddamn protestor, your hair hanging way down past your ass practically."

"I just protest," Vince confided, "when I don't get enough of those honeys in the backseat of my Chevy."

The barbers laughed like dinosaurs. A pleasant lifetime passed in the company of men.

"Hey," I piped up, stifling the little squeak that sometimes crept into my voice. "Let's change the music. Okay, you guys?"

"You want to listen to your Berkeley beatnik protester songs? You want I should find you some Joan Baez?"

"Gimme some James Brown," demanded Frankie. "Gimme that sweet soul music!"

"James Brown's gonna move to Sweden," announced Bert, "to get a sex change operation so he can marry Little Richard."

"God," groaned Vince, "I heard that in junior high."

"I read all about it, smart guy."

"*National Enquirer* don't count as reading, Bert."

"Big draft-dodging college student. You know everything now, don't you?"

Buddy stood up and padded slowly across the floor, taking care not to slip, and turned up the speaker volume. More clarinets and violins and whatnot.

"That's Felix Mendelssohn's 'Midsummer Night's Dream,'" announced Buddy. He pressed one hand against the wall and dipped his head towards the speaker, his cheek brushing its grill. "I listen to it on my eight-track when I'm cleaning sparkplugs in my garage."

"Felix? Like Felix the Cat?"

"Yes, Vincent. Felix the Cat wrote this beautiful music. I pity this world when you guys finally take over."

For a long dreamy moment, Buddy stared at the ceiling, the condensation forming droplets like a thousand pocky nipples, and though I swear to God I didn't want to, I couldn't help noticing that he had the longest eyelashes I'd ever seen.

✦ ✦ ✦

"Have you ever been, Mom?"

"Once. During the war." She peeked over my shoulder and smiled into the middle distance. "Some of the girls from Red Cross took a train from Boston to Montreal. Right at the start of winter, and you can't imagine—"

"This isn't the smelly cheese part of Canada," insisted Dad. "Not by a long shot. We're talking about Mr. John Bull. Pure English. Pure as you can get nowadays. You can tell by the name."

"British Columbia!"

"That's correct, son."

"How we going to get there?"

"How'd you two like to travel? Boxcar, bobsled?"

I looked to my mother for guidance. She was beaming over the prospects of this year's summer vacation, still months away. Usually, we drove to Reno for a long weekend, maybe stopping off in Sacramento to visit the Gold Rush display in the Capitol. Once we went to Lake Tahoe to spend a few days in a canvas-flap cabin. But more often, we settled for nowhere.

"Your father is going to take us on an airplane."

"We're going to fly?" I couldn't believe it. Dad was not an extravagant person—at least, when it came to money.

"Your father's been doing so much overtime lately. Really, Franklin, I wish you could take a rest."

"You tell the Navy brass. Tell General Westmoreland."

"General Waste More Land." I'd heard Mr. Karplonsky, one of our beatnik teachers from Berkeley, call him that.

"We get back from vacation," mused Dad, his hand brushing a rough patch on his cheek that his morning shave had missed, "I might sit myself down and write a letter to the president. Tell him to finish up this mess pronto."

"Tricky Dick."

Dad cast me one of his cautionary glares. "Still the president, son."

"When will we go?" I wondered. Anything seemed possible if we were going to climb into an airplane, head off into the skies, then land in a foreign country.

"I was thinking we'd be there for Canada Day."

"When's that?"

"You don't know when's Canada Day?"

I felt pretty certain that I didn't need to.

"He doesn't even know when Canada Day is."

"Just tell us, dear."

"The first of July. The two of you may be more familiar with the term 'Dominion Day.' No? Well, anyway. We might find ourselves smack dab in the middle of downtown Vancouver for the ceremonies, or maybe out in the woods somewhere near where your grandfather used to chop down the trees to build houses that frankly don't hold a candle to this one."

"We're not going to be camping," asked Mom, "are we?"

"Hell, we could travel all the way up to the Arctic Circle if we had a mind. Straight along the Porcupine River by birch-bark canoe and maybe locate Sergeant Preston of the Yukon. I have a bone to pick with that man about—"

"I don't like bugs," my mother said firmly. "You know that."

"Hell, sweetheart." He draped the big thick of his forearm

across Mom's shoulders, drew her into his chest, and pecked her twice on her puckered lips.

Sometimes, they astonished me.

✦ ✦ ✦

Dad used to talk about his boyhood on the prairie in the years before the soil blew away and his family lost everything. Without warning, he would lean back into his La-Z Boy recliner, strike up his pipe, puff clouds of gray toxic fumes in the direction of me and my mother, and then he'd be lost—returned to Chin's restaurant, the only restaurant in Colgate, Saskatchewan, in the year of 1919.

Outside, the winds shrieked across the prairie, bullying the shutters with an incessant tap-tap-tap-tap like some pathetic stranger begging entry, his sense whipped away, soon to freeze in his own tracks. The morning, like every morning towards the end of fall, was sunless, heavy, bruised and flattened by the pewter sky—unremarkable. As the men talked, Dad scooted closer to the hot breath of the potbelly stove, tempted to inscribe his back with the black iron curl of its legs and claw feet. A rancher spat against the stove wall and it hissed a warning to stay the distance.

Them damn Yanks, said one man. "Driving down the price of wheat."

Other men seated at the table grumbled their agreement.

"Them Yanks," he repeated, "all them people sitting so warm and comfortable down there in Kansas City and Bismarck, North Dakota..."

Them Yanks, talking about them damn Yanks all the time. Back then, Dad didn't have any idea what constituted a Yank.

"I got me a field full of stone bolts," said a farmer. "I'm going to load my wagon down and roll every one of them stones onto the Yanks' side."

Chin scraped off a layer of eggs and burnt noodles from his frying pan, serving the men around the table in random portions, damning them Yanks himself and winning the admiration of his new countrymen. Most of Colgate's citizens had themselves recently arrived from Germany, Norway, Sweden, the Ukraine. They ate without speaking, their forks battering their plates in syncopation to the rattling shutters; and then one man pulled out his pipe and tobacco pouch, and they all smoked and gossiped like women.

A fool boy from neighboring Goodwater had joined the Canadian army, gone for a soldier when he still might be useful on the farm. The Germans had shot him or gassed him or some such thing in Belgium. That seemed like a waste, the men agreed, since he was still needed at home. A young rancher from Colgate announced that he had made his first run into the States, peddling moonshine whiskey. He recounted how he had adulterated his septic brew with doses of plain Canadian water, making himself a bundle. "Damn Yankees," said somebody, laughing uproariously at the rancher's initiative. Damn Yanks, damn Yanks, damn Yanks...

A pair of Indians entered the restaurant. They stomped their way across the floor to the front counter, their heels clicking against the hard wood. The ranchers and farmers made a show of paying no attention. Indian ways, not worth bothering about, as long as they didn't steal or ask questions. Several minutes later, two Indian women appeared at the front door, hesitating once they had gained entry. "Blackfeet," whispered one of the ranchers, and the others responded with a disinterested nod. Blackfeet, the occasional allies and adversaries of the Oglala Sioux—friends to Sitting Bull, a Hunkpapa, who had made his home in Saskatchewan following the Little Big Horn. Dad thought: tomahawks, scalpings, smallpox blankets—everything he knew about the Blackfeet.

The Blackfeet interested Dad.

Indians, Dad knew from listening, were nearly as terrible as Yanks. Every spring, some band of Indians would drift into town, mixing their animals with the ranchers' herds so that cattle or horses might melt into the prairie along with the tribe.

To retrieve your property, you had to call the Royal Canadian Mounted Police. Yet nobody was afraid of Indians. It had been thirty years since the government hung Louis Riel, leader of the Red River Rising. The Indians did not even frighten my father. One day a cart and horse team appeared at the farm when his own father was off in British Columbia, logging for the season. The Indians had intended to water their horses, as custom prescribed, but his mother did not welcome them. Clara stood at the front door, cursing in English and then in Norwegian. She lifted the axe from the doorstep woodpile and fanned it across her face as though it didn't weigh an ounce. She promised to drive that axe straight through any head that needed it; but the Indians remained on their buckboard, contemptuously silent. Dad looked on, worried mostly that his mother was going to get herself in real trouble this time. Finally, the driver lashed his horse and the Indians drove away.

Now, from the front of Chin's restaurant, Dad puzzled over the Blackfeet, wishing he could interrupt his father to ask a question.

Dad scooted across the floor, silent and cunning. He thought to himself: like an Indian.

The Blackfeet women wore their leggings up to their knees, leather moccasins wrapping their feet. Their dun-colored hands waved above their chests and shoulders, fluttering like prairie fowl.

When Dad peered his head up under one woman's dress to satisfy his curiosity about whether their feet really were black—Oh, didn't she scream bloody murder!

✦ ✦ ✦

When the war came to Jefferson Manor, we did not rally around the cause. Who had heard of Viet Nam, and why should we give a rat's ass, anyway?

Veterans of Inchon, the Burma campaign, and Kula Gulf were now partisans of the suburbs. If consulted, they did not recommend the Asian continent as worth saving.

The old men ate monkey brains, their women were whores, and nobody even spoke English.

"Keep your head down," said Win. "Keep your mouth shut. It'll blow over soon."

"Fulfill your military obligations elsewhere," Mr. Ortiz advised me and Phil, once high school graduation moved into our sights. Mr. Ortiz recommended Germany.

They served good beer in Frankfurt, a city named after the hot dog, and the German girls spoke English. They loved Americans because we had saved them from themselves. This much we knew about the world.

But the war wouldn't go away. The war was fought each evening on the network news, animated by the thrust and boom of distant thunder in the land of Gog and Magog, the music of pandemonium. Very few citizens of Jefferson Manor perceived in the war an opportunity for distinction; almost nobody, a crusade. In the end, you did what you had to do.

Mostly, it was our friends' older brothers who got caught in the first draft, several returning home to the incurious sniff and subsequent disregard of their neighbors. Benny's cousin had trod upon a land mine, losing two toes. For a year, he corkscrewed down familiar streets, his hair flagging in the bay breeze as it inched halfway down the fatigue jacket that he now constantly wore for reasons which nobody could fully apprehend. Nicky LeRoux's older brother returned from the Air Force and screamed through the night for six months. In the morning he drifted into the kitchen, cheerful and contrite, bragging to us over pancakes which he prepared himself that he could kick back now, collecting his unemployment checks and enjoying a year of baronial leisure in his old bedroom since they would never find him civilian work in the trade for which he had been recently trained: aerial combat photography.

Ralph Studge, along with a few others, had drifted back to Jefferson Manor indignantly patriotic. Ralph would curse the draft dodgers, the college kids. But two minutes later he might turn around and offer sound, generous advice about how to make the Army doctors believe you were crippled, queer, drug addicted, deranged.

You just did what you had to do.

I longed to know what that might be. I ached. Sometimes it felt like my insides were going to boil over and I wanted to howl like some stupid mutt. But how could you tell? What words did you use to even raise the question?

What kind of dumbass pussy doesn't understand how a man's supposed to act?

I searched for help wherever I could find it. At home, we kept copies of *Life, Look,* and *The Saturday Evening Post* stacked on the coffee table, the weeks swelling into months with each year's pile stored eventually in the garage. Sometimes I'd flop across the couch and flip through a dozen magazines in a trance, recklessly detaching the pages from their center staples, my gaze ardent and insatiable. Olympic Charmer Peggy Fleming. Picasso, Apollo 7, and The Nixon Era Begins. The Raiders' Ben Davidson with handlebar moustache, straddling a Harley. Diet pills. London Bridge transplanted to Lake Havasu City in the Arizona desert.

Sandwiched between the stories I didn't care about and the advertisements I ignored were the black-and-white photographs of Khe Sanh, US field medics, interrogations, firefights, aerial targets, civilian casualties, US Congressmen Visit the Troops, Tet, Hue, Hanoi.

One photo I stored away for further scrutiny—evidence, I suppose, that the world was too terrible a place for anybody to comprehend.

I had stumbled across it in the garage one Saturday while cleaning my father's tool drawer, the full-page spread lining a box of awls and files. Moisture had thickened the paper and wrinkled its edges, though a lurid gloss remained. I just stared. Eventually, I slipped the photo into the back pocket of my jeans and when nobody was looking, I folded it into the previous month's *Saturday Evening Post*—"John Wayne Stars in True Grit." Whenever

I found myself alone in the house, I extracted the image from its hiding place and gaped at it like a Peeping Tom.

The monk was sitting cross-legged in front of an abandoned car on a main street in Saigon, the empty five-gallon container of gasoline positioned between him and the crowd. He held himself upright as the flames swept across his haunches, engulfing his robe, scorching his face. I'd study the way he had set his jaw and shut his eyes, and I'd try to imagine the crowd waiting for the screams that never came. It was like the fire kindled something inside of me, too—some seed of ingratitude that cracked open in the flames and flowered into a fear and longing so crazy and certain that I didn't dare give it a name.

✦ ✦ ✦

"Bomb 'em back to the Stone Age!" whooped Charlie Rivers.

Mrs. Waterman folded one arm over the other and suppressed a discreet snort as she stood beneath our classroom's languorous wall clock. She nodded gravely, as though she were contemplating the reasonable opinion of a sane person. She had long pale fingers sculpted from fleshy white palms—hands too large and awkward for most girls. Sometimes I thought of her as a girl. She had only been teaching for a year, which made her not that much older than the rest of us—especially the kids held back once or twice, like Charlie Rivers.

"All the way with Curtis LeMay!" bellowed Charlie. "Nuke the Gooks!"

Third-period Social Studies. Mrs. Waterman had directed us to rearrange our desks into a circle so that we could look our classmates in the eye and fully appreciate the mental flashbulbs popping off in staggered rhythm. Nicky LeRoux scratched the side of his nose with his middle finger pointing my direction. Frankie made goon faces at his cousin Kendall, who lived in one of the mobile homes at the edge of the bay. Most of the girls shielded themselves with expressions of glazed disregard, their mascara-laden tinsel eyes squinting into the void, their toes silently tapping as they waited for us to grow up. Still, Mrs. Waterman seemed interested in what we thought: amazing. It was boys from places like our town who were fighting the war. She had said so many times.

"Does it matter to you that Viet Nam is a civil war?" she asked. She slid between Charlie and Phil, occupying Debbie Hamsun's empty seat. At the beginning of class, Debbie had whispered some confidence to our teacher and taken refuge in the girl's restroom.

"North versus the South?" asked Charlie, suddenly the scholar with Mrs. Waterman radiating body heat right next door.

"That's right."

"Don't matter to me!" bellowed Nicky, and I could see that Charlie was pissed about the interruption.

"Me neither. That's their business."

"They oughta hang Robert E. Lee. No offense, Frankie."

"Hey, my family's Okies. Go ahead and string the dude up."

"It's the North that are the commies, you morons."

Charlie raised both fists above his head, reeled out his legs, and yawned obstreperously.

Obstreperous. A nice word. Dad had used it twice one evening after tripping over the meaning in a *Tribune* editorial. Then he immediately looked it up.

"Hey, Charlie resembles that remark."

"Shut up, Frankie."

"Or," Mrs. Waterman persevered, "that Ho Chi Minh, much like Robert E. Lee, is revered by many Vietnamese. They consider him the father of their country—like George Washington."

Nicky slumped into his chair and giggled. "Ho Chi *who?*" He let one eye scale the heights of Sandy Benito's enormous beehive, a monument to a half-hour's ratting and shellacking with Hidden Magic hairspray.

"*Hoo-chi coochy-coo.*"

"Shut up, Rivers!"

"I'll see you after school, man."

"Oh, I'm so scared."

I was going to make a contribution, but Phil beat me to it.

"Look," he intoned, his voice lowered gravely, his chin nodding in nervous contemplation, "if we don't fight them over there"—Phil set both elbows on his chair's armrest, leaned forward, and unleashed his most penetrating glare at the other side of the circle—"then we're just going to end up fighting them in the streets of San Francisco."

"Like you go to Frisco all the time, Barnes."

"I been."

"You just heard somebody say that stuff on television," objected Stacey Pastor. She had a clipped, peevish little girl's voice that seldom entered into current events, but her brother Ernie had just shipped out that fall.

"So what? If it's true..."

"Let's see them Viet Cong invade the Manor," said Charlie. "Henry Eagle and his boys will kick their asses back to the deserts of Viet Nam!"

"It's jungle there, dope!"

"Sure, the Eagle's already enlisted."

"Course he has. Did he join the Marines? I bet that animal is loving the Marines."

"National Guard."

Mrs. Waterman combed her brown hair in pixie bangs draped above bubblegum checks. They reminded me of a small child who had just run inside the house on a cold day and then stuffed her mouth full of candy. Her blue eyes were so bright and clear they made you think that she was always thinking about something secret and amazing. She was part of the Berkeley contingent of young teachers who carpooled fifteen miles to school each morning, riding in Mr. Karplonsky the math teacher's VW van or Miss Lewis the art teacher's VW bug. During our junior year, after Karplonsky heard that Frankie and I had spent the night in jail, he waved me over in the hall and, all sly-like, slipped a smudgy mimeographed booklet into my coat pocket. It was called "What to Do When You're Busted"—though Frankie and I had been trying to buy beer, not incite revolution. I never read it.

I knew that Mrs. Waterman lived in a brown shingle up in the Berkeley hills with her husband, a lawyer, who had graduated from one of those fancy colleges back east that everybody's heard of but nobody in Jefferson Manor would ever see. She might as well have come from the moon.

"Who has today's quote?"

I'd heard one of the other teachers call her Peg as they entered the faculty lunchroom. *Peg*. Short for Margaret. Margy. Marg. Peggy. Peg.

She rose from her chair and slipped up next to the blackboard, chalk poised for dictation. We could skip the Pledge of Allegiance if somebody brought in a quote from a famous dead American. Then we would discuss. Sometimes we would discuss for half the period. That meant no pop quizzes.

"Anybody?"

I didn't mind pop quizzes. I knew plenty of dates and practically all of the presidents—lots of stuff.

"I got one," volunteered Danny Andretti, his fingers clawing towards the overhead acoustic tiling. He vaulted a half-foot off his chair and hovered above his desk.

Mrs. Waterman nodded her assent. Danny plopped down in his chair and extracted a rectangle of loose-leaf binder paper from the pocket of his madras shirt. He flattened the edges.

A single, nervous cough.

"'If a man does not move in step with his fellows then perhaps it is because he hears the sound of a different drummer.'"

Then Danny pounded his desktop twice with the flats of his hands, stood all the way up to take a bow, dropped back into his seat, and launched into the drum pattern to "Wipe Out" by the Surfaris.

"That's lame, Andretti."

Danny kept beating out the rhythm with both palms.

"Andretti thinks he's Ringo!"

"The Beatles can kiss my ass," called out Danny. "Four dudes with haircuts like Moe Howard!"

"Now, who can tell us something more about Mr. Henry David Thoreau?" asked Mrs. Waterman. Peg.

"Must've loved the Beach Boys!" hollered Frankie above the drumming.

"The Beach Boys can lick my beach balls," sniped Charlie, who ran with a harder crowd.

"You'd like that, Charlie."

"Danny!" pleaded our teacher. "Please stop! Now!"

"Andretti, if you was a horse, they'd have to shoot you, you're so lame."

"I'll see *you* after school, man."

"*Rank*! He got you, Charlie."

Squeals of derision and insults and more hooting followed by threats of bodily harm…

Still, Mrs. Waterman managed to move us back onto the topic of Danny's famous dead American quotation. Why did most people conform, while some did not? Was there a benefit to society when an individual stood up and disagreed with everybody else? Was there a price we had to pay for the liberty of speaking our minds? Did we have the right to persecute Danny Andretti just because he was lame enough to deserve it? Mrs. Waterman claimed that we were now grappling with the big questions.

✦ ✦ ✦

Sometimes, I got restless. In the evening, just after my folks turned in, I'd hit the streets, covering the Manor like it was New York or Paris or someplace you read about where people just walk, certain there will be something to see.

I crossed Pond Street to Dartmouth Avenue ending at Meadow and then turning onto Princeton: everyplace the same, though now and then I remembered things. The smell of Phil's house some mornings when we were kids, the kitchen reeking of ammonia and lye like the Manor Beauty Parlor with its front door swung open when you walked past in the summer—and then I pictured Phil's mom in the kitchen wearing curlers and towering over a sink full of milk-soppy cereal bowls. I recalled coming home from school late with the windswept alarm of meat and fat frying: dinner in a dozen houses. The sight of Karl Connor's father, Big Karl, lying face-down dead-drunk on his front lawn at the corner of Colgate and Field on Christmas morning, and how funny and awful it seemed on the way to early Mass at St. Bernard's—and then after the first time, it was just what happened now and then.

I skirted four corners—the Chevron, Mobil, Shell, and Regal gas stations all open for business until stragglers from the graveyard shift at Caterpillar and the Coca Cola bottling plant pulled in to tank up, desperate to make it home again after eight to ten hours. Somebody I didn't recognize was working late in his own garage, chains wrapped around the rafters to sling a V8 above the yawning chassis of his family Ford, the engine's heads removed, the gaskets peeled away, a set of valves resting on the workbench ready for grinding.

I walked past the rusting cadmium-colored air raid tower that still sounded most days at noon.

A cactus garden presided over by a waist-high plaster statue of the Virgin of Guadalupe.

Sycamores rising thirty feet above the sidewalks with their peeling, mottled bark like giraffes' necks.

You couldn't tell any longer where our town ended and everything else began. The borders of one tract bled into another, and then another, then another. Jensen's Garage across from Foster's Freeze, the traffic light sputtering yellow with the red sometimes stuck forever, the sudden dip in the blacktop that had always been there—that's how you navigated, never paying attention to street signs. But new folks were now arriving in Jefferson Manor ignorant of the fact that a dairy farm, cherry orchard, or field of tules once covered the ground presently occupied by their house. For some folks, Jefferson Manor was just a place to wait until they could move somewhere else. Neither an achievement nor a terrible mistake. Just someplace ordinary, which I knew it was. But that didn't stop me from feeling sad or angry sometimes. Almost always, I couldn't tell the difference between the two. A few miles away, at the southern edge of town, they had built a shopping mall and filled it with strangers.

✦ ✦ ✦

"What do you mean?"

"You heard me. Now don't embarrass yourself by begging."

"Christ. I'm just asking—"

Mom ladled string beans from a bone-white serving bowl. "*Language*." They plopped onto Dad's plate, then mine, and just sat there.

"How come?" I pleaded. The airplane, a foreign country—something different for a change. She had said so herself.

Dad stabbed his fork into a hunk of lamb chop and filled his mouth. His wintry blue eyes throbbed with fatigue.

"They have the entire hangar working ten hours," Mom explained. "Honey, we're up every morning by four."

"But in the summer—"

"There's not going to be any summer." Dad gulped down a mouthful. "All leaves are cancelled until further notice." He drew his hands into his lap and rubbed his right with his left, each finger in succession.

"But we planned—"

"They just sent a crew down to El Toro for six months, and there's another headed to Whidbey come spring."

"But you said—"

"I'll be lucky if they don't send me to the Philippines. God-damn son of a bitching shithole."

"Language," reminded Mom, but gently.

Dad kept kneading his hands. They had swollen up and turned black at the fingertips from the solvents and adhesives the airbase was using to patch the F-4 Phantoms and A-4 Skyhawks shot down by Russian MiGs. The Navy retrieved the remains and shipped the fuselages back home.

"We can come with you. I don't care if I miss school."

"We're not going nowhere. Final."

Mom nodded, arms wrapped around her chest, striving to take his side. Whoever's side. They worked together. That had always been their arrangement, a strategy for prevailing on the suburban homestead. Mom filled each of our coffee cups. I dosed mine with Pream until it sloshed over the lip.

"You should quit."

I took a long gulp of hot, white coffee.

"What?"

I looked down at my plate. "Just quit," I muttered to my lamb chop. "I would. You could find another job. After we get back from British Columbia. You're not for the war anyway. You think it's stupid. And a waste. You said so. A lot."

"My God," said Dad, shaking his head hopelessly. He drummed four swollen fingers on the green Formica tabletop. "My God, what you don't know."

• • •

Gandhi beat the British by using passive resistance, which is tougher than it sounds. Basically, it means letting the other side kick your ass until they get too tired to keep it up and too embarrassed by the rest of the world thinking they're assholes. I once saw Henry Eagle coldcock a guy, then stomp him in the ribs until he could be pretty sure they were mostly broken. So I had some questions about passive resistance when you're on the receiving end of high-heeled, needle-nosed gray suede boots.

Gandhi got a lot of his ideas from Henry David Thoreau, who got some of his ideas from Count Leo Tolstoy of Russia, who said he got his directly from Jesus. Maybe. I'd have to look into that. But Thoreau wrote a whole essay about how he wouldn't pay his taxes for a war that he thought was wrong. He went to jail over it.

For a night.

I'd spent a night in jail. I didn't want to repeat the experience, but I wasn't going to write a whole long essay about it.

The book that really got to me was *Johnny Got His Gun* by Dalton Trumbo, which is a made-up name if I ever heard one. It's about this soldier who gets his legs and arms blown away, and his eyes messed up, and he can't talk or hear either. He can't even smell. He's a stump. The worst part is that he's so young, he's never done anything worth remembering. So he just lies there. He gets his rocks off when somebody moves him into the sun for a couple of hours. Eventually, this nurse figures out that his brain is still ticking and she communicates with him by tapping on what's left of his body. But she gets transferred.

Pretty grim.

I liked it a lot.

I read it through in two sittings and gave it back to Mrs. Waterman after the weekend.

I also handed back her Gandhi and Thoreau and a couple of other books about the history of Southeast Asia and so forth that I knew I wouldn't read unless it was me in the hospital with two legs blown off and time on my hands.

On the inside flap of Mrs. Waterman's copy of *Johnny Got His Gun* (even though it was just a cheap paperback with coffee cup stains on the cover), she had printed in block letters, just like a little kid: PROPERTY OF PEGGY LUNDBERG.

Which I figured was her name before she got married.

Lundberg.

Which meant she was a Swede.

Just like a quarter of me.

✦ ✦ ✦

"What if some guy's trying to rape your sister?"

"I don't have a sister."

"Then your mother."

"You're a sick sack of shit."

Frankie swallowed hard from his twelve-ounce Coke bottle and passed it to Phil. He had raided his parents' liquor cabinet to top off a base of Red Mountain burgundy with shots of rum and vodka, mixing us up something special for the occasion. The volume to his living room television was turned low. On the screen, Santa was sledding down a snowy mountain peak on top of a rechargeable razor with triple heads and a detachable cord. "Say Merry Christmas," ordered Santa, "with the Lady Norelco."

"What if Karol Kowalski was your sister? Use your imagination."

Phil interrupted. "I'm using my imagination. Right now, I'm imagining her lathering up in the shower. And I gotta brush my teeth. So I crack open the door, real quiet-like—"

"Say it's Bert and Buddy Benavides and they're both doing her."

"Those guys are homos," said Phil.

"Say that to their faces, Philip."

"I *would*."

Frankie took a big swig from the Coke bottle. "So you walk in your house and some psycho's on top of your grandmother."

"I'd tell him to stop."

"Hey, brilliant. I never thought of that. We should've just told Hitler to stop. I'm serious. Some biker caveman straight out of San Quentin is high on glue and gas fumes, and he's balling your little cousin with a gun in one hand and a knife in the other. So what're you gonna do?"

"I can't answer that. It's just hypothetical."

"How's he holding her down with his hands full?" wondered Phil.

"Meaning," said Frankie, "you're too big a pussy to talk straight."

"I guess I'd kick his teeth in. Take his gun away and shoot him in the face. Stab him in the belly fifty times and then cut off his balls. That make you feel better?"

"I feel better knowing you're not the world's biggest pussy."

I didn't know how to explain. I didn't understand myself.

Those magazines sitting on our dining room table, the bodies lying in ditches and the little kids screaming at the camera and baring their arms to the sky so you could see their burns—all that stuck between the ads for the Jolly Green Giant and the Frito Bandito, the Ty-D-Bol Skipper and the Pillsbury Doughboy.

"It's different with war, man. Maybe you don't have a choice when some assholes jump you or a criminal breaks into your house. But that doesn't mean I want to go halfway around the world to waste some motherfuckers that I don't have no beef with."

"You don't want to get wasted yourself. Is that what you're saying? I can understand that. But just say it straight out."

"I don't think the war's right."

Frankie's head flitted from side to side, trying to rattle my words into sensible order.

"It's wrong."

Both their faces were full of pity.

"So you're going to decide, hunh?"

"You know more than the government."

"Anyway, who says it's wrong?"

"His girlfriend. Mrs. Waterman."

Phil took a pull on the Coke bottle, started to gag.

"She's a lesbian," he coughed out.

"She's married, you asshole."

"I heard that she does it with hippies every weekend in the back of Karplonsky's van."

"I don't know, man. I'm just saying. I'm *thinking* about things, you know? That's all."

I felt an urge to get up and leave. Stagger home and hope my mom smelled the Red Mountain burgundy on my breath. Confess everything.

"Yeah, we know. You don't even got a sister."

Phil rose from the couch to fiddle with the television controls.

"I want to turn it up. Can I turn it up now?"

"Yes, Philip. Please, be my guest."

"I don't want to miss it."

"You're not going to miss it, Phil. Anyway, they know where you live."

Phil turned up the volume.

"Because of the CBS News Special Report which follows, 'Mayberry RFD' will not be presented tonight, but will return next week at its regularly scheduled times over most of these stations."

"Phil, get the fuck out of the way and let us watch, too."

Phil backed up onto the couch and plopped down between me and Frankie. He scooted a little too close, but I didn't mind. I could see that he was nervous. I would have been, too. Phil had been held back in second grade, which made him a year older than me and Frankie. He was eligible for the draft as soon as we all graduated in June.

A bunch of old men in suits moved into the camera's view, their faces emaciated and gray, their hair slicked back in stiff shiny wings with Brylcreem. One of the old guys inserted his hand into a wire cage, hesitated, then fished around until he latched onto an egg-shaped capsule. He handed the capsule to a lady with glasses who looked like an elementary school secretary sitting at her office desk. She didn't smile. She didn't look at the camera. When she cracked open the capsule, she didn't read the slip of paper contained inside. Instead, she handed it to another old man in a white shirt and tie who studied its message, chewed his upper lip, and announced: "September fourteenth."

Phil shot up from the couch like it had caught fire.

"Fuck!" he shouted. Then quietly: "Fuck."

◆ ◆ ◆

By 1923, they were all talking about getting out. Farmers had borrowed money on their property one bad year after another. Crops failed and markets collapsed. More borrowing, more failure. It took about six years to go broke, a slow choking on promises that the next year had to be better. First, the bank took the farm, and soon after, the house. Then, finally, it was all over.

My grandfather wanted to resettle on the Peace River territory in Alberta. The Canadian government had just opened hundreds of thousands of acres to homesteaders, but my grandmother insisted on a new country. My grandfather headed south to find work and the family followed.

The train delivered them to Kingsley, Idaho, the immigration center, where a uniformed man in a green military cap collected the head tax on newcomers. From the passenger car, Dad spotted a billion bright pockmarks of electric light rising off the city, and an artificial, weightless glow suffused the skies. Back on the prairie, Colgate had been lit by candles and coal-oil glass lanterns with baffled mantles that could hugely magnify the reflected flicker of a single tiny flame. In the black evenings of winter and fall, when nothing happened, the town managed without illumination. Kingsley, Idaho, city of lights, flared with the pride of wasted energies.

The rain commenced and Dad watched the water bounce off the hard surface of the station tarmac. He was puzzled. Then, after considerable cogitation, simply bewildered.

No mud!

In Saskatchewan, there was nothing but dirt roads, no pavement or sidewalk. Always, every season—mud, mud. His mother allowed him to scramble out of the coach so he could stand in the rain, his hands extended, open-palmed, to test the reality of American precipitation. The rain was real enough, no different than Canadian rain. He kicked his boot heel upon the surface of the hard ground and it did not yield. The water ran right off the pavement, it was no mistake.

Them damn Yanks.

Then on to Coeur d'Alene, Spokane, Walla Walla, and after that, Portland, a city swelled to an unbelievable size. At last, they reached Eugene. My grandfather had sent word about finding work in the nearest logging camp and he had located a home for the family at the far end of Willamette Street. The first day in town, trudging up the residential streets with the family's clothes trunk carted out on rollers and a wooden push frame, Dad stopped to gaze at the front of a two-story Queen Anne. Behind the home's wrought iron fence—a rust-repelling coat of blue paint covering the succession of impossible folds and squiggles that described the metal barrier—he spotted what he believed to be a tiny pasture.

From the fence to the stairway of the home, the ground was covered with a fine-mowed grass, the grazing area for some peculiar Yank beast. He inspected the other homes. Almost every one was surrounded by these manicured pastures. Most residents hadn't even bothered to erect a fence or string wire to pen in their animals. Dad thought about rabbits, who would certainly hop away, and then goats, who needed more ground to feed. He stood at the front of the house for a long time, waiting for something to emerge from the buildings and start grazing. He couldn't imagine what kind of animal it might be.

This, his mother explained, was what the Yanks called their "lawn." And someday he might have one of his own.

+ + +

"You're an idiot," declared Frankie. "Phil, you are a dumb shit."

"Asswipe," agreed Benny Chang.

The sky turned indigo and pitch, the illumination of our houses, and the houses built after our houses, dimmed by the jumbled canopy of Sicilian stone pines and Portuguese cork trees, palmettos and black acacia surrounded by castle walls of pollen-laden privet. The four of us strode past the empty tennis courts as their neon tower lights extinguished with an audible click as evening turned to night. We marched in the direction of the barbecue pits, where the twelve-foot windbreaks would permit us to convene in peace. Frankie carried the sack of Rainier Ale that his sister's boyfriend had bought us.

All along the dirt path, Phil kept talking about how a young man who had nearly achieved the rank of Eagle Scout could directly join the Army Rangers without stopping off for boot camp. He was also considering the Green Berets. In a few weeks it would be June, and then, before you knew it, graduation. Phil liked the hat.

"I'm going to kill me a million red commies!" Phil had already drained one can of evil brew in the backseat of Frankie's car, which was one can more than he usually drank. "They're just little fuckers."

"You're a littler fucker."

"A waste, Phil."

"The Cong'll waste Phil."

"'Cause he's got shit for brains."

"The man's bassackwards."

We cut across the baseball diamond where as a child I had devoted hundreds of hours to right-field daydreams of Cepeda, Mays, and McCovey. There, softballs lofted far above my head like comets and I stretched my arms as high as bone and sinew would allow, hoping the effort might help me to grow up faster.

"Shoot yourself in the toe. That's my recommendation. You get a .22, I'll be happy to do it for you."

"Better your friends, Phil, than some slope you don't even know. No offense, Benny."

"Fuck you, Frankie."

"Go to Canada, Phil."

"Tell 'em you're queer. They'll buy that."

We arrived at the barbecue pits and took refuge behind the windbreaks. I sat next to Phil on one side of a picnic table, the cement slab garnished with seagull droppings. Frankie passed out the Rainier and Phil tugged too hard on his pull-tab, spilling Green Death down the front of his shirt.

"You guys ever hear of the word 'duty'?" His voice had turned slurry, his brown eyes vague and glowering. "Who else do you think is going to step up? Some rich kids in the hills riding their polo ponies?"

"You ever even seen a polo pony?" demanded Benny, indignant on their behalf.

I tried to brush the droppings off the table, but they wouldn't budge. It was like the seagulls had welded them to the cement. The thought of seagull welders made me blurt out a laugh that sounded more like a fart. Frankie narrowed his eyes to slits and shook his head.

"You girls want to know my philosophy?" asked Frankie.

"Not particularly."

I fit my elbows between the squiggles of seagull deposit, lay my head in my hands, and let my eyeballs roll up at the moon.

"I don't look out for anybody but me." Frankie reached across the picnic table and patted Phil's knee. "That's my philosophy in a nutshell. I got my own problems. And even if I didn't, I'm probably going to screw things up in new ways as soon as I can figure out how. Everybody else in this world ain't none of my business. You understand what I'm saying?"

"He's saying wear your mother's underwear to your Army physical. There's no shame in that."

"You should be proud."

"Make sure your shoes and purse match."

Frankie withdrew a fat joint from his front pocket and dangled it between his thumb and forefinger. "Gentlemen?"

Benny whisked the joint away, plugged it into the side of his mouth, and sparked up.

"You guys notice," asked Benny, drawing deeply, holding it down, and then blowing a sweetish cloud into Frankie's face, "how peaceful things have been around here since the hard cases started getting high?"

It was true. Guys once destined for the penitentiary had cut back on the bloodshed with the advent of dope. Instead of downing a few cans of Old English 800 and then brawling until heads cracked and the police arrived, they now staggered into a serene and passive muddle, nodding out for the evening in the backseat tuck and roll of a '63 Chevy Impala or sprawled across our high school's front lawn. The Age of Aquarius.

"I feel like a swim."

I checked Phil out to make certain that he was serious. As a rule, Phil wasn't a rule breaker. It didn't give the rest of us any choice.

Frankie stuffed the Rainier into its sack and we cut pass patterns across a rolling field, tossing the last six-pack like a pigskin until we reached the other side of the park. Alongside the municipal swimming pool, we assembled at the foot of the wire mesh fence. For a moment, we stood there dumbly. The bay's humid breath blew in our faces. "C'mon, girls," commanded Frankie. Then he scrambled up and over. Benny and I followed. The three of us landed on a patch of cement painted marine blue where throughout the summer the mothers of young dogpaddlers blistered themselves crispy while worshipping the sun. Phil still languished on the other side of the fence. He gawped at us through the mesh like a resident of the monkey house.

"C'mon!"

Phil inserted his fingers into the wire, inched his way up, and then tossed one leg over, followed by the other.

Frankie had already torn off his shirt and shorts, kicked his Keds across the concrete. I slipped out of my own jeans and t-shirt just in time to watch him land in the center of the pool with a metallic splash, the news of its sting rippling across the water. I cannonballed into the deep end, my knees tucked under my chin. In the dark, the journey to the bottom felt endless, and for a panicky moment I thought I might have slipped in sideways or something—it made no sense, but that's how you think sometimes—and then my toes scraped the familiar bottom and I immediately began to rise.

I scissors-kicked to the surface and crawled lazily to the edge of the pool, gripping the gutter with one hand. Phil had stepped onto the diving board. In the moonlight, his skin looked as white as milk, the contours of his muscles like polished stone. He took one, two, three steps, and then glanced off the platform's edge and sailed into the air, outstretched arms tapping his shins so that in silhouette the jackknife of his naked body seemed to swallow the moon and then spit it back out. He speared the water at an angle, then skated along the bottom until surfacing at the far side of the pool in a single breath.

This perfect creature in his moment, ready to do harm and filled with nonsense—too young, unprepared, bereft of guidance like us all.

We sprawled across the blue concrete and drank another Rainier under a cloudless sheet of stars. Benny crawled to the shallow end of the pool and daintily threw up. Time passed with random speculations, insults, execrations. We downed more beer. That made the climb back over the fence harder, but we got it done. Doing a job that needed doing.

Men.

We slugged one another on the shoulders, called each other "brother." Then everybody felt embarrassed because there wasn't anything else to say. We shambled out of the park and drifted home to our mothers and fathers.

A few minutes later, I was slipping through the front door of our living room as quietly as I could. I didn't want to wake my father, who was working Saturdays and did not appreciate an early reveille. Edging my way carefully down the hallway and trying not to lose my balance, I allowed my eye to catch an old black-and-white photograph hanging on the wall. Its borders blurred and swayed and almost made me sick. I fixed my feet to the carpet and stood perfectly still. I concentrated on the photo. It showed Dad and some buddies patching an airplane outside their hangar, back when they were all still in the Army. I eased the photo off its single nail and carried it into my bedroom.

I sat on the corner of my bed and slipped off my shoes, then my socks. I placed the photo in my lap and stared at it for a very long time. The bed rocked. I closed my eyes. When I opened them, Dad was leaning against the side of the plane with one of his pals goofing alongside the propeller. Another was stationed in the cockpit, where you could plainly tell he didn't belong. I felt something squirm in my guts. The Green Death. I turned the photo over to check for names or dates on the back. Instead, I found my father's neat hand-printing in faded pencil. I squinted it out.

> Dr. Robert Hutchins, president of the Univ of Chicago, has said: "There are works of permanent value with which every person of cultivated mind should be familiar, which he should be trained to understand and enjoy."

And below that, Dad had written:

> "To be cultured—a capacity for being at home in the large world." So says the President of Wesley College in Dover Delaware.

The old man, not too many years older than me at the time, trying to figure out how to make his way in the world. Maybe there had always been a hole in his life, and now it was passed down to me.

Maybe it was the beer.

I rose carefully from my bed and retraced my steps back down the hall. The door to my parents' bedroom was left open a crack. I eased it forward another few inches. My parents both asleep. I realized that I'd never seen them in bed together, eyes shut against the world, dreaming whatever they dreamed. I felt terribly old. That same stout moon poured into their bedroom and seemed to chill my father's face, his bald baby's head, one eye twitching over some interruption of the peace. Defenseless.

"You okay?" My mother scooted herself upright, awakened by instinct. She was buttressed by either elbow, her whisper penetrating the dark.

"Yeah."

She glanced at the window shade, the evidence of night. "You go to bed now. It's late."

"Okay."

The old man stirred, snorted, flipped to his opposite side. He had spent his life getting here, this warm bed shared with my mother, the house they might own free and clear someday. Did he sense some faltering of these promises in his deep and honest sleep? I cannot claim for him, for any of us, knowledge or prescience. But from where I stand today, this foothold of privilege and dispensation that has compelled me to write what will now stand as their story: this book of mine that I could only dream into being because of their steadiness and sacrifice, I know that it was a fine life that they had prepared for me without an inkling of what it might entail or how far it would remove me from them. The green radium dial of their radio alarm clock read 12:45. Everything would change.

"Mom. I'm sorry."

She studied me in the darkness. "You go to bed."

I paced slowly back into my room, settled myself on the edge of my bed. I didn't know what I was going to do when the time came. I felt terrible, the copious Green Death churning in my guts, crawling up my throat. I could taste the upchuck on the back of my tongue.

The war was wrong.

If I got drafted, I didn't think I'd go. Maybe I'd just wait and let them try to find me. Maybe I'd leave for Canada.

The war was wrong. Not like our fathers' war. They had rescued the world, given us everything. Not that you could trust what anybody had to say about that.

The war was wrong. I wasn't even sure what I meant. But I thought it was probably true.

Maybe that made me a pussy, a coward, a punk, a traitor. I didn't know about that, either. Finally, you had to decide for yourself. Wasn't that what everybody's advice boiled down to? Our fathers and uncles, our teachers and neighbors, even Bert and Buddy Benavides demonstrating how to execute a proper bench press while stumbling over the facts of life at the gym. *Here, kid—take this. It's a gift—the rest of your life...*

Everybody was scared. They got by, day to day, without

guidance or advice they could trust or even comprehend. Nobody was prepared for whatever came next.

I threw up on my bare feet.

+ + +

The way you got to know a place was by walking, walking, eyes wide open. Nobody walked the Manor.

One night in the beginning of spring, I found myself striding down the oil-stained blacktop long after the rest of our neighborhood had gone to bed. With time running out, I forced myself to inspect what had always been there and what I'd only sometimes noticed…

Leaning towers of backyard citrus festooned with grapefruit and tangelos. Metal storage shacks turned by rain and time to shades of fur brown and madder. Stone bunnies guarding brick-and-slab planter boxes, shoulder to shoulder with plaster angels—and on one front porch, a four-foot stump of redwood chain-sawed into the shape of a grizzly cub. I spotted at least a half-dozen American flags hoisted above their porches. A Marine Corps banner flapping against a two-story pole alongside the garage. This is what I'd remember someday.

Years before, they had built our neighborhood out of nothing but the possibility that the country was ready for someplace, many places, exactly like ours. Our own frontier. Down the street, around the block, in every direction, convoys of trucks had greased their way across the newly paved fields, dropping off carpenters, masons, electricians, plumbers. The crews picked up their tools and waved into existence a park, a swimming pool, stores, and churches—and soon after, an elementary school, a junior high and high school, some bars and restaurants, a library.

They slapped up the power lines above, the sewer lines below, and our life began to take shape.

I arrived at Billy Sweet's old house—new people lived there now—and I remembered how in sixth grade a drunk lady had ploughed through his living room picture window, and the next morning Billy bragged at school that he'd slept through everything. The ambulance, police, even a fire engine. I crossed into the park. At the far end of the baseball diamond, I listened to the roar of the Admiral Chester W. Nimitz Freeway dividing our neighborhood from the one next door. A stranger might look at the two places and fail to see the difference. Neon-lit exit signs the size of a two-car garage door peeked above the rooftops to announce the distant goals of Fresno, Merced, San Jose.

I would miss Indian summer most when I left home: when I discovered what came next. Indian summer, Dad had told me, was the time of year in the colonial days when hostile tribes might launch a final attack before the snow fell. In Jefferson Manor, Indian summer was a week or two of warm evenings when folks listened to the ball game on their transistor radios while raking the leaves and maybe risked one last backyard barbecue before the rain.

I broke into a run. I ran until my heart beat like crazy, the wind smacking my face. After a few minutes, I found myself padding across the last acre of landfill at the far end of town, the ground yielding a soppy squish with each footfall. Seagulls circled above the cyclone fence, flecks of white burnished in starlight. I followed the dirt path to the water's edge. For almost a half-hour, I sat on a large smooth rock shaped like a varnished burl, but cold, very cold. I caught a whiff off the bay, the scent of salt and garbage.

I tipped back my head to gaze at the moon, its radiance brutally illuminating all the little orphans of Earth. The water drew a ruffled line across the horizon—nearly invisible in the dark, though I could hear it shushing, the waves pulling closer and drawing back.

That's China out there somewhere, I told myself.

Out there somewhere, something, someday.

I felt very afraid.

I rose, turned back towards the lights, the empty streets and the similar houses. Here people made themselves righteous and peculiar in all the ways that people must, uncertain if their lives might shine like beacons. Here people were ordinary—which is to say, they were beautiful. As slowly as possible—one foot after the other, my stride along the sidewalk so deliberate that I thought I might totter and fall—I walked back home.

On Manor Boulevard, something fluttered past my nostrils and then vanished just as quickly—a trace of jasmine, early for the season. I filled my lungs until they ached, greedy for what I could capture in this moment. For what I hoped to hold inside myself forever. I caught a remnant of that fleeting scent, a hint of what would swell and spread over the next few weeks and flood the air—and I thought I knew what my parents must have felt in their pioneer years with the perfume of a thousand gardens coursing across the unblemished streets and sidewalks and the sky so full of promise it could make you weep.

I kept walking.

Acknowledgments

Thanks to my friends and colleagues who generously helped in so many ways throughout the writing of this book:

Mark Greenside
Dawn Hawk
Gena Corea
Kim Bancroft
Mike Caple
Clyde Leslie Hodge III
Martha Nichols
Anne Fox
Mitchell Schwarzer
Marjorie Schwarzer
Lonny Shavelson
John Raeside
Marilyn Waterman
Bill Mastin
Susan Felter
Lee Hope Betcher
Kristen Tsetsi
Jocelyn Bartkevicius
Jenine Bockman
And, as always, Ann Van Steenberg

For the loan of their family photographs, I thank Mike A'Dair, Scott A'Dair, Dan Suzio, Francesca Suzio, Linda Fleming, Bob Bezemek, Nick Bezemek, and Mitch Coffman.

Thanks, too, to the Hayward Area Historical Society for assistance with photo research, as well as Nick Lammers and the *Hayward Daily Review.*

The Vermont Studio Center was the perfect place, long ago, to begin writing. In particular, I thank Jon Gregg, Gary Clark, and Neil Shepard.

Thanks, finally, to Malcolm Margolin, Gayle Wattawa, Lorraine Rath, and Jeannine Gendar—along with the rest of the remarkable staff at Heyday—for their counsel, professionalism, and friendship.

About the Author

Fred Setterberg is the author of *The Roads Taken: Travels through America's Literary Landscapes,* winner of the AWP prize in creative nonfiction. He cowrote *Under the Dragon: California's New Culture* with Lonny Shavelson (published by Heyday), and edited *Travelers' Tales America.* His essays and reporting have appeared in *The Iowa Review, The Southern Review, The New York Times, The Nation, Utne Reader, The Boston Phoenix,* and scores of other journals and magazines. He is the recipient of an NEA fellowship, the William Faulkner–William Wisdom essay prize, fiction awards from *The Florida Review, Literal Latte,* and *Solstice Literary Magazine,* and numerous journalism awards. A former staff writer for the *East Bay Express,* he lives in Oakland, California.

About Heyday

Heyday is an independent, nonprofit publisher and unique cultural institution. We promote widespread awareness and celebration of California's many cultures, landscapes, and boundary-breaking ideas. Through our well-crafted books, public events, and innovative outreach programs we are building a vibrant community of readers, writers, and thinkers.

Thank You

It takes the collective effort of many to create a thriving literary culture. We are thankful to all the thoughtful people we have the privilege to engage with. Cheers to our writers, artists, editors, storytellers, designers, printers, bookstores, critics, cultural organizations, readers, and book lovers everywhere!

We are especially grateful for the generous funding we've received for our publications and programs during the past year from foundations and hundreds of individual donors. Major supporters include:

Anonymous; James Baechle; Bay Tree Fund; B.C.W. Trust III; S. D. Bechtel, Jr. Foundation; Barbara Jean and Fred Berensmeier; Berkeley Civic Arts Program and Civic Arts Commission; Joan Berman; Peter and Mimi Buckley; Lewis and Sheana Butler; California Council for the Humanities; California Indian Heritage Center Foundation; California State Library; California Wildlife Foundation/California Oak Foundation; Keith Campbell Foundation; Candelaria Foundation; John and Nancy Cassidy Family Foundation, through Silicon Valley Community Foundation; The Christensen Fund; Compton Foundation; Lawrence Crooks; Nik Dehejia; George and Kathleen Diskant; Donald and Janice Elliott, in honor of David Elliott, through Silicon Valley Community Foundation; Federated Indians of Graton Rancheria; Mark and Tracy Ferron; Furthur Foundation; The Fred Gellert Family Foundation; Wallace Alexander Gerbode Foundation; Wanda Lee Graves and Stephen Duscha; Alice Guild; Walter & Elise Haas Fund; Coke and James Hallowell; Carla Hills; Sandra and Chuck Hobson; G. Scott Hong Charitable Trust; James Irvine Foundation; JiJi Foundation; Marty and Pamela Krasney; Guy Lampard and Suzanne Badenhoop; LEF Foundation; Judy McAfee; Michael McCone; Joyce Milligan; Moore Family Foundation; National Endowment for the Arts; National Park Service; Theresa Park; Pease Family Fund, in honor of Bruce Kelley; The Philanthropic Collaborative; PhotoWings; Resources Legacy Fund; Alan Rosenus; Rosie the Riveter/WWII Home Front NHP; The San Francisco Foundation; San Manuel Band of Mission Indians; Savory Thymes; Hans Schoepflin; Contee and Maggie Seely; Stanley Smith Horticultural Trust; William Somerville; Stone Soup Fresno; James B. Swinerton; Swinerton Family Fund; Thendara Foundation; Tides Foundation; TomKat Charitable Trust; Lisa Van Cleef and Mark Gunson; Whole Systems Foundation; John Wiley & Sons; Peter Booth Wiley and Valerie Barth; Dean Witter Foundation; and Yocha Dehe Wintun Nation.

Getting Involved

To learn more about our publications, events, membership club, and other ways you can participate, please visit www.heydaybooks.com.

Heyday is committed to preserving ancient forests and natural resources. We elected to print this title on 30% post consumer recycled paper, processed chlorine free. As a result, for this printing, we have saved:

7 Trees (40' tall and 6-8" diameter)
3 Million BTUs of Total Energy
772 Pounds of Greenhouse Gases
3,485 Gallons of Wastewater
221 Pounds of Solid Waste

Heyday made this paper choice because our printer, Thomson-Shore, Inc., is a member of Green Press Initiative, a nonprofit program dedicated to supporting authors, publishers, and suppliers in their efforts to reduce their use of fiber obtained from endangered forests.

For more information, visit www.greenpressinitiative.org

Environmental impact estimates were made using the Environmental Defense Paper Calculator. For more information visit: www.papercalculator.org.